Praise for The Cue Ball Mysteries

"Fast-paced reads with humor and mystery blending together to create the perfect story."
Socrates Cozy Café

"Humor, believable dialogue, extremely likable characters, and just the right amount of romance—everything I love in a story."
Linda Lovely, author of *The Marley Clark Mystery* series

"Cindy Blackburn's great author voice shines through."
Morgan Mandel, author of *Her Handyman*

"Bright and breezy, easy reads that kept me laughing."
ValleyGal

"Even if you've never played pool in your life this really is a mystery series you need to pick up."
Melissa's Mochas, Mysteries, and More

"I knew I was going to like Jessie right away! She is smart and fun, and I would love to hang out with her and shoot a little pool."
Escape With Dollycas Into A Good Book

"The humor sparkled on the page. I highly recommend the Cue Balls to lovers of cozy mysteries. You won't be disappointed."
Dorothy St. James, author of *The White House Gardener Mysteries*

"Jessie Hewitt seems prepared to handle anything life throws her way."
Joyce Lavene, author of The Missing Pieces Mysteries

Also by Cindy Blackburn

Playing With Poison
Double Shot
Three Odd Balls

Four Play

by
Cindy Blackburn

A Cue Ball Mystery

Four Play

Published by Cindy Blackburn
www.cueballmysteries.com

ASIN(Kindle): B00H4OUWGW
ISBN-13: 978-1494314019
ISBN-10: 1494314010

This one's for my critique group:
For Joanna, who tells me what’s good work and what isn’t.
For Jane, who laughs in all the right places.
For Bob, who gave me the title for number four.

Acknowledgements

Four Play wouldn't exist without the help and encouragement of lots of people. Here are a few of them: Joanna Innes, Jane Bishop, Bob Spearman, Megan Beardsley, Sharon Politi, Kathy Powell, Joy Kamani, Jean Everett, Betsy Blackburn, Kathy Miller, Louise Sobin, Traylor Rucker, Barbara Tucker, Teddy Stockwell, Karen Phillips, Anne Saunders, Linda Lovely, Ellis Vidler, Polly Iyer, and my friends at Sisters in Crime. And most all, thanks to John Blackburn, my husband, my techno-geek expert, my partner in crime, my hero.

Chapter 1

"It's been five months, Jessie. Let's just do it."

I knew exactly what Wilson wanted us to "just do," but asked anyway. "Do what?"

"You know what. Let's get married and get it over with."

I blinked twice. "That is not the most romantic of proposals, Mr. Rye."

"We already did romance. Five months ago." He reached over and tapped my engagement ring. "You forgetting Hawaii?"

Well, no.

I glanced down at the diamond Wilson had given me that night—on the beach, under a full moon, Christmas Eve. And yes, in Hawaii.

"The whole nine yards of romance," he muttered impatiently. "Some women would even call this romantic." He waved at the scenery, and I tore my eyes away from my ring.

Okay, so the man did have a point. Lake Lookadoo was indeed lovely. And if you're into the rustic-rural thing, Wilson's lakefront shack would charm your hiking boots off.

But I'm not into rustic, or rural. Yes, I might enjoy the occasional glass of champagne on his screened-in porch, but I am far less enamored with the supposed house that porch is attached to. Evidently the person who built the place sixty years ago considered indoor plumbing a passing fad. And the furniture? Let's just say the Adirondack chairs we were presently utilizing were the crowning glory of the décor.

"Lake Lookadoo is romantic as hell." Wilson glanced down at his cats. "Right guys?" he asked, and Bernice and Wally stopped supervising the ducks a few yards away to look at me.

I rolled my eyes and dutifully agreed Lake Lookadoo is romantic as hell.

"So, what do you say, Jessie? Let's set a date for our wedding."

I promised we would set a date.

"Soon," he said.

"Soon," I mumbled and went back to watching the ducks.

***

"It's been five months, Miss Jessie."

"Oh?" I looked up from the phone and cringed at my cat. "Frankie Smythe," I mouthed, and Snowflake's whiskers twitched.

"Don't you remember?" Frankie was asking. "It was right after I got my license. You said I could borrow it for a special occasion."

"Oh?" I tried again.

"Miss Jessie!" He emitted an exasperated sigh, and I confessed that I did remember.

I mean, how could I forget? My young friend and former neighbor had been begging to get behind the wheel of my Porsche since he graduated from kindergarten. So when Frankie finally got his driver's license, I lost my head and agreed to let him drive my car. This complete lapse of good judgment happened right after I got engaged, when I was feeling rather elated with life. That will teach me.

At least I had demonstrated a little common sense. I insisted Frankie would need a very special occasion to drive the Porsche and somehow assumed his wedding day would be that occasion. Considering the child is only sixteen, I thought my car would be safe for years. Maybe even decades.

But apparently Frankie had a different understanding of very special. And apparently taking his girlfriend Lizzie to the Junior Prom qualified.

"What do you say?" he asked again. "Can I use your car?"

I closed my eyes and prayed for strength, and whispered a barely audible "Yes."

"Yes!"

Frankie held his hand to the phone, but I could still hear him proclaim the good news to what had to be the entire junior class of Clarence High School. "The Porsche, the Porsche!" he yelled. "I've got Miss Jessie's Carrera for the Cotillion!"

Eventually he remembered me. He thanked me a few hundred times, and much to my dismay, made arrangements to pick up my car the following day.

"I'll be careful," he promised. "I'll drive real slow and park way in the back of the lot. No dents, no scratches, no nothing."

I told Frankie I had the utmost confidence in his driving skills and hung up. Then I rushed over to my file of important papers and double checked that my car insurance was paid up and current.

***

Kirby timed it perfectly. "When's the wedding?" he asked just as I took aim at the four ball, and of course I missed the shot.

"Sorry," he said.

"Yeah, right." I made sure he saw my smile and pointed him to the stripes. Then I stepped back to contemplate the situation.

Okay, so the situation was dire—I was about to lose a game of eight ball to Kirby. That's Kirby Cox. The worst pool player at The Stone Fountain, and likely the worst pool player in all of Clarence, North Carolina.

Camille came up from behind me. "Your game is pitiful," she said, and I thanked her for noticing.

At least Gus offered a little sympathy. He put an arm around my shoulder and insisted Kirby had practically cheated. "Everyone knows not to mention your wedding."

Actually, everyone knew just the opposite. All my buddies knew the sure way to throw me off and beat me at the pool table was to mention my engagement.

Kirby knew, and the eight ball fell.

I winked at Gus and stepped forward to congratulate the victor.

***

"That was kind of sad," my best friend Candy told me.

"It was pathetic." My other best friend Karen was a bit more blunt. "You lose all the time lately."

"Well, I have an excuse tonight." I plopped myself down on my favorite bar stool. "I'm distracted."

Candy offered a knowing nod. "By Wilson."

"No. By Frankie. He has my Porsche."

My friends exchanged another knowing nod. "By Wilson," they said in unison.

I gave up and waved to Charlie. "Champagne?" I asked, and bless his heart, the bartender made an effort to help. He came over, bottle in hand.

Considering my mood, you might find this odd. But champagne became my beverage of choice a year earlier when my divorce became final. Trust me, every day without my ex-husband is a day worth celebrating. Even days when my game is off.

"Matthew and Gina have been talking about you," Charlie said as he handed me a glass. He tilted his head towards the proprietors of The Stone Fountain, who were busy at the other end of the bar. "They're worried about you."

"No one needs to worry," I said, but Charlie had already wandered off.

I sipped my champagne and watched Matthew Stone load his wife's serving tray with a round of drinks.

"Gina, I would expect." Karen was also watching the Stones. "But it's got to be bad when Matthew starts worrying."

"No one needs to worry," I tried again.

"They're right to worry," Candy said. "Jessie's lost more games this week than in the entire time we've known her."

I groaned out loud. "Can we change the subject, please?"

"Good idea. Let's talk about your writing." She glanced around me and spoke to Karen. "She's starting to call it 'the dreaded W-word.'"

"Writing?" Karen asked.

"The dreaded W-word." I curled my lip.

"Come on, girlfriend. You love your job. What about the Romance Writers Hall of Fame?"

"That's what's so surprising." Candy tapped me with a hot-pink fingernail. "Their most recent inductee can't write anymore. Jessie—I mean, Adelé Nightingale—hasn't written a decent sex scene in weeks!"

"What!?" Karen stared at me aghast. "No sex?"

I rolled my eyes and reminded my friend she had never actually read one of my books. "And even if you had, there's no need to worry."

"Are you kidding? Everyone knows that you, or Adelé Nightingale, or whoever you want to call yourself, write the world's best sex scenes."

"And plenty of them," Candy said. "But so far *A Singular Seduction* has no sex scenes whatsoever. Zero!" She snapped her fingers. "Zip!"

"Zero?" Karen gasped. "Zip?"

I again rolled my eyes. "Perhaps Adelé Nightingale is in a slight slump," I said. "But I have suffered from plot plight before, you know?"

"This isn't any old plot plight," Candy said. "This is sex scenes."

"A sex-scene slump and a pool-playing slump." Karen shook her head. "Oh boy."

"We all know what the real problem is," Candy said.

"Okay, here we go!" I threw my hands in the air. "Have at it, ladies. Knock yourselves out."

And so they did. Yadda, yadda, yadda. Veritably channeling Wilson Rye himself, my friends enlightened me as to my real problem.

"Wedding," Candy said. "That's the real dreaded W-word."

"Or Wilson," Karen added. "Another W-word."

"Wilson's wedding." Candy again. "You're stalling, Jessie."

"I am not stalling."

"But you keep saying you're waiting for spring."

"I am waiting for spring."

"It's May!" That was Karen.

"Well then, I'm waiting for summer."

"You're stalling, girlfriend."

"Oh, and you're one to talk. You've never even been married."

Karen shrugged. "So what's your point?"

"And you." I faced Candy. "You've been engaged so many times we've lost track."

Candy shrugged. "So what's your point?"

I scowled and tried to remember the point.

Karen patted my knee. "Cheer up, Jess. Once you marry Wilson all your slumps will disappear. The whole town is waiting for this wedding."

A fact that didn't exactly cheer me up, but she was right. Like it or not, Wilson and I were local celebrities. Wilson, because he's a prominent cop. And me, because of my writing career.

Several of Adelé Nightingale's most recent masterpieces had become bestsellers, and Jimmy Beak, our local TV station's star reporter, had a thing against romance fiction. Or at least he had a thing against me. He made a point of denouncing me and my career at every opportunity.

On a more flattering note, and our local newspaper had recently run a piece about my induction into the Romance Writers Hall of Fame. To add to the human-interest angle, the *Clarence Courier* had emphasized my engagement—my own "personal romance."

"People I don't even know stop me on the street to ask about the wedding," I said.

"There now, you see?" Candy asked. "Everyone wants you to get married. And soon."

"You're not getting any younger," Karen added helpfully.

I folded my arms and glared. "I'm over fifty, so therefore I should rush into things?"

"Rush?" they said.

"What is the rush, anyway? Wilson's after me twenty-four-seven, and now you two."

"I think it's sweet he's in such a hurry," Candy persisted. "His little cottage sounds so romantic."

Okay, so I may have snorted. "It's a shack. It's anything but romantic."

"It sounds pretty nice to me," Karen said.

"Shack," I repeated. "You should see the supposed décor. And don't even get me started on the plumbing."

"Come on, Jess. You don't have to pee in the woods, do you?"

I whimpered slightly and admitted there was an actual toilet. And upon further inquiries, also had to agree the hot water worked. "Nearly half the time!"

"There now, you see?" Candy said.

***

My friends were busy discussing Wilson Rye's plumbing when my cell phone rang. I glanced down at the number. Speaking of the devil.

"Where are you?" he greeted me, and I told him.

"You know where your car is?" he asked.

"An old friend borrowed it. Well actually, Frankie Smythe isn't old at all," I corrected myself. "I've just known him his entire lif—"

"Where's this Smythe character right now?" he asked.

I blinked twice. Why was my beau the cop—make that, my fiancé the cop—questioning me about Frankie? Or my car?

"Where are you?" I said. "And where's the Porsche? Don't tell me he's totaled it? Is Frankie okay? What about Lizzie? Oh, my Lord, Wilson! What's happened?"

"I have no idea what happened to Frankie, but your car looks fine."

I breathed a sigh of relief as he continued, "It's the dead lady on top of it I'm a little concerned about."

Chapter 2

"What is it with you Hewitts and dead bodies?" Karen asked as she drove us out to the high school. "You guys are like corpse magnets."

"It's weird," Candy said from the back seat.

Unfortunately, I had to agree. The previous summer Stanley Sweetzer, one of Candy's many fiancés, had seen fit to die on my couch. And then at Christmas a bartender named Davy Atwell dropped dead in my mother's vacation bungalow. In Hawaii of all places. And now this—a corpse on my car.

I mumbled something about yet another murder as Karen downshifted for a red light.

"We don't know it was murder," she said.

"Excuse me? Wilson is there."

She cringed. "Oh that."

"Wilson Rye, the homicide guy," Candy said.

The light turned green, and as Karen took off, I warned my friends the homicide guy would not be pleased to see us.

"In fact." I cleared my throat. "He might have ordered me to stay away."

Karen gave me a sideways glance. "Might have?"

***

As Wilson would say, everyone and his brother was at the high school when we arrived.

Karen tried to nonchalantly maneuver her van around the police barricade and into the parking lot, but a uniformed cop jumped in front of her and she was forced to stop.

Luckily I recognized Officer Leary.

I rolled down the window and re-introduced myself. "Jessie Hewitt—Captain Rye's fiancée?" I stuck my hand out the window for a nice friendly shake. "Remember me, Jenna?"

She frowned at my extended hand. "Captain Rye said you'd pull something like this."

"Pull somethi—?" I recoiled my hand and regrouped. "Well, that is excellent!" I lied. "Then you already know the car in question is mine." I gestured toward the flashing lights at the far end of the parking lot. "I'm needed out there."

If possible, Officer Leary's frown got frownier. She held her ground and told me she was not about to let me anywhere near the place. "Captain's orders."

I remained calm and pointed to the hundreds of vehicles, and people, already in the lot. The place was swarming with an unlikely combination of cops, emergency personnel, and teenagers dressed to the nines.

"Everyone and his brother is in that parking lot," I said, but Officer Leary wouldn't budge.

I was gearing up for further argument when Karen started backing away.

I waved a few fingers at the cop. "Nice seeing you again, Jenna," I chirped and closed the window. I lost the fake smile. "Okay, now what?"

"You're forgetting, girlfriend." Karen shifted into drive. "Both Kiddo and I went to this school."

"Faculty parking," Candy suggested.

"On it." Karen rounded the corner and found a spot in the empty lot out back. Another car pulled in behind us, and we all climbed out of our vehicles about the same time.

"There's strength in numbers," I said, and would have led the way, but the middle-aged woman from the other car beat me to it. She stormed off at something akin to a gallop as the guy who had driven her struggled to catch up.

My friends and I did the same, but unfortunately we ran into another barricade. And another cop—a rather large specimen I was not familiar with.

Before I even had time to think of a strategy, the woman leading our pack commenced scolding the cop. "I am in charge here," she announced. "I am Superintendent Gabriella Yates."

Ah, yes. I knew she looked familiar. Dr. Yates was more of a local celebrity than Wilson and I combined. Our school superintendent made headlines in the newspaper at least once a week as she endeavored to resolve the many and varied controversies the school board managed to get into. The most memorable of those controversies, at least for me, was when Dr. Yates had gotten her nose broken in the line of duty. The Clarence School Board meetings are, shall we say, rather heated gatherings?

I recollected the elementary school desk debacle and studied the superintendent's nose. It looked as good as new.

"I am responsible for this campus," Dr. Yates continued scolding the cop. She pointed to the barricade. "Kindly remove this obstacle."

"But the Captain said."

"Captain-Schmaptain! I am not accustomed to waiting." She turned on her heel and gestured toward the portly guy who had driven her. "Gordon!" she commanded, and the man hopped to attention.

He heaved the barricade aside, and Superintendent Gabriella Yates took off. "Gordon!" she called back, and said Gordon jogged into position beside her.

Candy Poppe was on it. "We're the superintendent's secretaries," she told the stupefied cop. "We're here to take notes." She grabbed Karen and me by the elbows, and we slipped around the barricade, close on the heels of Superintendent Yates.

"I will burn in hell before I let that asinine Jimmy Beak get to the scene before me," the superintendent told Gordon, and I stopped dead in my tracks.

"Beak?" I squeaked.

***

"The car!" Jimmy Beak screamed. Oh yes. Channel 15's finest was smack dab in the thick of things. "Get footage of her car!" he ordered his cameraman.

The good news? The vast majority of the car Jimmy was so keen on was covered by a tarp, and the body was nowhere in sight.

The bad news? My rear license plate was clearly visible. Especially since one of Jimmy's minions was pointing a high-wattage spotlight at it while the cameraman filmed.

Jimmy pointed at my vanity plate. "Adelé!" he screamed. "That's Add-a-lay!" He emphasized the pronunciation. "This is Jessica Hewitt's car." Some flapping of unnaturally long arms. "The borderline pornographer is involved in yet another murder!"

I squeaked again, and Wilson, who swears he doesn't believe in intuition, caught my eye. He offered me a quick cop-like look and turned away to deal with Superintendent Yates. While she barked questions at him from one angle, Jimmy Beak stood at his other side, microphone in hand.

"We're out of here," Karen said.

Candy yanked my arm, and we beat a hasty retreat. We sprinted past the cop from earlier, cleared that pesky barricade in what must have looked like a choreographed leap, and made a beeline for Karen's van.

***

"Do you think he saw us?" Candy asked.

I strained my neck to look, but was propelled backward as Karen stepped on the gas.

She checked the rear view mirror. "He's not following," she said. "No Channel 15 vans."

"Thank God," the three of us said in unison.

Trust me, my friends and I are seldom so easily intimidated. But this was Jimmy Beak. The man who had delighted in accusing me, and then Candy, of cold-blooded murder during the Stanley Sweetzer murder investigation. He'd given poor Karen a hard time, too. She was guilty simply for associating with me.

"Did you guys hear him?" Candy was asking. "Add-a-lay! Add-a-lay!"

"I'm beginning to rue the day I thought of that pen name."

Karen stopped at a red light. "It does describe your books, Jess."

"But Jimmy doesn't have to harp on it. And I am not a borderline pornographer. No matter how often he claims otherwise."

This, too, went back to the Stanley Sweetzer fiasco. Borderline pornographer this, borderline pornographer that.

Jimmy loved insulting me. And he had resurrected his borderline pornographer routine when I was asked to judge a writing contest for local teenagers.

"He got me fired from the Focus on Fiction contest last month," I reminded my friends. "He claimed I was morally unfit to judge teenagers. Morally unfit," I sputtered. "I've been boycotting Channel 15 ever since."

Karen glanced in her rear view mirror. "Should we tell her?"

"Tell me what?"

"Umm, Jimmy has kind of been talking about you again," Candy said. "He's been calling the Romance Writers Hall of Fame, the Hall of Shame. Do you get it?"

I looked at Karen.

"Every night for a week now," she said.

"Why have I not been informed of this?"

Karen told me not to blame the messengers, and Candy reminded me I was boycotting Channel 15. "We figured you didn't want to know."

"Maybe," I said. "But now he's found some brand new fodder to torment me with." I stared out the window. "Let's hope Superintendent Yates will distract him this time."

"Yikes," Karen said.

"She does seem rather scary."

"No, Jess. Yikes is her nickname."

"Jimmy calls her Superintendent Yikes," Candy said. "You get it? Yates-Yikes?"

I squinted at the street lamps as Karen turned onto Sullivan Street and headed for home. "The *Clarence Courier* doesn't call her Yikes."

"The newspaper has some class," Candy said.

We were assessing Jimmy Beak's complete lack of class when my cell phone rang.

"Wilson's gonna kill you," Karen said.

And yes, she did know who it was. It's uncanny, but I swear my cell phone takes on a particularly angry ring tone whenever Wilson has something to kill me over. Let's just say, it's happened before.

***

"What the hell were you doing?" he asked me. "Didn't I tell you to stay away?"

"It's my car," I said. "And you know I don't follow orders very well."

He sputtered something I didn't quite catch and commenced scolding me for butting in where I wasn't needed.

Yadda, yadda, yadda. I let him get it out of his system and interrupted only when he insisted I shouldn't have brought my friends along. "Earth to Captain Rye," I said. "I don't have my car. Karen had to drive."

He went back to sputtering incoherently.

"We're home now anyway," I told him as Karen turned into our parking lot. "We left the school the second we saw Jimmy. Why didn't you tell me he's been defaming my character again? Hall of Shame, my foot."

"Believe it or not, I don't give a damn about Beak's opinion of you." Wilson paused. "Neither do you, right?"

"Right." I climbed out on the van. "Was it really murder, Wilson? How? Why? Who was she?"

"Name's Miriam Jilton. She was an English teacher—one of the chaperones for the Junior Prom. Strangled. Keep that to yourself, please."

"On the top of my car?" I asked as my friends and I entered our lobby.

Wilson told me the victim had likely been killed closer to the school itself, but was carried to my car.

"Why?" I asked.

"That's the million-dollar question."

We dropped Karen off at her door. She whispered goodnight, and Candy and I started climbing the stairs.

"Another million-dollar question," Wilson continued. "Concerns your friend Mr. Smythe. What was his role in this?"

"I'm sure Frankie had nothing to do with it."

"How do you know that? How do you even know this kid?"

I waved Candy goodbye at the second floor. She blew me a kiss, and I headed back to the stairs. "He was my neighbor on Maple Street. Back when I was married to Ian."

Wilson harrumphed.

"I assume you've talked to Frankie?" I asked. "And Lizzie? She's his date."

"No. And no. I've got three hundred kids swarming around out here, and none of them is Frankie. Or his girlfriend. What possessed you to give him your car?"

"I didn't give him my car. I merely loaned it to him for a special occasion."

Another harrumph.

"I've known Frankie since the day he was born, Wilson. He's a responsible person."

"Well then, where is he?"

Okay, good question.

"I can go look for him," I said as I reached the top floor. "I could borrow Karen's van."

Needless to say, Wilson told me to stay put. "Call me if this Smythe character shows up on your doorstep."

I said goodbye to a dial tone and opened my door.

To my credit I blinked only twice before returning to my cell phone.

Wilson answered after half a ring. "Let me guess."

Chapter 3

"He's not on my doorstep," I said. "He's on my couch."

But not for long. Frankie sprang up and was hovering over me before Wilson could utter even one four-letter word.

Hindered by her strapless gown and four-inch heels, the girl on my couch took a little longer to get to her feet. Lizzie, I assumed. I watched her totter over, and was trying to remember where I had seen her before, when Wilson started asking questions.

At least I could answer the first one. "No, they did not break into my condo. Frankie had a set of my keys. They must have let themselves in?"

I glanced at the teenagers for verification, and they nodded a few hundred times.

With Wilson bombarding me with questions from his end of the phone, and Frankie and Lizzie bombarding me with more questions and even a few answers, it got a bit confusing. At some point I grew tired of being the middleman and suggested I hand the phone over to the teenagers.

"No!" Wilson said in no uncertain terms. "I want their parents present and a court-appointed social worker. Detain them while I round up the troops."

Detain them?

I frowned at the six-foot-two Frankie Smythe, who kept apologizing for ruining my car, and at his much shorter girlfriend Lizzie, who continued to explain that, like, this whole thing was, like, nothing she ever expected to happen, like, in a million years!

Somehow I knew it was going to be a very long night.

***

"Tea," I said for the fifth or sixth time as Frankie repeated for the fifth or sixth time how he hoped I didn't mind they had let themselves in.

For the fifth or sixth time I assured him I did not mind and physically steered him and his girlfriend back to my couch. I pointed emphatically, and they finally sat back down.

That herculean task accomplished, I moved on to the tea preparations.

Frankie, meanwhile, moved on to the tangent of how he and Lizzie had expected me to be home when they arrived. And how they had waited for me to come back home so they could explain. And how he had expected me to be home. And how, since I wasn't, he wasn't sure what to do, and so that's why he let himself in, and he hoped I didn't mind, but they didn't know what else to do, and the taxi had already left, and so they decided to stay until I got home, and he really hoped I didn't mind.

Testimony to my infinite patience, I listened. And listened. At some point, I even managed to serve tea. I calmly sipped my beverage, hoping that my own serene aspect might rub off. Lo and behold, eventually Frankie did have to breathe.

He shut up, but that only gave Lizzie a chance to get rolling. "It's, like, all my fault, Ms. Hewitt. It was me who wanted to go out to the car in, like, the middle of the dance. We were in line to get our picture taken and I was, like, 'I lost my lipstick,' and, like, I thought maybe I dropped it in the car, and so Frankie was, like, 'Let's go look for it,' and so we went back to the car, and that's when we saw Ms. Jilton, and she was, like, dead."

I was relieved she put a period there, but before I could get a word in edgewise, Lizzie was, like, talking again.

"And then Frankie, like, panicked and started running away, and I was, like, trying to keep up but I couldn't go fast in these shoes." Lizzie picked up the corner of her red satin dress to display her ruby red stilettos. "But then Frankie noticed I wasn't keeping up, and he, like, stopped and by then we were three blocks from the school, and we tried to figure out what to do next. I was, like, 'Maybe we should go back to the school,' but Frankie was, like, panicking about your car. So, like, he called you, but you didn't answer!"

Lizzie stopped long enough to frown, and it occurred to me Frankie only had my land line number.

I got up to check my messages as she continued, “Frankie was, like, all afraid you’d be mad at him for wrecking your car, and I was, like, ‘Why don’t we go tell her what happened in person?’ But then we remembered we didn’t have a way to get here, since, like, we didn’t think it would be a good idea to take Ms. Jilton off your car and drive it.”

She looked at me for verification, and I agreed that yes, it probably was best they had not moved the body.

Lizzie continued, “So then Frankie was, like, ‘I have my father’s credit card tonight,’ so we called the cab company and, like, neither of us had ever called a taxi before, but, like, we figured it out, and then the cab came, and we got here, but you weren’t home!”

She stopped. But it took me a moment to realize she had finished and was expecting a response.

“Umm,” I said.

***

“Elizabeth!” Lizzie’s mother shouted from my doorway. She was the last of those troops Wilson had promised me to arrive. The last, but certainly not the least.

She propelled herself into my living room as Frankie’s parents, Greg and Laura Smythe, caught my eye. “Rita Sistina,” they told me as the newcomer bounded over my coffee table and landed in front of her daughter.

Lizzie was again having trouble standing up, but her mother paid no attention to the cut of that dress. She yanked her daughter to her feet as Lizzie desperately tried to keep her strapless gown in position. But the person who would have been interested in the peep show missed it. Indeed, Frankie had moved rather quickly out of Rita’s way and was headed for the door when Wilson blocked his path.

“Sit,” he ordered. “Everyone sit,” he said, and everyone scrambled to obey.

Everyone except the cat and I. We chose to stay out of the fray. Snowflake found a spot on top of the fridge to watch the musical chairs, and I escaped behind the kitchen counter.

Greg and Laura, both as thin as their son, settled themselves into one of my overlarge easy chairs. The social worker, whose name I never did catch, ended up in the other easy chair, and Wilson and his right-hand man Lieutenant Russell Densmore grabbed the two bar stools.

Rita Sistina took another yank at Lizzie's dress, and mother and daughter plopped onto my sofa, where Rita continued pulling and tugging at Lizzie. The girl tolerated what might have passed for a hug and stared forlornly at my front door.

Frankie was the last to sit. He shrugged at Wilson, perhaps implying there were no spots for him. Wilson pointed toward the couch, and Frankie frowned at the space remaining next to the older Ms. Sistina. The kid braced himself visibly and took a seat.

This distracted Rita from her interminable hug. She let go of her daughter to face Frankie. "What have you done to my daughter?" she demanded.

Wilson cleared his throat and insisted he would be the one asking questions. An argument ensued as Ms. Sistina pointed to Frankie and insisted she had a right to know what "this stupid goofball" thought he was doing.

"Goofball?" Greg Smythe said.

"Stupid?" Laura Smythe asked.

But Rita was only interested in the youngest Smythe. "Ms. Jilton is dead!" she said, and Frankie flinched. "Murdered!" More flinching. "On your car!"

"Actually, it was Miss Jessie's car," Frankie said quietly, and Rita re-directed her wrath.

"Your car!?" She glared in my direction. "What were you thinking!?"

Bless his heart, Wilson rescued me, and reminded everyone he was the one asking questions. No doubt Rita would have argued some more, but the social worker sided with Wilson. He explained the process—why the parents were there, and why he was there. "The police need to ask you some questions," he told the teenagers. "But no one is in trouble, okay?"

"Okay!?" Rita shrieked. "Then why is my daughter under arrest!?"

"Arrest!?" the teenagers shrieked.

"No one is under arrest." Wilson did not shriek, but his voice was loud and firm. He looked directly at Rita. "No one," he repeated, and the woman positively glowered.

"My daughter intended to go to law school," she hissed. "But this!" She waved a hand in Frankie's face and raised her voice considerably. "This boy and his shenanigans have ruined Elizabeth's chances for a career in the law. What's she going to do now, Captain Rye? Answer me that!"

I do believe my beau the cop—make that my fiancé the cop—was at a loss for words. But Lieutenant Densmore helped him out. "Your daughter can still go to law school," he said, all calm and rational. "She's not under arrest, Ms. Sistina. At this point she's not even under suspicion."

"Suspicion!" Rita grabbed her daughter's hand. "Your father will hear about this. Sistinas do not tolerate police brutality."

Wilson rolled his eyes and turned to me.

"May I get you an Advil?" I asked him, and several hands shot up.

***

I chalked it up to decades of dealing with hardened criminals, but by the time I found the Advil, Wilson had actually managed to move the interview along. He and Lieutenant Densmore, with the occasional clarification from the social worker, asked questions, Frankie and Lizzie answered, Laura and Greg Smythe popped pain relievers, and Rita Sistina interrupted. A lot.

Even so, Wilson got the basic story out of the kids. And they had made it all the way to the critical juncture when Frankie had started running away from my car before Rita was back at it.

"You ran away?" she screamed. "How stupid can you be!?"

Laura Smythe shot forward in her seat. "If you call my son stupid one more time."

"He is stupid!"

"No one is stupid," Wilson said. "The kids were in shock, Ms. Sistina. Running away might not have been the best idea—" Laura made as if to argue, but he held a hand up to stop her, "—but many adults would have done the same."

"At least they didn't tamper with the crime scene," Lieutenant Densmore said. "They could have done a lot worse. Isn't that right, Captain?"

Wilson agreed, but the wrath of Rita sent Frankie back into apologizing mode.

He looked at me and recommenced a litany of regrets—apologizing for borrowing the Porsche, for driving the Porsche, for parking the Porsche, for ruining the Porsche, et cetera, et cetera.

I whimpered only slightly, and in my most soothing voice, asked him to please stop apologizing.

"Why are you apologizing to her?" Rita's voice was anything but soothing. "It's my daughter's life you've ruined. Elizabeth planned on going to law school!"

"I think you mentioned that," Greg Smythe mumbled.

"There's no reason Lizzie can't go to law school," Wilson said.

"Elizabeth," Rita corrected.

"Lizzie," Lizzie corrected.

"Elizabeth!" Rita repeated.

"Lizzie," Lizzie said.

"Eliza—"

"Stop!" Wilson ordered, and everyone froze. Everyone but Rita, that is. She sputtered out something about police brutality.

Wilson ignored her and returned to the kids. "Tell me about Ms. Jilton."

Frankie and Lizzie leaned forward to get a glance of each other around Rita, shrugged in unison, and sat back.

Frankie looked at Wilson. "She was a teacher."

"Like, our English teacher," Lizzie said.

Wilson took a deep breath. "What else?"

"Huh?" the kids asked.

The social worker helped out. "Elizabeth and Frankie," he said and waited until they both looked at him. "As Captain Rye has already explained, Ms. Jilton was murdered. Do either of you know anything that could help him?"

"Like, about Ms. Jilton?" Lizzie seemed truly perplexed at the notion.

"She was our English teacher," Frankie said.

"What about tonight?" Wilson asked. "Was there anything unusual going on?"

"The dance," Lizzie said helpfully.

Wilson tried again. "Was Ms. Jilton acting strange tonight?"

"She was a teacher," Frankie said as if that clarified everything.

Poor Wilson gave up and spoke to Russell Densmore. "Verify the time they left the dance. And talk to the cab driver." The lieutenant nodded, and Wilson returned to the teenagers. "You two understand why?"

They nodded mutely.

"You should have called 911," he told them.

They hung their heads, and I remembered how hard it was to be sixteen.

***

Wilson endured one more remark about police brutality from you know who before declaring that the interview was over. Everyone seemed more than ready to leave, except for you know who.

Rita sprang up and blocked Frankie's path. "You are not to see my daughter again," she spat. "Elizabeth has a future. But you! You stupid idiot!"

"I told you not to call my son stupid." Mama-Bear Smythe elbowed her son out of the way to block Rita, and I do believe the fists would have flown if Lizzie hadn't intervened. She finally figured out how to stand up without losing half her dress, and moved quite swiftly to get between her mother and Frankie's.

"Moooom," she said. "Like, please stop."

"Stop!? Your future is at stake Elizabeth Maria Sistina. I will not stop!"

"Well then, we need to leave," Lizzie said, and the rest of us stared aghast. Had the child had actually uttered an entire sentence without one single like?

While we adults recovered from the shock, Lizzie propelled her mother out the door. Making sure to block Rita's re-entry, she turned in the doorway. "Sorry," she said. Her eyes met Frankie's, and she closed the door.

Laura and Greg waited until the elevator dinged in the hallway before beckoning to their son. Frankie followed them toward the door, but remembered something, and stopped.

"Sorry," he told me, and I made every effort not to groan.

The social worker exhibited a bit less self restraint. As the door closed behind Frankie he emitted a prolonged sigh, requested an Advil for the road, and rushed off to catch the elevator with the Smythes.

"Jimmy Beak, Superintendent Yates, and Rita Sistina." Russell looked at his boss. "Why am I thinking the murder is the least of our problems?" He didn't wait for an answer but headed for the exit. "I'll meet you at the station?" he asked.

"Soon," Wilson said, but then he caught a glimpse of me. "Sooner or later," he corrected himself.

Chapter 4

"I have some questions," I said the moment the door closed.

"What a surprise." Wilson pulled the bar stools back to the kitchen counter and took a seat. Snowflake jumped into his lap.

"Let's start with Lizzie," I said. "I know that girl from somewhere."

"Peter Harrison."

"Ah, yes." I nodded as I started the tea kettle. Lizzie was one of Peter's piano students. My elderly neighbor, who lives across the hall from Karen, gives lessons in his condo. "I must have seen her in the lobby."

"Yep," Wilson said. "And Rita knew exactly where to come tonight. Lucky me."

I thought about Rita's winning personality. "I assume she's divorced?"

"Oh, yeah." Wilson informed me the Sistinas had been in court the previous year, about the same time as Ian and I were. "Their divorce was even uglier than yours."

"Hard to fathom," I said. "Was there a custody battle?"

"An ugly one."

I asked how Wilson knew that, and he told me Ray Sistina is a prominent lawyer.

"Lots of cops knew Ray from criminal court," he said. "So the divorce got discussed."

"I thought he must be a lawyer," I said.

"So you caught the threats about police brutality? Rita might want Ray's help now, but during the divorce she accused him of being crooked."

I poured the tea. "Is he crooked?"

"Not when he worked in Clarence. He was a partner in Tony DeSousa's law firm."

"He's good then," I told Snowflake. Unfortunately, I knew from personal experience Tony DeSousa was the best criminal defense lawyer in Clarence.

"Sistina practices in Atlanta now," Wilson was saying. "He left town after the divorce."

I sipped my tea and studied my cat. Wilson studied me.

"Do not start thinking," he ordered. "Ray Sistina had nothing to do with this murder."

"But if he's a criminal defense lawyer?" I said. "And Lizzie found the body?" I wiggled my fingers. "Connections?"

Wilson gave me one of his stern cop-like looks.

I moved on to Frankie and Lizzie. "Please tell me you don't suspect them."

"I don't suspect them," he said, but continued with the stern stare. "This stays between you and me?"

"Absolutely."

"In particular, the kids' names stay out of the media. And how Jilton was killed."

"Absolutely," I repeated. Believe it or not, I do know how keep a secret. Especially secrets involving Wilson's work. And keeping the method of murder a secret was almost always part of his strategy. If only the murderer and the cops knew the details, the culprit might slip and say something incriminating.

"You'll be happy to know Lizzie isn't tall enough to have done this," he told me. "Jilton was as tall as you, Jessie."

I winced. "Lizzie couldn't have reached her neck?"

"Your friend Smythe could have."

"Wilson!"

"Relax," he said. "That kid doesn't seem capable of swatting a fly, much less killing a teacher."

I agreed that Frankie is a very sweet boy. "But he wasn't very helpful, was he? He didn't know anything about his teacher."

"You noticed? And he's not the only one. I questioned everyone at that dance. All the kids are clueless."

I asked who had called 911.

"The other chaperone. The gym teacher realized Jilton was missing and went looking for her."

"In the parking lot?"

"She went out to take a phone call." He looked up. "And that's where things get interesting."

"Let me guess. Her phone's missing."

"Yep. And that's not the only thing that's interesting." He reminded me, quite unnecessarily, that my car was interesting also.

"The million-dollar question." I frowned. "Have you figured out why she was left on my car?"

"How about your license plate? We assume the victim was having an affair, and the killer was making a statement."

"Okay, so here's my million-dollar question." I got up to clear the tea cups. "You somehow managed to hide the body and my car from Jimmy Beak and his cameraman. But not my license plate? Why, oh why, didn't you cover that up?"

"You realize you just answered your own question."

I blinked twice. "You couldn't cover up my license plate, because it would look like you were covering up evidence. To protect me."

"Very good."

"And let me guess," I said. "Forensics now has my car."

"You'll be without wheels for a while."

I sighed dramatically, but Wilson told me to look on the bright side. "No distractions, right? You can stay home and concentrate on *Singular Sensation*."

"*Seduction*," I corrected. "I suppose it will give me an excuse to hide at home when Jimmy Beak starts accusing me of murder." I hesitated. "Again."

"He won't accuse you of murder."

"Come on, Wilson. You know the history. The man has it in for me."

"I had a little talk with Beak before I came over here."

"Oh?"

"I threatened him with a libel suit."

"Wilson!"

"Actually, I threatened him with you. I said you'd sue him, and Channel 15, if he accused you of murder again."

"You didn't?"

"We can't hide the fact your car played a role in this. But you sure didn't."

I smiled at the baby blues. "Have I mentioned I love you?" I asked, and he grinned.

"But we should call Beak's boss." Wilson took his cell phone out and looked up a number. "Name is Cal Ransom. He owns Channel 15."

He turned his phone to face me and pointed to my land line. "This threat needs to come from you. And you have to mean it, Jessie. Would you be willing to sue if Beak accused you of murder again?"

I thought about Jimmy's various and sundry denunciations of yours truly—the Stanley Sweetzer fiasco, the Focus on Fiction fiasco, the Romance Writers Hall of Fame-slash-Shame nonsense—

I picked up my phone.

"Be a little scary," Wilson said as I tapped in the number.

"No." I pictured Jimmy hyperventilating over my license plate. "I'll be a lot scary."

***

"Hello?" Presumably Cal Ransom answered, and presumably I had woken him. "I swear, Beak. If that's you again, you're fired."

"It's Jessica Hewitt," I said, and Mr. Ransom dropped his phone.

At least that's what it sounded like. I waited while he rustled around grumbling a few vague obscenities.

Seemingly recovered, he cleared his throat. "What can I do for you, Ms. Hewitt?"

I glared at Wilson to get into the proper spirit. "You can make sure that stupid reporter of yours doesn't accuse me of murder," I said.

"Reporter?"

"Jimmy Beak," I snapped. Go figure, but being scary was surprisingly easy. Especially when dealing with the person who paid Jimmy a salary to be Jimmy. "If I hear so much as one mention that I was the cause of Miriam Jilton's death, I will sue him, Channel 15, and you. Is that clear, Mr. Ransom?"

He hesitated. "Umm, did you kill Miriam Jilton?"

"No!" I said, and I do believe he dropped his phone again.

"Beak knows the deal," he said when he recovered.

"What deal?"

"Beak knows accusing you of murder is off limits."

"And what will happen if he forgets?" I asked.

"I'll fire him. And you'll sue me."

"Count on it," I said and hung up without further ado.

Snowflake purred, and Wilson grinned.

I shrugged modestly. "I can be a little scary when I want to be."

He grinned some more. "No joke."

Chapter 5

I broke my own self-imposed boycott. The next morning I subjected myself to the Weekly Wrap Up, Channel 15's "award-winning" Sunday morning news program. No big surprise, Jimmy Beak's report on the murder was the top story.

First we were treated to a few choice scenes from the high school parking lot, where my Porsche, or more specifically, my license plate, figured prominently. Eventually even Jimmy grew weary of screaming my pen name. He moved on to the arrival of Superintendent Yates and the verbal assault she had seen fit to give Wilson. Ever-helpful, Jimmy had held the microphone to her lips to capture every word.

"Miriam Jilton was a fine educator," Dr. Yates said. "She deserves justice!"

"Justice!" Jimmy repeated.

The superintendent jabbed Jimmy in the ribs and stepped closer to Wilson. "The exemplary students of this fine school deserve justice also," she said. "I insist you get to the bottom of this murder! ASAP!"

"Does she really think Wilson isn't going to get to the bottom of this?" I asked Snowflake.

The two of us were sitting at the foot of the bed. While I watched my seriously-outdated twelve-inch TV, Snowflake conducted her morning toilette. She was cleaning her left front paw when the program cut to the Channel 15 studio.

"You heard the superintendent," Jimmy told the anchorwoman. "Dr. Yikes will not rest until this culprit is caught! And I know who the culprit is!"

"Don't say it, Jimmy," I told the screen as someone behind the cameras yelled, "Cut! Cut to commercial!"

"My threat worked," I said as Snowflake switched to her right paw. "Jimmy is not allowed to accuse me of murder."

Indeed not. When the Weekly Wrap Up returned, it was obvious, at least to me, that he had been scolded during the commercial break. The man was visibly pouting.

"Channel 15 has learned from reliable sources that Jessica Hewitt, the borderline pornographer with the Add-a-lay license plate, is not a murderer," he said. He was rolling his eyes and looking generally skeptical when I turned off the TV.

"There now, you see?" I asked the cat. She twitched her whiskers, and I had to agree Jimmy's report was still a bit less than flattering.

***

"Are you okay?" Karen asked when she called a few minutes later. "Did you watch the Weekly Wrap Up?"

"I did. I broke my boycott."

"Do you need some company, girlfriend?"

I thanked Karen for her concern but explained I was already expecting company. I looked at the kitchen clock. "Roslynn must be running late. She's coming over for a sex-scene session."

"Say what?"

"You know Roslynn, my fellow romance writer? She and I are going to brainstorm in the hopes of convincing Willow LaSwann and Kipp Jupiter to hop in a haystack together. Have I mentioned *A Singular Seduction* is a western?"

Karen skipped a beat. "Speaking of company, who were all those people I heard traipsing in and out of here last night?"

"Only everyone and his brother," I said. "Cops, social workers, parents, kids."

"Frankie?"

I asked Karen to please forget Frankie's name and told her only the barest basics about the murder. She understood the deal. Secrets are standard in Wilson's line of work.

"Don't worry," she said. "I don't remember Frankie's last name, even if you have told me. So who killed her, Jess?"

"As yet, we know nothing."

"We?" Karen asked.

"Okay. Wilson knows nothing."

"Jimmy Beak thinks he knows."

"The man is desperate to accuse me, correct?"

"I could just see it on the tip of his tongue," Karen said. "Jessica Hewitt! Murderer!"

"Won't happen," I sang.

"You sure about that? We're talking about Jimmy Beak."

I explained the reason for Jimmy's uncharacteristic caution, and Karen was duly impressed. In fact, she promised to testify on my behalf if I ever did end up suing.

Bless her heart, Candy was equally supportive. She called soon after I hung up with Karen, I filled her in on the latest, and she also assured me I wouldn't have to face Jimmy all alone in a courtroom.

"Or even on TV," she said. "Come down here at five and we'll watch the news together. I'll invite Karen, too."

"I'm not sure I want to see Jimmy on that wide-screen of yours."

"My TV is only fifty inches, I have champagne, and I'll ask Karen to bring Oreos."

Needless to say, I accepted Candy's kind invitation.

***

"Give me title, plot, and characters," Roslynn Mayweather demanded the moment I opened my door.

I blinked at her highly-glossed lips. "I have the title?"

"That was a question, not an answer." She brushed past me, the heels of her impeccably polished pumps clicking across my wood floors. She stopped, deposited her briefcase on the coffee table, and pivoted. "Since when does Adelé Nightingale have this much trouble writing a story?"

I walked over and shoved the laptop I was holding into her hands. "Since now," I said. "Read." I pointed her to the couch and went to fetch the coffee.

I had added milk to my cup, and was stirring the requisite two teaspoons of sugar into Roslynn's, when I glanced up. Ten-thirty on a warm Sunday morning and the woman was dressed to the nines—tailored skirt suit, Chanel scarf, sheer hose—the whole nine yards.

As for my own attire? Quite a few yards were missing. I was barefoot and clad in my standard writing uniform—a pair of cutoff jeans and one of Wilson's old dress shirts.

I braced myself and hazarded a glance at Roslynn's face. The woman was frowning, nay scowling, at my computer screen.

"What's in the briefcase?" I asked.

She leaned over and pulled out a large and dog-eared tome. "Look familiar?"

I groaned out loud as Roslynn displayed a copy of *Sensual and Scintillating: The Sex Scene Sourcebook for Today's Romance Writer* by Maxine Carlisle. *Sensual and Scintillating*, *S and S* for short, is the industry standard. A Sex Scenes 101, if you will. I keep my own dog-eared copy on my nightstand.

"I'm listed in the acknowledgements," I said, and Roslynn raised an unimpressed, if perfectly plucked, eyebrow.

I tried again. "Maxine quotes extensively from both *A Deluge of Desire* and *Windswept Whispers*. She couldn't have written *Sensual and Scintillating* without Adelé Nightingale's input."

Mumbling something about that was then and this is now, Roslynn placed the book on the coffee table. Snowflake sniffed the cover and promptly decided it was an ideal platform for napping.

"Did you see the Weekly Wrap Up?" I asked. Anything to avoid talking about sex scenes.

"It's why I'm late getting here." Roslynn spoke distractedly and kept reading from my computer. "I'm surprised Jimmy didn't accuse you."

"He wanted to, but I threatened to sue."

She looked up. "You did what?"

"I agree it's extreme, but it's working." I explained my threat of a lawsuit. "Jimmy won't dare blame me for murder this time."

"I guess not." Roslynn said. "But let's not worry about inconsequential nonsense."

"Murder is inconsequential nonsense?"

"Nooo. But Jimmy Beak certainly is. And we have other things to think about." She tapped my computer and reminded me she was still waiting for title, plot, and characters.

I picked up our coffee cups and stalwartly marched over to the couch.

"I actually do have two of the three," I said. "*A Singular Seduction*, starring Willow LaSwann and Kipp Jupiter." I nodded. "That's a good start, no?"

"Plot!" Roslynn demanded, and I jumped accordingly.

"That's kind of what's giving me trouble."

"Kind of?" she said and went back to reading and frowning.

Oh how the mighty have fallen, I thought to myself. Once upon a time Adelé Nightingale had been instrumental in launching Roslynn Mayweather's romance-writing career. I gave her a few editorial suggestions on her first novel *The Sultan's Secret* and introduced her to my literary agent Louise Urko.

And Louise, fondly known as Geez Louise in the publishing industry, had landed Roslynn her first book contract with Perpetual Pleasures Press—the most respected name in romance fiction.

But now? But today? Lord help me, I was the one seeking assistance. Geez Louise had demanded it. "Get help!" she ordered me over the phone. "Get Roslynn!" she had said. "And get some sex on the page! Sex, sex, sex!"

"Sex," I muttered forlornly, and Rosylnn looked up from the computer.

Her face softened considerably, and she assured me our brainstorming session would do wonders. "We'll get this plot rolling, Jessie. I promise."

"But I've lost my touch, Roslynn. No sex scenes. Zero." I snapped my fingers. "Zip."

"Zero?" She gasped. "Zip?"

"The problem is my premise," I said. "But I swear it's a good premise. Willow LaSwann is masquerading as a man."

"No!"

"Yes! As you can imagine, the situation is most harrowing. Willow even cut her hair! She wept as her lovely golden locks dropped to the floor, but what else could she do? She's impersonating a rancher."

Roslynn cringed at the horror of it.

"She's been wearing men's clothing for weeks," I explained. "And of course the poor girl has to bind herself up."

"Let me guess. To hide her figure?"

"Correct," I said. "Willow is endowed with a most womanly physique. But she's determined to keep her ranch, and she knows the law. Women are not allowed to own land in Wilcox County. Her dearly-departed Uncle Hazard knew the rules, too. When he left Willow his ranch, he made sure to identify her, not as his favorite niece, but as his nephew. Will!"

I threw my hands up. "So therein lies the problem."

"Huh?"

"Don't you see? The owner of the neighboring ranch, the ruggedly handsome Kipp Jupiter, doesn't know Willow's a woman. So how the heck do I write a sex scene into this mess?"

"How?" Roslynn shooed Snowflake from *Sensual and Scintillating* and began searching the index. "Adelé Nightingale doesn't write gay romance, correct?"

"Correct. Adelé has nothing against that genre, but I doubt she could pull it off. And it gets even trickier since Will-slash-Willow really is female. Kipp Jupiter would have to be bisexual if he were to seduce Will-slash-Willow in his—that's Kipp's—current state of ignorance." I shook my head. "And I doubt Adelé's fans would accept that."

I watched Roslynn rifle through her reference material. "I've searched in there a few hundred times," I told her and continued the saga. "Willow finds herself exceedingly attracted to Kipp. But if she reveals her true identity, she's afraid Kipp will report her to the sheriff and confiscate her land. Willow-slash-Will readily handles the duties on the ranch. But Kipp?" I shook my head. "She's losing sleep over him."

"Sooo?" I asked my guest. "Any ideas?"

Roslynn blinked twice. “Do you happen to have an Advil?”

Chapter 6

I located the Advil and hauled out my own copy of *S and S*. And Roslynn, Snowflake, and I were wracking our brains, trying to resolve Willow LaSwann's conundrum, when Wilson called.

I hadn't expected to hear from him that morning. "Shouldn't you be looking for the killer?" I asked.

"Where are you?"

"You called me on my land line, Wilson. I'm home. Roslynn came over for that brainstorming session I told you about."

"I guess it's fitting you're working on sex scenes."

"Not yet. We're still deciding how Kipp will learn Willow's true identity. We're thinking an accident. Willow will get gored by a bull, and Kipp will find her—who he thinks is a him—and somehow her-slash-his shirt will need to be removed to administer first aid. And voila! Breasts."

"Huh?"

I gave Roslynn a thumbs down and spoke to Wilson. "It's too bloody, isn't it?"

He took an audible breath. "Have you looked out your windows lately? Go check Sullivan Street."

"Why must every phone conversation we have fill me with dread?" I asked as I headed across the room.

Roslynn and Snowflake followed, and soon the three of us stood at the windows, staring at the scene below. Two police cars were parked in front of The Stone Fountain, and a crowd was gathering in the street. As more and more people congregated, traffic at the corner of Sullivan and Vine became heavier and heavier.

"What in the world? What's going on, Wilson?"

"I was hoping you'd tell me."

I leaned toward the window to get a better view. "Is that Alistair Pritt down there? What's he doing?"

"You mean, you actually know the guy? You recognize him?"

"I do. That's Alistair Amesworth Pritt." I explained Alistair owns a coffee shop in my old neighborhood. "And yes, I recognize him. He's a rather large, bald specimen, no?"

"I'll take your word for it. So his business is near your old house? Maybe that explains it."

"Explains what?"

"Does Ian know this guy?" he asked, and my sense of dread continued to grow. "Or maybe Amanda is friends with him," he added as my blood pressure hit the stratosphere.

Why was Wilson wondering about my low-down, no-good, cheating, and altogether despicable ex-husband Ian? Or his equally despicable new wife Amanda?

I handed Roslynn the phone and hunted around in the nearby desk for my binoculars. I lifted them to my eyes and spit out a string of four-letter words.

"What?" Rosylnn asked. She set the phone down next to Snowflake, and we wrestled each other for the binoculars until I noticed Wilson was still talking.

I gave up on the binoculars and returned to the phone.

"What?" I said irritably.

"Is it as bad as the dispatcher says?" he asked.

Roslynn stumbled backwards into the chair at my desk, and I rescued the binoculars as they slipped from her grasp.

"Yes," I said. "I do believe it is."

***

"Borderline Pornographer!" one poster read. "Ban Bad Books!" read another. "The Queen of Smut!" Alistair Pritt's poster even had a red arrow pointing upward, evidently at my condo and yours truly.

"Jessie!" Wilson said, perhaps for the second or third time. "Would you please tell me what's going on."

"I think it's a book-banning demonstration. I think it's against me."

"What?"

"Against me and my books. Apparently they're smut." I returned the binoculars to my eyes and quoted the most noxious placards for Wilson's edification.

He let the words sink in, and again asked if Ian knew Alistair. "Did he set him up to this?"

I was considering my ex when Roslynn started to stir. She reached for the binoculars, and we silently agreed to switch places.

"Jessie?" Wilson asked, and I told him Ian definitely knew Alistair.

"But Ian would never encourage something like this."

"Let me guess. His new wife the social-climber wouldn't allow it."

"As much as Amanda loves it when I get bad publicity, she hates it more if I get any attention whatsoever." I shrugged at Snowflake. "She called me about it just last week."

"What?" Wilson asked, and I noticed Roslynn was listening also.

I explained that the new Mrs. Crawcheck had scolded me about the Romance Writers Hall of Fame. "She claimed I got myself inducted just to destroy her social standing. I told her that was an extra perk I had not anticipated."

"You're sure she didn't mastermind what's going on down there?" Wilson asked, and I insisted Amanda didn't have the brains to mastermind anything.

I stood up next to Roslynn. "No," I said. "I think Alistair came up with this all on his own. He's always disapproved of my books."

"How do you know that? And don't say intuition."

"It's more than that. He refused to let me write in his shop."

"What?" Wilson asked.

"What?" Roslynn scowled.

I shrugged. "This was years ago," I told them. "I went into the Hava Java for a latte, but when I sat down with my laptop, Alistair told me to turn it off." I imitated his voice. "'I know what you have on that computer, Missy. This is a family-friendly establishment, Missy.'"

Roslynn shook her head and resumed scanning the scene below.

I returned to my own voice. "It was so odd, I still remember it. Alistair kept calling me Missy and kept pointing to a picture of his family he keeps behind the counter. He has no children, but apparently there were plenty of nieces and nephews who needed protecting from the likes of me."

"I hope you set him straight," Wilson said.

"Not really. I got sick of arguing and left after about the tenth Missy. Trust me, the latte wasn't that good."

I was distracted by a gasp from Roslynn, glanced down to where the binoculars were directed, and repeated my string of four-letter words.

"Let me guess," Wilson said. "Beak just showed up."

"Lucky me."

He hesitated. "Maybe it is lucky."

"Excuse me? Jimmy Beak is down there."

"But you said it yourself last night, Jessie. You have no car, and now you can hide from Beak, and Pritt. Three good reasons to stay home."

"Lucky me."

Wilson ignored the sarcasm. "*Singular Sensation* will get done in no time."

"*Seduction*!" I snapped and hung up.

***

I tossed the phone onto my desk. "That man!"

"Is darling," Roslynn said. "When's the wedding?"

"Can we change the subject please?"

"Good idea. *A Singular Seduction* awaits." She dropped the binoculars on my desk, and we headed back to the couch.

"I've lost my power of concentration," I said as I plopped down.

"Well you better find your power of concentration. Your job depends on it."

"Yeah, right." I reminded my colleague I had just been inducted into the Romance Writers Hall of Fame. "It's not like I'm about to lose my publishing contract."

"That's not what Geez Louise says."

Okay, so I suddenly recovered my power of concentration. "Excuse me?"

"I probably shouldn't say anything." Roslynn grimaced. "But Geez Louise."

"What about Geez Louise?"

"She's worried you're about to lose your contract with PP—"

"What!?"

"—P," Roslynn finished.

"PPP!?" I repeated. "Perpetual Pleasures Press is about to dump me?"

"Not yet," she answered, which didn't exactly relieve my anxiety.

***

Roslynn handed me her copy of *Sensual and Scintillating* as she was leaving. "Two copies are better than one," she said. "And you need all the help you can get right now."

I thanked her for her support and saw her to the door. Then I made a nice tidy stack of *S and S*'s on my coffee table and joined Snowflake at the window.

Speaking of needing help.

The crowd below had gotten thicker. Not with more demonstrators, necessarily. But there were plenty of onlookers. Especially disconcerting, Roslynn was down there. In fact, she was making a point of confronting Alistair and Jimmy.

"Is she actually smiling at Jimmy?" I asked the cat. "I thought he was inconsequential nonsense."

But by the time I re-adjusted my binoculars Roslynn had left, and Candy Poppe and her dog were in the fray. Candy definitely was not smiling, but she had to walk her dog. Trust me, Puddles has a lot of piddle in him.

Candy did her best to sidestep the demonstrators, but she tripped over Puddles' leash and ended up bumping straight into Jimmy Beak. He shoved his microphone under her nose, but bless his little canine heart, Puddles saved the day. He lifted his leg and aimed, and Jimmy backed off.

"I always did like that dog," I told Snowflake.

Chapter 7

Roslynn Mayweather was not alone. As Wilson Rye would say, everyone and his brother visited me that day. Let's start with Frankie Smythe, who arrived while Puddles was still deciding between the nearby fire hydrant and Jimmy Beak's pant leg.

"You gotta help me out!" he said as I buzzed him in.

I assumed he was in a rush to get away from Jimmy, but he repeated the same exact thing when he got upstairs to my condo.

The dregs in my coffee pot temporarily distracted him, and he made a beeline for the kitchen. "That looks good," he said, and I had to chuckle. I'm not much of a cook, but Frankie Smythe has always managed to find something of interest in my kitchen.

I made a fresh pot, decaf this time, and Frankie and Snowflake settled themselves on the couch. When he told me how much sugar to ladle into his cup, I wondered how he would ever manage to sit still. But never fear—he found Roslynn's copy of *Sensual and Scintillating*.

"What's this?" he asked, and I stopped shoveling sugar to rush right over.

"Oh, nothing," I sang. I yanked it away and tossed it back on the table, upside-down.

"Do you use those for writing your books?" Wide-eyed, Frankie pointed to the sex manuals. "Like, a two-volume set?"

I ignored the question and served the coffee while my young friend insisted he's not a kid anymore.

"I do know what sex is." He frowned at Snowflake. "In theory."

I tried not to laugh out loud. "All in due time, Mr. Smythe." I patted his knee and waved at the books. "And yes, I use those for reference material. But whatever you do, don't tell the people outside."

"That I'm a virgin? Trust me, Miss Jessie, I don't advertise it." He shook his head. "What's Mr. Pritt doing out there anyway?"

I choked on my coffee, but of course Frankie would know Alistair from the old neighborhood. Keeping in mind he isn't a kid anymore, I explained the situation.

Frankie seemed unfazed. "I was wondering what the Queen of Smut sign was all about." He reached for the nearest *Sensual and Scintillating* and nonchalantly sped-read through who knows what.

"Frankie." I put my hand out, and he relinquished the book. "Let's talk about your problems," I said. "What do I 'gotta' help you with?"

"Who," Frankie corrected. "You've gotta talk to Ms. Sistina for me."

"I do hope you mean Lizzie."

"I mean her mother. She was serious last night, you know? She won't let me see Lizzie."

Apparently Frankie had borrowed his father's Jeep to visit his girlfriend that morning. But Rita had answered the door and refused to let him in.

"She told me to go away, Miss Jessie. She told me to never come back."

The child looked truly pained, but all I could do was suggest patience. "Let Captain Rye catch the killer," I suggested. "Then maybe Rita will let up."

"But what if she doesn't? Lizzie and me." He hesitated. "We need to see each other more than just at school." His gaze met mine, and it dawned on me that Frankie Smythe was in love. Call me a sentimental fool, but I could not keep the smile off my face.

Frankie smiled, too. "You'll do it, won't you? You'll talk to her?"

"I hardly know the woman, Frankie."

"But she likes you."

"Excuse me?"

"Lizzie says so."

"You just told me you're forbidden to see Lizzie."

"Texting." He held up his phone. "Come on, Miss Jessie. Can't you tell Ms. Sistina I'm a good kid?"

"But I have no car," I said. "The police have it."

"I have the Jeep. I can drive you!"

Now there was a concept even more terrifying than facing Rita Sistina.

"What about the demonstration?" I waved behind us, indicating Sullivan Street. "I don't want to face Jimmy and Alistair in person."

"I'll protect you!" Frankie slapped his chest, and what could I do but praise my young friend for his valiant courage?

He shrugged modestly. "Ms. Sistina will listen to you, Miss Jessie. You're old!" He saw the look on my face and corrected himself. "Older," he said. "People listen to you. You can tell Ms. Sistina how you've known me my whole life, and how we've been friends forever, and how smart I am, and how much you trust me, and—"

"If I say yes, will you shut up?"

"Yes!" Frankie held up an open palm and waited until I thought to high-five him.

He stood up, and I do believe he expected to drive me over to the Sistina household right then and there.

I quickly disabused him of the notion. "First of all, I'm not dressed for such an encounter." I pointed to my cut-offs.

"So get dressed." He sat back down. "I'll wait."

"Frankie! I can't just barge in on the woman. I'll call her first. We'll set up a mutually convenient time and then get together for a nice cordial chat."

He looked puzzled. "I don't think Lizzie's mother has ever been cordial."

***

Apparently I was not to be trusted. Notwithstanding our sixteen years of friendship, Frankie insisted I make the call in his presence. He fetched my phone from the kitchen, tapped in Rita's number, and jammed the instrument into my hands.

Rita answered on the first ring. "I was just looking you up," she said.

"You were?"

"We need to talk. My daughter's career is in crisis, and I need your help."

I skipped a beat. Then I agreed a meeting was just the thing and asked when would be convenient.

"Today. Immediately. Now! Why are you stalling?"

Perhaps because I wasn't quite up to facing Rita on such short notice?

"I can't meet you today," I lied. "I don't have a car."

"Because your brute of a boyfriend confiscated it!" she said.

Meanwhile Frankie pounded on his chest and mouthed, "Jeep. Jeep."

I stood my ground and suggested the following day. "Perhaps around five?" I said, and Frankie nodded enthusiastically to that alternative also. Indeed, we had already decided that Monday after his baseball practice would work well.

"This can't wait," Rita said. "I'll come to you."

"What!?"

"We have a crisis on our hands! Don't you know what crisis means!?"

Much to my chagrin, I heard the jingling of car keys.

"And if you think that ridiculous demonstration is going to stop me, you don't know Rita Sistina!"

I let out a silent scream as Rita informed me Channel 15 had broadcast a midday news bulletin about Alistair's book-banning campaign. "It's what prompted me to get in touch with you," she said.

I heard a car door slam shut, and the line went dead.

"What did she say?" Frankie asked me.

"She's on her way over."

"Here!?" he shouted. "Now!?" he screamed."Thanks a million!" he said over his shoulder and flew out the door.

So much for valiant courage.

***

The intercom buzzer had never sounded quite so agitated.

"Get me out of here!" Rita shouted when I answered.

I buzzed her in, and Snowflake found her safety spot on top of the fridge.

"Coward," I said, but the cat did have a point. Soon Rita Sistina was knocking, incessantly and impatiently, on our door.

"Lunatics!" she offered by way of greeting.

"Jimmy and Alistair?" I asked.

"Who else?" she said as she marched her feet toward my couch. "I had half a mind to stay down there and tell those ignorant maniacs exactly what I think of them!"

"Won't you have a seat?" I suggested rather belatedly.

"What's this?" she asked, and before I could stop her, Rita Sistina had *Sensual and Scintillating* firmly in hand. "*A Sex Scene Sourcebook*," she read out loud and started rifling through the pages. "Boy, could I use this."

"A book on sex scenes?"

She glanced up and waited.

"Ah, yes." I nodded knowingly and asked if I could get her anything.

"Coffee." Her nose was back in the book. "Black."

Ever the gracious hostess, I poured the last cup from the pot and set it before her. "Frankie likes coffee, too," I said as I took an easy chair.

Rita ignored me and continued reading. Clearly she and Frankie also shared an interest in *S and S*, but I thought it best not to mention that.

Eventually she tore herself away from her studies. "Now then," she said. "Let's talk about Elizabeth."

"Yes, let's," I said, all pleasant-like. "Let's discuss her relationship with Frankie."

"Frankie!?" she shrieked. "Relationship!?"

"Correct," I said calmly and proceeded to offer this, that, and the other complimentary assessment of Frankie Smythe's character. I concluded with a basic, "He's a good kid."

"He's not right for Elizabeth," Rita said. "And they're way too young."

I conceded that they were young. "But their feelings are real, Rita. You should give Frankie a chance."

"No."

"Keeping them apart will only draw them closer together. The Romeo and Juliet Syndrome happens all the time in my books."

"The what?"

"Remember what happened when the Montagues and Capulets tried to keep Romeo and Juliet apart."

Rita gasped. "They both died!"

I waved a hand. "No, that's not what I meant. I meant they got married."

"Married!?" she screeched. "I swear, I will take that kid and cut off his—"

"Nooo!" I waved both hands that time and waited for Rita to calm down. "Okay, so let's forget about Romeo and Juliet," I said. "Instead, let's think about the phrase 'forbidden fruit.'" I pointed to the stack of *Sensual and Scintillating*. "Maxine Carlisle devotes a whole chapter to that topic."

Rita stared at the books. "I'm adding fuel to their fire," she said eventually. She looked up and actually asked me what she should do.

"Let it be," I suggested. "Maybe they really are meant for each other."

"Over my cold dead body! Now then! Let's get to the real issue."

I sighed dramatically. "And what, pray tell, might that be?"

"The crisis! The emergency! Elizabeth's career! Haven't you been listening?"

Testimony to how much I care about Frankie Smythe, I chose not to throw this woman out of my home, and instead asked what I could do to alleviate the "crisis."

"Solve the murder!"

"Excuse me?"

"You know perfectly well your boyfriend is out to destroy my daughter's future. He plans on accusing Elizabeth!"

"Excuse me?"

She jerked a thumb toward my windows. "And isn't it convenient Jimmy Beak is right outside? I have a good mind to march down there right this minute and expose the truth. I know police brutality when I see it!"

Rita glared with all her might. But trust me, I'm an expert at that maneuver also.

"You should write fiction," I told her. "Your imagination is even more outrageous than mine."

She huffed and puffed.

"As you well-know, Lizzie has suffered zero police brutality."

"Elizabeth."

"Zero," I repeated. "You should be grateful to Wilson. He's keeping Lizzie's name out of the news."

"Elizabeth."

"One assumes you, too, would like to keep Lizzie off of Jimmy Beak's radar?"

"Elizabeth," Rita mumbled. She shifted uncomfortably and looked over my shoulder. "What's your cat's name?" she said, and I knew I had made my point.

I asked why she expected me of all people to solve the murder. And she dove into a long-winded rigmarole about how she wouldn't rest easy about Elizabeth's future until the murder was solved.

"I pay attention to what goes on in this town," she said. "You're an excellent detective. You've helped that brute—"

"Rita!"

"You've helped Captain Rye solve several cases, and you have a stake in this one. It was your car." She again gestured to my windows. "Chances are, when we stop hearing about your car and your license plate, we'll stop hearing from that fool Pritt."

"Which brings up another point," I said. "I can't go sleuthing. My car has been confiscated."

"By that brute!"

"Rita!"

She took a deep breath and tried again. "Rent a car," she said. "Borrow one. Have the Smythe kid drive you around for all I care. But solve this murder. Please!"

A thought occurred to me, and I sat forward. "Let's make a deal," I said. "I'll work on the murder, and you'll allow your daughter and Frankie to keep dating each other, or whatever. Deal?"

Rita frowned at the stack of sex manuals. "It's the whatever I'm worried about."

Chapter 8

The good news? Thanks to our rooftop garden, Snowflake and I weren't cooped up inside all afternoon. Invisible to the street below, we could putter around to our hearts' content. Snowflake chased a few dead leaves. I tended to my flowers.

The bad news? Although the protestors couldn't see us, we could definitely hear them. "Ban bad books!" they chanted as I deadheaded the marigolds.

I moved on to the petunias as a new slogan wafted up from below. "Smut, smut, smut! Queen of Smut!" It sounded like they were clamoring for, not against, the Queen of Smut, but perhaps I misunderstood.

I unwound the hose and had started watering when I heard the unmistakable voice of Jimmy Beak drowning out everyone else. "Jessie Hewwwitt?" he sang. "Come out, come out, wherever you are. Where are youuu?"

"Watering the roses," I sang to my flowers as the demonstrators again changed their tune.

"Come out to play, Add-a-lay." They, too, were singing.

"The Beatles, they are not," I told Snowflake, but she still jumped onto the railing at the edge to get a better look.

"They'll see you," I warned. But even so, we were four stories overhead, and the door into our building was locked and secure. Feeling all safe and smug, I turned off the water and walked over to join my cat.

The circus below looked about the same as earlier. But Jimmy had replaced his microphone with a bullhorn, presumably to get the attention of yours truly. This worked of course, and Jimmy was positively beside himself when he saw me. He screamed, pointed, and jumped, and I waved a few fingertips at the camera far, far below.

"Get down here!" he bullhorned up at me. "The public has a right to know what you have to say for yourself! The public demands answers!"

He waved at the crowd, but from where I stood no one looked all that demanding. Except for the actual demonstrators, that is. They jerked their posters up and down and revved up their "Come out to play" theme song.

I changed the fluttering of fingertips to the royal wave.

Alistair handed his poster to a neighboring idiot, stepped out of the circle, and made a gesture to indicate silence.

"Quiet!" Jimmy screamed into the bullhorn. "Mr. Pritt has something to say! Quiet! Quie—"

He shut up when Alistair began wrestling him for the bullhorn. But Jimmy was not about to relinquish control.

"Get me another one!" he bullhorned to the Channel 15 van, and someone tossed out another instrument.

It hit the cameraman in the head and bounced into Alistair's hands.

Alistair was ready. "I know why Jessie Hewitt won't come down to face us!" he bellowed into his bullhorn.

"Why!?" Jimmy asked. "Why!?"

"Because she's ashamed!" Alistair directed his bullhorn upwards. "Ashaaamed," he repeated.

"Borderline pornographer, borderline pornographer," the placard-bearing group chanted helpfully.

"It's just like a pornographer," Alistair continued.

"What's just like a pornographer?" Jimmy asked.

"To go into hiding the minute someone questions the waywardness of her wicked ways."

I reached over to pet Snowflake. "Nice alliteration," I said.

"But usually!" Alistair again. "Usually she flaunts her wicked ways!"

"How!? How!?" Jimmy again.

"In her books, of course! And think about her car."

"You mean her Add-a-lay license plate?" Jimmy asked, and I began to wonder if they had rehearsed the whole dialogue.

"I mean murder!" Alistair said, and Jimmy abruptly dropped his bullhorn.

He grabbed at Alistair's, but Alistair is a big guy, and Jimmy is skinnier than Frankie Smythe.

"Maybe this wasn't rehearsed," I told Snowflake.

"Murder on the Queen of Smut's car!" Alistair managed before Jimmy finally confiscated the bullhorn. He seemed startled, but Jimmy leaned in and whispered something, and they both glanced up at me.

I smiled sweetly and again offered the royal wave.

***

"You need champagne." Candy answered her door, a bottle of Korbel in hand.

"You need Oreos." Karen held up an unopened package of cookies.

"You need to play," Puddles the poodle may as well have said. He dropped his "Baby" at my feet and insisted I find the squeaky spot.

"I need to get out." I squeaked Baby and tossed him over Candy's shoulder. "Except for the roof, I haven't left the building all day."

"Who can blame you?" Candy said as she gestured me inside.

It wasn't the same as leaving the building, but Candy's place was a nice change of scenery. She has the same brick walls and huge windows as I do. But her condo is half the size and boasts a small black dog instead of a large white cat. The bright pink sofa is also fun to visit.

We broke open the champagne and cookies and found our spots on the couch, all the while marveling at how much worse the situation had become since we had spoken earlier—back when we thought we had only Jimmy Beak and a mere murder to contend with.

"But now we have Alistair, too." I pointed to the windows and told my friends how I actually knew the man from my previous life. I explained the history, they demonstrated adequate indignation, and Candy turned on her TV.

"Tonight's top story!" Anchorwoman Belinda Bing's face filled the screen. "Jimmy Beak reports, live from Sullivan Street! Home of the Queen of Smut!"

"I can't believe he's still out there," I said as Channel 15 cut to a commercial.

Candy hopped up to check. "Everyone's still there," she said from the window. "Jimmy's combing his hair."

"Getting ready for the live report." Karen handed me another cookie, and we were soon treated to a close up of Jimmy's well-combed coif on the huge TV.

"Jimmy Beak, reporting live from Sullivan Street! Where a large group of concerned citizens has given up their entire Sunday to come out and voice their objections to Jessica Hewitt."

The camera shifted to Alistair Pritt and his cronies.

"Where did Alistair get all those people?" Karen asked as we listened to the various chants.

I suggested she check again. "It's mostly just onlookers," I said, and Candy confirmed there were only twelve actual demonstrators.

"Puddles and me counted," she said. "And I bet most of them are related to Alistair."

"Good guess," I said as the enthusiastic face of Ms. Bing returned to the screen.

"Looks like Jimmy and Alistair had a busy day!" she said. "Let's take a look at the highlights!"

"Let's!" I said as a montage of images from the day's festivities began rolling.

I can't speak for everyone, but the true highlight for me had to be Jimmy's impromptu interview with Roslynn Mayweather. I reminded my friends who she was as Roslynn's perfectly-polished figure appeared on the screen.

"She was here earlier to help me with *A Singular Seduction*," I explained.

"How did it go?" Candy asked, but Karen shushed us in order to hear Roslynn touting the virtues of yours truly.

Roslynn reached into her briefcase and pulled out a copy of *The Sultan's Secret*. "I am proud to say Jessica Hewitt, a.k.a. Adelé Nightingale, is my mentor," she told Jimmy.

She held her masterpiece to the camera, and we were treated to a close up of the semi-nude sultan and his equally undressed lady friend, entangled in an altogether passionate embrace.

“Oh boy,” Karen said, and Candy wondered if Channel 15 could get in trouble for showing that kind of stuff on TV.

Roslynn continued, “*The Sultan’s Secret* would never have been published if Jessica-slash-Adelé had not given me her expert advice.”

“You’re a writer also?” Jimmy asked.

“For Perpetual Pleasures Press,” Roslynn said. “Jessica Hewitt is their most-seasoned author. And I, Roslynn Mayweather, am their rising star!”

I rolled my eyes. “Put the book down, Roslynn,” I said.

She lowered *The Sultan’s Secret* and smiled demurely for the camera.

***

I was still rolling my eyes when Jimmy Beak returned after a brief message from his sponsors.

“Our protesters are packing up for the evening,” he announced. “But Alistair Amesworth Pritt has graciously agreed to answer a few questions.” He frowned ominously. “Because the public has the right to know what is lurking in our midst.”

“Did he just call me a ‘what?’” I asked.

“Maybe he’s talking about your book.” Candy pointed, and sure enough, Alistair was displaying *Temptation at Twilight* for the camera.

“Temptation was my first hardback release,” I said as Alistair opened the book and turned it toward the camera. “He’s tearing the dust jacket.”

“What’s all that yellow?” Karen asked.

“I’ve taken the liberty of highlighting all the pornographic parts.” Alistair answered and flipped through the pages.

“That’s a lot of yellow,” Karen said.

Alistair began reading one particularly well-conceived passage as someone off-camera handed Jimmy a stack of my paperbacks. This third invisible person handled the microphone. And one-by-one, Jimmy held up each book for the camera, displaying each cover—each pair of semi-nude lovers in various stages of impassioned ecstasy.

“Your covers look nice,” Candy said.

"That's a lot of yellow," Karen added as Jimmy flipped through the pages.

Meanwhile Alistair continued reading from *Temptation at Twilight*. But right as he came to the most inspired segment of Rolfe Vanderhorn and Alexis Wynsome's most glorious romantic encounter, we were back to watching commercials.

"Darn!" Candy said. "He was just getting to the good part."

***

"That was a lot of yellow." Karen remained on topic even after Candy switched off the TV. "When did Alistair find time for all that highlighting? He's been demonstrating all day."

I suggested Channel 15 likely had a staff for that sort of thing. "They probably call themselves researchers."

"That was a lot of research."

"It's ironic, isn't it?" Candy said. "Them calling you the Queen of Smut even though you can't write sex scenes anymore?"

"Temporary," I said.

"What's temporary?" Karen asked. "Your sex scene slump, or Alistair Pritt giving you a hard time."

"Can I hope for both?"

"Maybe one problem will solve the other," Candy said as she refilled our glasses. "As long as Alistair keeps you inside, you can concentrate on *A Singular Seduction*."

I asked if she'd been speaking to Wilson and insisted Adelé Nightingale did not like being trapped.

"Well Adelé Nightingale better get used to it," Karen said. "It doesn't look like Alistair's going to let up anytime soon."

"Tough." I took a defiant sip of my beverage and told my friends I refused to be intimidated any longer. "I'm venturing out tomorrow. I plan to solve this murder."

Karen's Oreo-bearing right hand hovered in midair. "Say what?"

I explained the logic. "Alistair only came up with this silly idea because of all the publicity Jimmy's been giving me and my car. Once I solve the murder, Alistair will go away."

"Try again, Jess." Karen waved her Oreo at the TV. "They didn't even mention the murder. And you already told us Jimmy isn't allowed to blame you."

I pursed my lips. "Nevertheless."

"Won't Wilson find the murderer?" Candy asked.

"I'll help him." I ignored the disapproving frowns and explained my vow to help Frankie, and my deal with Lizzie's mother.

"Frankie's depending on me," I said. "And I definitely got the better end of the bargain with Rita. She'll stop her accusations of police brutality and let Lizzie see Frankie. Meanwhile all I have to do is solve a murder."

"Gosh," Candy said. "You get in trouble just sitting around your house."

"Wilson's gonna kill you," Karen agreed. She took a gulp of her champagne. "He's gonna kill me, too."

"Oh?" I asked.

"You have no car, girlfriend. The murder happened at the high school, right? So won't you need a ride out there?"

Okay, good point. I hadn't actually developed a sleuthing strategy, but luckily Karen was way ahead of me.

"Kiddo here has to work tomorrow," she said. "It's up to me to taxi you around."

I reached out to hug her, but she pushed me away. "You'll want to hug me again when you hear what else I have to say."

"What's that?" I asked.

"I have a hall pass."

"Excuse me?"

"A permanent hall pass for all Clarence schools."

"Gosh." Candy was clearly impressed, but I was still confused.

"Earth to Jessie Hewitt." Karen waved an Oreo at me. "This is the Twenty-First Century. You can't just waltz into a school and start harassing people."

"I won't harass anyone. I'll just ask a few questions."

"But schools have rules now," Candy said. She turned to Karen. "Why do you get a hall pass?"

“Maintenance.” Karen explained how she helped the custodial staff whenever something needed fixing at any of the public schools. In case I haven’t mentioned it, Karen Sembler is the all-around handy woman of Clarence, North Carolina. She builds custom furniture for a living. But she’s also the person to call when anything, anywhere, breaks.

“People will probably recognize you,” Karen told me. “But we’ll say we’re friends, which we are, and that I need an extra pair of hands.” She groaned at her own cleverness. “I even have an extra tool belt to loan you.”

Candy bounced a little. “You’ll look all handy, too, Jessie!”

“This will work?” I was skeptical.

“The high school always needs an extra pair of hands with their plumbing,” Karen said. “The situation in the boys bathroom is even worse than at Wilson’s cottage.”

“Shack.”

“Jack will be glad to see me,” she continued. “Jack MacAdoo’s in charge of the custodial staff.”

“And the janitor is a great place to start sleuthing! And you were right.” I reached out. “You do deserve another hug.”

She again pushed me away. “I was right about something else, too,” she said. “Wilson’s gonna kill us.”

Chapter 9

"I'm headed right back out," I told Snowflake when I arrived home. "It's time for a walk."

Indeed, the evening was lovely, it was still light out, and Sullivan Street was blessedly free of Jimmy Beak and Alistair Pritt. But the intercom buzzed while I was lacing up my left sneaker. So much for being rid of Jimmy.

I clicked on the intercom. "Don't you ever take a night off?" I asked. "Go away, Jimmy."

"Jimmy?" an indignant female voice answered.

I blinked twice. "You're not Jimmy Beak."

"I most assuredly am not."

I tried to place the voice. "Superintendent Yik—I mean, Superintendent Yates? Is that you?"

"Dr. Gabriella Yates, yes. I need to speak to you. Allow me entrance, please."

"Umm." I glanced forlornly at my sneakers. "I wasn't expecting company."

"Company-schmompany! This is important, Ms. Hewitt. And I am not accustomed to waiting."

"Heavens, no," I mumbled and buzzed her in.

***

"Gabriella Yates." Dr. Yates had her hand extended as I opened my door.

"Jessica Hewitt." I shook her hand. "Won't you please—" my guest swept into the room—"come in."

"Your shoelace is untied," she informed me.

I thanked her for noticing and gestured her toward the couch. "Would you like some tea?" "This is not a social call, Ms. Hewitt. Now sit down." She patted the seat beside her, and I had to work to remember we were in my home.

Feeling rather defiant, I took the easy chair opposite.

"I need your help," she said as she reached for a copy of *Sensual and Scintillating.*

"Doesn't everyone," I mumbled and leaned over to tie my shoe.

"Look at me when I'm speaking to you, Ms. Hewitt."

Excuse me?

I took my sweet time with the sneaker. Then I looked up and told Dr. Yates I was not accustomed to being treated like a recalcitrant teenager. "Especially by someone who barges into my home on a Sunday evening." I pointed to the manual she was holding. "Return the book and change the attitude."

She skipped a beat. "What is wrong with me?" she asked. "I am so sorry! I know it is no excuse for my rude behavior, but I have just endured the most harrowing twenty-four hours of my life, Jessica. May I call you Jessica?"

"Jessie."

"And I'm Gabby." She tilted her head. "Forgive me?"

I pointed to the book she still held. "Be nice to me, and I'll let you keep that."

Was that a giggle?

"I'm married to Gordon." Dr. Yates—I mean Gabby Yates—returned the book from whence it came. "Trust me. It's hopeless."

"Well then, at least let me get you that tea."

"Tea would be lovely." She hesitated. "But a bourbon on the rocks would be even lovelier."

It was my turn to laugh. I informed the superintendent I don't keep hard liquor in stock and suggested champagne instead. She told me she didn't feel much like celebrating, I told her to trust me, and soon we were sipping some bubbly.

"Now then," I said. "What can I do for you?"

"You can solve this murder."

I raised an eyebrow at Snowflake, who stood on the back of the couch, hovering over the superintendent's left shoulder.

Gabby reached up and stroked the cat under her chin. "You don't seem very shocked at my request," she said.

"Believe it or not, you're not the first person to ask."

"Oh, I believe it. Everyone knows you have a knack for these things."

"Everyone except Captain Wilson Rye."

"Don't be modest," she said. "Your fiancé knows you're talented, and this murder is right up your alley."

I raised my other eyebrow. "Oh?"

"Many petty intrigues and jealousies. Ms. Jilton was an excellent educator, but." Gabby paused. "But I'm fairly certain she was having an affair."

"With someone at the school?"

"I don't know. I can't get a clear answer from my principal out there, and I doubt he'll open up for your fiancé, either. That's where you come in."

"Oh?"

"You can talk to him, Jessie! His name's Richard Dempsey. And while you're at it, you can talk to the other faculty and staff. People will trust you."

"Are you kidding? People will not trust me, Gabby." I pointed toward Sullivan Street. "You do know about the demonstration today?"

"Which is exactly why people will talk to you. Educators disapprove of book banning. And no one likes the way you're being bullied."

"Oh great. So people will talk to me because they feel sorry for me?"

"What difference does it make why?" she asked. "Won't you at least try?"

I watched Gabby sip her champagne, and for the first time noticed she was in quite a disarray. Like my first guest of the day, my latest visitor wore a business suit. But while Roslynn Mayweather had been clean, crisp, and pressed, Gabby Yates was anything but. Somewhere along the line she had slipped off her pumps, her hose had a run, and her hair looked something like Karen's does on an average day.

"You've had a rough day," I said.

"An understatement. And you?"

I offered a brief summary of my trials and tribulations, and Gabby did the same.

"First an emergency session with the school board," she said. "Then the *Clarence Courier* called, then the mayor. Then I had a three-hour meeting with the state education commissioner. I barely had time to watch Jimmy Beak's report this evening."

She gave me a sideways look. "At least the book-banning demonstration kept him out of my hair. Thank you."

"Don't mention it," I mumbled.

"I thought I was home free for the evening, but then our Congressman caught me on my cell phone on my way over here."

"Wow," I said. "You really do need some bourbon."

Gabby held up her champagne glass. "This is quite nice," she said. "And please don't get me wrong, Jessie. I love my job—I embrace my responsibilities. But I can't concentrate on education until this useless tragedy gets cleared up."

"You care a lot," I said.

"I didn't earn my nickname for nothing."

"The nickname doesn't bother you?"

"The Dr. Yikes label means I'm doing my job. Just like the Queen of Smut label means you're doing yours."

I harkened back to something I had read in the paper, and congratulated Gabby on the latest SAT scores for the county.

She smiled broadly. "I am so proud of our high-schoolers! And our grade-schoolers. Our fourth-grade reading levels are among the highest in the state this year!"

"Thank you, Dr. Yikes."

"You're very welcome. But if you really want to thank me, you'll solve this murder."

She rummaged around in her purse and pulled out an ID badge. My heart skipped a beat when I saw the photograph.

"Where did you get that?" I asked.

"From the back of *My South Pacific Paramour*." Gabby rummaged some more and whipped out a lanyard in Clarence High School's purple and orange colors. She attached my ID and dangled it in front of me. "Here you go. Your hall pass!"

I grabbed it just as Snowflake got interested. I jiggled it in front of the cat and spoke to Gabby. "You didn't actually read *My South Pacific Paramour*?"

"Of course I did. But *Windswept Whispers* is your true masterpiece."

I pointed to *Sensual and Scintillating*. "That one got high marks from Ms. Carlisle also."

"Please don't tell anyone I read romance, Jessie. It could ruin my reputation."

My face fell. "Oh no," I said. "That kind of attitude is the problem."

To her credit, Gabby understood immediately. "I'm being a hypocrite, aren't I?"

"Sorry, but yes. Many intelligent people read romances. But as long as they do so behind closed doors—"

"—people like Alistair Pritt get away with their insults," Gabby finished for me. "Let's make a deal, Jessie. I'll proclaim to the whole wide world, or at least to Jimmy Beak, that I read your books and am proud of it. And you'll solve this murder." She smiled slyly. "Deal?"

I smiled slyly. "Deal," I said and retrieved my hall pass from the cat.

***

The intercom buzzed, and I jumped about ten feet.

"Who's that?" Gabby looked alarmed.

"Jimmy Beak." I winced, scowled, and made other unhappy faces, but my guest seemed relieved.

"There's no time like the present," she said. "Invite him up, and we'll discuss my reading habits."

I glanced at Snowflake. "Jimmy will be much less scary with Dr. Yikes on our side."

"Scary-schmary." Gabby pointed to the intercom as she put her shoes back on. "Answer that."

I buzzed in my next guest. "Come on up, Jimmy!" I said brightly.

"I'm not Jimmy, but thanks," a female voice answered. "I'm on my way."

I squinted at Gabby. "Who's that?"

She shrugged and shook her head, and insisted she should be going. "I'll track down Jimmy Beak tomorrow," she said as she stood up. "I know where to find him." She winked and was gone.

I listened in my open doorway as Gabby made her way down the stairs, and my next visitor made her way up the stairs. They exchanged a greeting on the second story landing, and soon my mystery guest stood before me.

She held out her hand and identified herself. “Dianne Calloway,” she said.

And I fainted.

Chapter 10

A bit melodramatic, you're thinking?

Well, let me fill you in. Dianne Calloway is Wilson Rye's former fiancée. Dianne Calloway is a convicted killer. Dianne Calloway bludgeoned her ex-husband to death with a broomstick. So yes, I fainted. I mean really.

In addition, the woman standing before me—make that, standing over me—had fingered Wilson for the murder. Wilson proved his innocence and sent Dianne to prison.

My eyes fluttered open. "You're out of prison."

"Duh."

Snowflake sniffed around my nose and mouth, but the other figure hovering above me had my full attention.

No visible weapons. No purse, even. And definitely no broomstick.

"Are you, or are you not, going to let me in?"

Okay, so clearly "not" would have been the better choice. But I was exceedingly flustered. And by the time I thought of responding, Dianne had already stepped over me.

She found her way to the couch, I struggled to my feet and took an easy chair, and Snowflake sat on my lap. Bless her heart, I appreciated the moral support, but I almost wished she had positioned herself at her safety spot on the refrigerator.

I kept my eyes on Dianne, ready for any sudden movement.

She reached out, I jumped ten feet in the air, and Snowflake flew to the refrigerator.

"Geeeez!" She sat back, a copy of *S and S* in hand. "I'm not going to hurt you. I didn't even bring my broomstick."

"What do you want?" I snapped.

Dianne pretended to be engrossed in *Sensual and Scintillating*. "I could use a bourbon on the rocks," she said without so much as looking up.

Trust me. I wasn't that flustered.

I did, however, get up and move to the kitchen. An excellent place, in close proximity to the phone, and the knives.

"What's that number?" I asked Snowflake as I grabbed the phone. "Nine." I made a production of hitting the nine. "One." Another production. "One." I glanced over, my finger poised to push.

"Okay, okay." Dianne dropped the book. "I'll talk to you."

"Gee thanks." I put the phone down.

She pointed to the easy chair, but I assured her I was quite content in the kitchen. "I keep my knives over here."

"Oh, and you're really prepared to protect yourself with a paring knife?"

I frowned at my knife block. "Maybe."

"Maybe you need to come up with a better threat."

"How about, I have Wilson on speed-dial."

Now that got a reaction. My guest emitted a rather creative string of four-letter words.

"That was educational," I said when she came up for air.

"Prison was good for something."

"I enjoy learning new words," I said for lack of anything better. "I'm a writer."

"I know who you are. A copy of *Everlasting Encounter* floated around my cellblock for over a year. I read it four times."

"Thank you."

"There was nothing else to read."

I folded my arms and glared, and told Ms. Calloway she had a choice. "You can tell me why you're here, or I can call Wilson, or I can threaten you with my paring knife. Take your pick."

"Would you give me a break?" She let out an elaborate sigh. "I was curious about you, okay? Haven't you been curious about me?"

I swallowed a sigh of my own, mumbled something about regretting this later, and went back to the living room. "Don't you live in Raleigh?" I asked.

She did. But apparently she was in Clarence for the day, visiting an uncle.

"Uncle John is the only person in my family who's still talking to me," she said. "He keeps me posted on Wilson and you."

My mouth dropped. "You're spying on us?"

She told me not to flatter myself. "I'm only here to see my uncle."

"You're in my home, Dianne. And you've already admitted you're curious."

"Jimmy Beak certainly thinks you're curious."

"Would you please leave?" I said cordially.

I meant my condo, but Dianne pretended to misunderstand. She told me she was due back in Raleigh the next day. "I have rules to follow, you know?"

No, I didn't know. But I assumed the rules had something to do with parole. "Well then!" I stood up. "You need to go home and get some rest."

She remained seated.

I swung my arms back and forth toward the door to clarify my intensions.

She remained seated.

"When's the wedding?" she asked, and I dropped my arms.

She smirked. "You're stalling."

"Speaking of which, you can leave now."

"I don't blame you for stalling. When it comes to Wilson, you should be cautious."

I folded my arms and glared. Or maybe I was already doing that.

"Nooo," she sang and pretended to assess her manicure. "I don't see you guys marrying at all. And I have excellent intuition about these things."

"You need to leave," I said.

She was busy with the smirking, and I was busy trying to quell the nausea, when the phone rang.

"Saved by the bell!" she chirped as I stepped away to answer. "I bet that's Wilson."

"Yes, Dianne." I picked up the phone. "You're downright brilliant."

***

"Who's brilliant?" Wilson asked.

"Umm. Snowflake."

"You two feel like company?"

"Two?" I blinked at my unwanted guest.

"You and Snowflake. Are you okay, Jessie? Did I call too late?"

I told him that wasn't exactly the issue and asked where he was.

"At the corner. I'm on my way up," he said and clicked off.

***

"Shiiiiiit!"

I repeated the sentiment several times and gestured frantically for Dianne to stand up. "Would you get out of here, already!" I said, and the woman finally got the hint.

She stood up and strolled—and I do mean strolled—toward my door.

I rushed ahead, opened the door, and waved both arms. Maybe the air current would move her along.

"You have got to get out of here," I said in case it still wasn't clear. "Wilson is on his way!"

"I knew that." She tapped her temple. "Intuition."

"Yeah, right." I pushed her over the threshold. "Even my cat could tell you what's going on here."

In fact, Snowflake jumped onto the kitchen counter, presumably to have a better view of the world war that promised to ensue if Wilson Rye found Dianne Calloway on my doorstep.

"He uses the stairs," I said as I none-too-gently prodded her into the elevator. I pushed the down button and said a little prayer of thanks when the door closed.

"What are you doing pacing around out here?" Wilson was on the top step when I twirled around.

"Oh!" I exclaimed and then caught myself.

"Ohhhh," I tried again. "Umm, I was acting out a scene from my book." I waved a hand at nothing in particular. "Trying to get the timing just right."

"It must be some fast-paced timing," he said as he stepped inside my condo. "You're all sweaty."

***

I laughed nonchalantly, or perhaps hysterically, and was even more giddy when Wilson made a beeline for my coffee table. Surely my supply of *Sensual and Scintillating* would distract him. It had all my other guests.

But no. He stood over the table, his back to me, and I remembered the incriminating champagne glasses Gabby and I had been using.

"Candy was here earlier," I lied.

"She give you this?" He turned around with my Clarence High School Hall Pass dangling from his fingertips, and I made a giant leap across the room.

I grabbed the lanyard and whisked it away to the kitchen.

"What is that?" Wilson was following me.

"Oh, nothing." I rummaged around in my junk drawer looking for a place to hide the stupid thing. "It's my Hall of Fame badge." That sounded good. "Roslynn delivered it this morning. You remember? She was here this morning?"

"Your what?"

"My Romance Writers Hall of Fame badge." I concentrated on maintaining a straight face. "Perpetual Pleasures Press asked Roslynn to present it to me. They didn't want to put it in the mail. It's quite an honor, you see."

"No, I don't see." He was struggling to get a view around me. "Especially since you're hiding it under your hammer."

I slammed the drawer shut.

He backed off and studied me. I concentrated on looking innocent.

"What is that thing?" He pointed to the kitchen drawer but kept his eyes on me. "Who's been drinking your champagne?" He pointed to the glasses on the coffee table. "And who was in the elevator?"

"Elevator?" I asked. "What elevator?"

He rolled his eyes. "I'm so happy you don't have a car right now. Whatever you're up to, you're home and staying out of trouble."

I had news for the guy.

But deftly avoiding the what's-Jessie-been-up-to tangent of conversation, I steered him toward that popular spot on my couch, and pointed out the nearest copy of *S and S*. And lo and behold, he picked up the book.

I winked at Snowflake and headed back to the kitchen. "Champagne?" I asked.

"What I could really use is some bourbon."

***

He got champagne.

"How was your day?" I asked as Snowflake and I sat down. "Did you find the killer?"

"I found nothing." Wilson frowned at his bubbly. "There's no motive. Miriam Jilton was well-liked and a good teacher. Pretty tough, by all accounts."

"So I hear—" I cleared my throat. "Could a disgruntled student have killed her?"

"Densmore's looking into it." Wilson caught my eye and told me there was another possibility involving students. "It has a connection to you."

"Oh?"

"Miriam Jilton was the judge for that essay contest you got fired from."

It took me a moment to figure out he meant Focus on Fiction.

"It wasn't essays," I corrected. "It was fiction—short stories to be exact." I shook my incredulous head. "Miriam Jilton ended up judging that?"

"Interesting, huh?"

I agreed the coincidence was astonishing, and Wilson explained the details. Apparently there had been some controversy about the winner. Ms. Jilton picked three finalists, but only one student won the thousand-dollar scholarship for college.

"The two runners up were pretty unhappy," he said.

"And one of them killed her? That seems pretty far-fetched."

"That's the problem. It's not much of a motive. And we've checked them. And their parents."

I cringed. "Maybe it's a good thing I got fired."

Wilson agreed being the town pornographer did have its advantages and mentioned my license plate. "That's still the million-dollar question," he said. "Jilton was having an affair. And the killer was making a statement."

"Have you found her phone?"

He shook his head and told me Lieutenant Densmore was checking her phone records and e-mails instead. "We'll have the answer soon enough." He groaned. "But not nearly soon enough for Superintendent Yikes and Rita Sistina."

"Have they been in touch?" I asked oh so casually.

"Pestering me all day. You'll be happy to know Dr. Yikes is not acc—"

"—accustomed to waiting," I said.

Oops.

Wilson stared at me. "What have you been up to?"

"On, nothing," I said. "But I think I read somewhere that Dr. Yates is rather impatient?"

He kept staring. "Rita Sistina's not much on patience, either. You might be a little scary, but that woman's a lot scary."

Speaking of which, Dianne Calloway popped into mind, and I whimpered slightly.

"What are you up to?" Wilson repeated, and I wondered if I should ask him the same thing.

***

I suggested it was time for bed and stood up to clear our glasses. "I assume Loretta is on cat-care duty at the shack?"

"It's not a shack, and yes." Wilson stood up and stretched, and we agreed how lucky he was to have a cat-loving neighbor. Loretta Springfield adored Bernice and Wally, and the feeling was mutual. Good thing, since Wilson had to leave his cats alone a lot.

"If you lived with me, Bernice and Wally wouldn't be cooped up all alone," he said as we got ready for bed.

"They have each other, and Loretta, and their cat door onto the porch," I said. "And if Snowflake and I weren't here, you'd be driving out to the boondocks right now."

"If you lived out in the boondocks, you wouldn't have to worry about Alistair Pritt protesting outside your door."

I thought of a retort as we brushed our teeth.

"If you arrested Alistair, he wouldn't be able to protest," I said as we climbed into bed. "Does he even have a permit?"

"Not today, he didn't. It's Sunday."

I refused to lie down. "I can't believe you let him stay out there illegally! You should have done something."

"Think, Jessie. What would happen if someone from the department cleared Pritt off the street?"

I had to agree it would only give Jimmy Beak more ammunition against me. He'd have a field day claiming the police were offering me undeserved protection due to my relationship with Wilson.

"And it's not like Pritt's a violent criminal," Wilson said. "I had Sergeant Sass check."

"I'm surprised you bothered. Alistair must be low on your priority list right now."

Wilson reminded me he doesn't like coincidences. "This sudden book-banning craze at the same time as the murder? I don't like it."

"I'm not too crazy about it either," I said. "Did Tiffany learn anything incriminating?" Dare I say, I was hopeful? Sergeant Tiffany Sass is a good cop, and very thorough.

But unfortunately Wilson shook his head. "Pritt's a law-abiding citizen, with lots of law-abiding family. No connection to Jilton."

I sighed dramatically and slipped under the covers. "I assume all those law-abiding family members are helping him with his protest?"

"Yep. According to Sass, they're also manning the coffee shop. He'll have plenty of free time to harass you again tomorrow."

"Oh goody," I said and turned off the light.

Chapter 11

Willow LaSwann stood at the edge of her property and gazed at the house in the distance. Kipp Jupiter's house. She sighed dramatically and her bosom strained its bonds. Pretending to be a man was so very difficult. But what choice did she have?

Willow recollected Uncle Hazard's final warning.

"Beware!" he had written in his last missive. "Guard your true identity, my dear Willow, or the varmints who call themselves your neighbors will eat you alive. They'll seize your property and drive you out of town. That is, if you're lucky!"

Willow shuddered at the thought of it.

Kipp Jupiter couldn't be one of those varmints, could he? Why, that very morning he had come by for a nice neighborly chat. "About the water situation," he said.

But as Mr. Jupiter started explaining the problem with her well, Willow felt herself blushing and had shooed him away. Indeed, she had treated him as if he were nothing more than a vicious hornet pestering her cattle!

But what if Uncle Hazard was wrong? What if Kipp Jupiter wasn't a varmint at all?

Willow vowed to find out. She would saddle up her horse Sparkle and ride into town that very day! Surely someone in Hogan's Hollow could tell her the true nature of Kipp Jupiter's character.

Willow strode over to her barn with new resolve. Today was the day! The day she would learn whether Kipp Jupiter was a good guy or a bad guy.

"I hope he's a good guy!" she exclaimed to Sparkle.

***

"Oh, for Lord's sake, Willow! Of course he's a good guy!" I hit the off button on my computer with far more gusto than necessary, and Snowflake tore her eyes from the scene below to glance over.

I curled my lip at the bad guys on Sullivan Street and phoned Karen.

"Ready for some sleuthing?" I asked her.

"I'm surprised you're still up to it. I take it you didn't watch Jimmy Beak's report this morning?"

I blinked twice. "Why?"

"Girlfriend! Haven't you heard of keeping your friends close and your enemies even closer?"

I reminded Karen my enemies were close enough. "Right below my window, to be exact."

"Which is exactly where they were when Wilson left this morning."

"Excuse me? Wilson left at six a.m. to get back to work. Surely Alistair didn't start that early?"

"No, but Jimmy Beak and his cameraman did. They were in our parking lot when Wilson got out there."

I rolled my eyes. "And let me guess. This encounter made it onto the news?"

"Oh yeah. Jimmy made a big deal about catching him red-handed—spending the night with you without the benefit of wedlock."

"He actually said that?"

"You think I could make this stuff up? He accused Wilson of cavorting with the enemy, and then accused him of illicit and licentious behavior."

I scowled. "I'm surprised Jimmy knows how to use licentious in a sentence."

"That's exactly what Wilson said."

***

"Lookee what I have." I stood in Karen's doorway proudly jiggling the hall pass dangling from my neck. "Gabby Yates herself gave it to me."

"Yates as in Yikes?" Karen seemed skeptical, but I insisted it made perfect sense and explained the deal Superintendent Yates and I had brokered the evening before.

"So you see?" I said. "Everyone wants me to solve this murder. Even Gabby."

"I can't believe she lets you call her Gabby?" Karen motioned me into her condo while I outlined the plan.

"You'll use your hall pass to talk to the janitor, and I'll use mine to interview the principal and some teachers. We'll make an excellent team."

"Speaking of which, Kiddo feels left out."

"Not anymore. I called her at work and gave her an assignment." I grinned. "A task that has Candy Poppe written all over it."

"You're a little scary," Karen told me.

I pointed to the huge dining room hutch and table parked in the middle of her living room and argued the same could be said for her. Karen's condo is in reality her carpentry workshop, replete with tools, power tools, and—

"What is that smell?" I asked.

"Varnish." She went around the room switching several industrial-sized fans to high. "The first coat's always the worst," she yelled over the din. She took off her tool belt and hoisted it over her shoulder. "Let's get out of here."

"I hope you're okay with taking time away from your work," I asked as we stepped out to the lobby.

Karen explained her latest project as she locked her door. "The Fister-Bickerson wedding is this Saturday," she said. "Between their parents and the bride's extended family, the happy couple will have every piece of furniture ever invented by mankind. In size large."

"And let me guess. You're in charge of building it all."

"I can handle it. But I can't handle them." She pointed to the outside door looming before us, and presumably to the bad guys on the other side. "What's your getaway plan?"

"Let's do it the old-fashioned way," I said.

She turned slowly and glared. "Meaning we'll make a run for it and hope for the best."

"You know we can outrun Alistair."

"Yeah, and what about Jimmy?"

I had to agree Jimmy was far more nimble on his feet. "But his cameraman is almost as clunky as Alistair," I said optimistically. "By the time he gets the camera rolling, we'll be halfway down Sullivan Street."

Karen shook her head. "Your getaway plan stinks," she told me.

***

Maybe so, but it worked.

We peeked out the door, and when Alistair turned his back, Karen and I made a run for it.

Ace reporter that he is, Jimmy Beak saw us, or else he heard Karen's tool belt clanking. He raced right over and reached us just as we dove into the van.

Karen threw her tool belt at me and locked the doors while I complained that hammers hurt when they hit your lap.

"The public has a right to know!" Jimmy rapped on my window.

Safe behind locked doors, I smiled and displayed the hammer.

Jimmy retorted with an altogether rude gesture and ran around to Karen's window.

She watched him jump up and down for at least half a second before checking her rear view windows and starting the engine. The cameraman arrived as she put the van into reverse. He and Jimmy stepped directly behind the vehicle, and Karen mentioned something about suicidal tendencies as she ever so slowly began backing up.

I twisted around and reported they were not moving.

"They'll move." Her eyes never left her rearview mirror.

And so they did. Then they followed along each side of the van as Karen inched her way to forward.

"I've a good mind to report you for hazardous driving," Jimmy yelled at her.

I couldn't believe it when she opened her window to speak to Jimmy. "You have exactly one second to get out of my way," she said and hit the gas.

Talk about a little scary.

Chapter 12

"I don't suppose you have a plan?" Karen asked as we entered the high school.

"We amateur sleuths like to play it by ear," I said, and she mumbled something I didn't quite catch.

I stopped short. "Is that a cop?" I jerked my head to the man who was clearly a uniformed cop guarding the entrance to the main office.

"They're called resource officers," Karen informed me.

"Things sure have changed since I was in school. Do you think he knows Wilson?"

Karen rolled her eyes. "Do you think we should have planned this better?"

She didn't wait for an answer, but marched over to the cop, who might as well have worn a sign saying "Informant for Wilson Rye."

I caught up as Karen greeted Officer Poleski. He was not the friendliest of people. With nary a hello, he held out his hand and demanded picture IDs. Apparently our hall passes weren't adequate.

We produced our driver's licenses and held still while Officer Poleski examined those, the hall passes hanging from our necks, and our faces. We held still again while he lined us up against the wall and took what amounted to a mug shot of each of us.

These pleasantries completed, he led us through the glass door and into the office. "Sign in and state the purpose of your visit with Ms. Chen," he ordered, and we obediently approached the secretary's desk.

But I'm showing my age again. According to the placard on her desk, Jodi Chen was not the principal's secretary, but the school's administrative director.

"Jessica Hewitt!" Ms. Chen seemed friendly enough. "We've been expecting you. Dr. Yates called first thing this morning to prepare us for your visit."

I blinked twice. "Umm. I'm glad she did that, Ms. Chen."

"Jodi," she said. "I think it's terrific you want to teach here this fall."

"I do?" I shook my head. "I mean, you do?"

"A creative writing course for our honors students is just the thing. But I can see why you'd want to visit first."

"You can?"

"Dr. Yates explained it." Ms. Chen gave the slightest sideways glance toward Officer Poleski, who remained stationed in the doorway. "You need to see the school before committing to anything."

"Oh?" I said, and Karen jabbed me in the ribs. "Oh!" I changed my tone. "Right you are!"

Jodi opened the guest book on her desk and tapped a blank line. "Sign in and put 'prospective English instructor' where it asks your purpose."

While I was doing as directed, the efficient Jodi Chen spoke to Karen. "Hey, girlfriend. I suppose you're here about the plumbing in the boys lavatory?"

"What else." Karen pulled the book away from me and signed on the next dotted line. "And Jess needed a ride. We're neighbors, and she's without wheels right now." She handed the roster back to Jodi. "We thought we'd kill two birds with one stone. Jess can check out the teaching opportunities while I hang out in the boys bathroom."

She asked where she could find Jack MacAdoo and was told he was working on the air conditioning unit in Corridor B. She wished me luck, saluted Officer Poleski, and slipped around him out the doorway.

I turned back to Jodi. "Is Principal Dempsey available?" I asked.

"I'll let him know you're here."

Jodi got up to speak to the principal, and Officer Poleski and I studied each other and listened to the conversation emanating from the principal's office. My name was mentioned, and a most decided "What the hell does she want?" from the male voice inside.

Resolute, I kept on smiling at the resource officer as Jodi reminded Principal Dempsey about the creative writing course. He snapped something about how he couldn't care less about next year's curriculum, Jodi mentioned Dr.

Yates, Principal Dempsey harrumphed, and Jodi stepped out.

"Dr. Dempsey will be pleased to see you now," she told me.

***

Dr. Dempsey didn't bother standing up when I entered his office, and he ignored my outstretched hand.

"I know why you're here, and you can forget it," he said. "Sit!"

I sat and watched while he pretended to read some paperwork on his desk.

"So you aren't looking for a creative writing teacher?" I asked after a second or two.

"I'm not hiring any teachers." He looked up in order to cackle. "Ever again!" Cackle, cackle. "And I'm not telling you anything. And I don't care who sent you—Yikes or your boyfriend."

"My boyfriend has nothing to do with my visit."

"Yeah, right. He just left."

"Oh?"

"Don't play dumb with me. The timing's too perfect. First Yikes, then Rye, and now you." He tapped his watch. "And each visit ten minutes after the last. Right on schedule."

I told the principal I had no idea what he was talking about and reminded him I was there to discuss the creative writing course."

"Save it. And tell Yikes she won't get away with this. One month before I'm due to retire, and she tries to get me fired? I don't think so. I've sacrificed my entire life for this school district. Twenty-five years!"

"Congratulations."

"Save it! Save it 'til next month. I have plans, you know? My roses!"

I again told Dr. Dempsey I had no idea what he was talking about.

"My retirement! My roses! I know what's going on here."

"That makes one of us, sir."

He pursed his lips and considered me. "You're good at playing dumb. You know that?"

Maybe. But at least I was smart enough to realize the teaching premise was not flying. So I did something altogether drastic—I resorted to honesty.

"Dr. Yates did send me," I said. "But I'm certainly not here to get you fired. I'm here to learn about Miriam Jilton."

"It was your car," Dr. Dempsey said.

"Which is why I'm so concerned." I sat forward. "As I'm sure you are. Since it happened in your parking lot?"

"Not my parking lot! I wasn't even here that night. But I know!"

"You know what?"

"Yikes will use this to get rid of me. I've sacrificed twenty-eight years of my life to this school system."

I blinked twice, but decided not to quibble over Dr. Dempsey's exact tenure. "That's a long time," I agreed. "So what do you know about the murder?"

"It had to happen during the last month of my last school year." He shook his head in disgust. "Thirty years I've spent upholding the highest standards of education in this city, and now this. What was Miriam thinking? Doing this to me?"

It was time to quibble. "Ms. Jilton did not get killed just to annoy you," I said. "She was the victim."

The principal smirked. "As Yikes would say, victim-schmictim."

I squinted. "What are you implying?"

"How should I know? Thirty-three years I've given this school system, and this is what I get for it? Cops, the school board, Superintendent Yikes, and now you? The Queen of Smut?" He waved for me to stand up. "Get out of here."

"Out of where?" I asked.

"What!?" he snapped, and I explained my question.

"Are you throwing me out of the school, or just your office? Because I would like to talk to your faculty, if I may."

"Absolutely! Whatever Yikes wants, Yikes gets! Don't you know that? You really are good at playing dumb."

***

Jodi Chen looked up from her desk. "How many years was he sacrificing before he kicked you out?"

"Thirty-three."

"He's gotten as high as thirty-nine with me," Officer Poleski said from the doorway.

"That's nothing," Jodi said. "This morning he told me he's put in forty-two." She stood up. "And now you'll want to talk to the faculty," she said and led me toward the door.

We tried to skirt around Officer Poleski, but he held his ground. "I'll show her around," he said.

"Dr. Yates specifically requested I escort Ms. Hewitt," she said. "I'm to personally introduce her to the teachers."

"You got proof of that?"

"No. But you can call Dr. Yates to verify."

The cop winced and stepped aside. And Jodi and I hastened out the door and down Corridor A.

"Thank you," I whispered as soon as we were out of earshot.

"My pleasure." She made a sharp left down Corridor D, and I tried to keep up. "Gabby Yates called me at home last night with the plan. She said you'd need a viable premise to get past Bruce Poleski."

"I'm glad someone planned ahead." I frowned as we passed the boys lavatory. "Because I sure didn't."

"Gabby is the Queen of Plan Ahead." Jodi shot me a sideways glance. "Which can't be nearly as much fun as being the Queen of Smut."

We passed a classroom with an open door, where a teacher was giving a power point lecture. "High school certainly has changed since I was sixteen," I said.

"But the faculty lounge hasn't." Jodi stopped short and pointed to the door on our left. "It's still the Command Center of Bitch, Moan, and Gossip." She checked her watch. "And it's lunch hour. Your timing is perfect."

She turned to leave, but I caught her elbow. "I thought you said you'd introduce me?"

"Trust me, Jessie Hewitt. You need no introduction."

"Swell," I said, but Jodi had already disappeared down Corridor—I looked for a sign—E.

I clutched my hall pass, knocked twice, and entered the Command Center of Bitch, Moan, and Gossip.

Chapter 13

All conversation ceased, and ten or so sets of eyes came to rest on me.

"I have my hall pass," I said and jiggled the stupid thing.

"Well, whoop-dee-doo," a woman with bright red hair responded.

I took in my surroundings. Whoop-dee-doo pretty much summed it up. The room was beige. The metal table everyone sat around was beige. The metal folding chairs everyone sat on were beige. The sandwiches everyone ate were beige.

I tried smiling. "I'm here about the teaching job," I said. "I'm Jessie Hewitt."

"We know who you are." The redhead shoved her lunch aside. "What job?"

I related the story Gabby had concocted for me.

"Let me get this straight," a youngish guy with glasses said. "Miriam gets dumped on your car, so Yikes offers you a job?"

"That's right. Gabby—I mean, Superintendent Yates—and I hit it off right away. But I'm a bit nervous about teaching, so she suggested this visit."

Blank stares.

I swallowed and pointed to an empty chair. "May I join you?"

No one said no, so I sat between the redhead and the guy in glasses.

"I can't wait to start teaching." I directed that particular lie to the redhead, and she frowned accordingly.

"And pigs fly," she said.

I sighed dramatically and glanced around. "Is this story even remotely plausible?" I asked.

"It's nonsense," an older woman sitting across the table answered. "I'm Doris Carver, the English department chair." She folded her arms and glared. "Yikes wouldn't dare add new curriculum without my approval. Are you even certified?"

"Excuse me?"

"To teach."

"Of course she's not certified," Ms. Redhead answered for me.

"Did your fiancé put you up to this?" the guy with the glasses asked. "He just left, you know?"

"Of course she knows," Ms. Carver said.

"When's the wedding?" a young woman at the far end of the table asked.

I cleared my throat and suggested we stick to the topic.

"Which is?" Ms. Carver asked.

"Miriam Jilton," I said, and no one skipped a beat. I added that I was interested in identifying her killer, and no one skipped a beat about that either. The young woman at the end of the table reminded me I have a reputation for that sort of thing.

"Okay then. So what can you tell me?" I directed my question at Ms. Carver, the English department head, but the redhead next to me answered.

"Miriam was a great teacher," she said.

Everyone nodded, except Ms. Carver.

"You don't agree," I asked her.

"She made her students write a lot."

I scowled. "But isn't that a good thing?"

"Students don't like writing. Not everyone gets to be Adelé Nightingale. And," she said ominously.

"And let me guess," I said. "She made them read, too?"

"You want to hear this or not?"

I humbly admitted that I did want to hear.

"Miriam was having an affair." Doris seemed happy to inform me. "With a married man."

"How do you know that?"

"Because she went out to lunch a lot. But never with anyone from school."

I shook my head. "She went out to lunch, so she was having an affair?"

"I followed her one day," Mr. Glasses volunteered.

"Isn't that kind of—" I searched for a diplomatic way to say it.

"Nosy?" Ms. Carver helped me out. "Kind of like you?"

Mr. Glasses ignored her. "I didn't recognize the guy," he told me. "No one knows who he was."

I looked around, and everyone shook their heads in ignorance.

Ms. Carver smirked. "So much for the Command Center of Bitch, Moan, and Gossip," she said.

***

The bell clanged, and everyone jumped. Chairs were shuffled, lunches were cleared, and everyone made haste. I also rose to leave, but Mr. Glasses told me to stay put. Apparently a second group of faculty was due in any minute.

"Good luck." He smiled kindly and disappeared out the door and into what sounded like a stampede of raging cattle from Kipp Jupiter's ranch.

Despite the ruckus, I caught tidbits of conversation as the faculty traded places. Thus neither I, nor my purpose, needed any introduction as round two of the faculty took their places in the Command Center. Things went about the same. Most people were friendly, some were not, some even offered me part of their lunch.

Yadda, yadda, yadda—we got to know each other. I was crazy to actually like Dr. Yates, Miriam Jilton was a great teacher, everyone agreed she was having an affair, no one knew with whom, and last but not least, everyone inquired as to my wedding date.

I was beginning to think I was wasting my time, when it dawned on me the guy sitting beside me was a gym teacher. Unlike the other male teachers, he wore a polo shirt, no tie.

I dove in. "Were you the other chaperone on Saturday?" I asked, and he put his sandwich down.

"How do you know?"

"I know the person who called 911 was a gym teacher." I gestured to his orange shirt with the purple CHS embroidered on the chest. "Sorry, but that shirt has gym teacher written all over it."

Bless his heart, Mr. Polo Shirt laughed out loud. "Guilty as charged," he said and held out his hand. "I'm Jason Bell. And yes. I'm the one who called the cops. But that doesn't make me a killer."

I assured Mr. Bell I knew that and asked what he could tell me about the dance.

"Jason's already gone over it a million times." That was the Ms. Cordial of this group, a Spanish teacher. "He was just doing his job. Cotillion duty is hard enough without this kind of harassment."

"Would you shut up?" Jason said. I am happy to report he was speaking to the Spanish teacher. "No one's harassing me, okay?" He turned to me. "Everything was normal. As normal as it gets at these things."

"What's normal?"

"The guys were trying to look cool, the girls were trying to look sexy. Standard cotillion stuff, right down to the couple hiding a six-pack under their table, which I confiscated." He shrugged. "Nothing unusual."

"Miriam Jilton was killed," I said.

"Well, yeah. That was unusual."

"So when did things start getting unusual?"

Jason gave it some thought. "When we were lining the couples up for the photographer. I was keeping an eye on the boys, and Miriam was on hairdo patrol with the girls. Everyone was out-of-control nervous." He glanced around the table. "Trevor Ploof was threatening to puke."

All the teachers groaned, and a math teacher informed me Trevor threatened to puke on a regular basis.

"Try having him in biology lab," the black guy across from me said, and several people got up to trash the remains of their lunch.

Jason turned back to me. "That's when Miriam got a phone call."

I sat forward and asked what he had heard.

"Not much since I was busy with Trevor. But I distinctly remember Miriam saying, 'She's fine! Would you stop worrying?'" Jason shrugged again. "She must have raised her voice, because it caught my attention."

"She said 'She's fine,' not 'I'm fine?'" I tilted my head. "Who was fine?"

"I have no idea. I was too busy getting Trevor to the boys lavatory. And that's the last I saw of Miriam."

"Alive," the black guy corrected him.

"Alive," Jason said and stared at the beige table.

***

Who was fine, I wondered as I meandered my way back to the office.

"Something wrong?" Officer Poleski asked, and I jumped ten feet in the air. He seemed happy to have startled me, but at least he held the office door open.

"Has anyone seen my friend Karen?" I asked as I entered.

Jodi informed me Karen and the janitor were down in the gym discussing the basketball court. "The floor needs re-varnishing over the summer, and Jack wanted Karen's advice." She addressed the cop. "Why don't you go see how they're doing?"

He was reluctant to leave, but Jodi persisted, and he finally got the hint.

She waved me to a chair. "What's the news from the Command Center?" she asked.

I pointed to the principal's closed door, but Jodi told me not to worry.

"Dempsey's taking a long lunch." She raised an eyebrow. "He deserves it after his forty-five years of sacrifice."

I relaxed and pulled up the chair. "You don't happen to know who Ms. Jilton was seeing?" I asked.

Jodi shook her head. "I wish I did. I'd like to help you."

"I'm sure you can help," I said and tried to think of a good question for the school's administrative director. "Tell me about Doris Carver, the English teacher," I asked. "She seems almost as hostile as Dr. Dempsey."

"Doris hated Miriam."

I asked why, and Jodi said petty jealousy. "Miriam was stellar, and Doris isn't. You won't believe it, but some of this involved you."

"Let me guess. The Focus on Fiction contest?"

"Bingo. When you got fired, Dr. Yates told Dr. Dempsey to choose a replacement. He chose Miriam, Doris got mad."

"Don't tell me Doris wanted to judge the thing?"

"Oh, heck no. But she wanted to be asked, and she used any excuse to give Miriam a hard time."

"I understand the contestants also gave her a hard time."

"And their parents. You should thank Jimmy Beak for getting you out of it."

"I'll be sure to do so when pigs start flying," I said. "But what about the Junior Cotillion? How did Ms. Jilton get picked for that?"

"Dr. Dempsey again." Jodi explained how the principal assigned extra-curricular events. "He tries to be fair by rotating the faculty." She started tapping at her computer keyboard. "Here's the schedule," she said, and I leaned over to glimpse an elaborate Excel spreadsheet.

"It goes back three years," Jodi explained. "That way Dempsey can keep track from one year to the nex—Well now, that's interesting."

"What?" I tried to decipher the column she was pointing to.

"MJ." She ran her finger across the screen. "And another MJ. Miriam Jilton chaperoned at last year's cotillion, too."

"But what about the rotation?" I asked.

"That's just it. Dempsey would never assign her two years in a row."

"So she volunteered?"

"Maybe. But no one ever volunteers for cotillion duty." Jodi looked up at me. "Ever."

Chapter 14

"Stellar," Karen said as we drove home, and I agreed that was the general consensus.

"Miriam Jilton even volunteered for cotillion duty," I said. "But she was also having an affair. Or at least I think she was. No one could tell me anything specific."

Karen stopped at a red light and offered a sly smile.

My mouth dropped open. "Mr. MacAdoo knows something?"

"I have news for you, girlfriend. Janitors always know something."

"What did he say?"

"Don't get too carried away." The light changed and Karen started moving again. "Jack couldn't give me a name, but he did see the guy pick Miriam up one afternoon. I guess her car was in the shop."

"And?" I asked impatiently as Karen made a left turn.

"She was seeing a parent."

"Of one of her students? Who?"

"Jack doesn't know," Karen said. "But that's his theory. He says the guy doesn't work at the school since he didn't recognize him. But he also knows there had to be a reason Miriam was so secretive."

"The other faculty assume the guy was married."

"Jack says no way." Karen glanced over. "It goes back to that stellar thing."

I thought about the implications of Miriam's behavior. "I wonder if there are rules against a teacher seeing a parent?"

"Jack wasn't sure. But he thinks Miriam would keep it to herself, either way."

I considered my chauffeur. "For a reluctant sleuth, you're pretty good at this stuff."

"Yeah, and wait 'til you see this." Karen reached over to my lap and tapped a compartment on her tool belt. "Look in there."

I reached in and pulled out a slip of paper. "You took notes?" I was impressed, even before I saw the details—a list of twenty or thirty people, each with a G or B next to their names.

"Good guys and bad guys?" I asked, and she nodded.

"The faculty according to Jack MacAdoo," she said. "He's not judging their teaching. It's more like how they treat people—the kids, the staff. Especially the custodial staff."

I scanned the list. "Wow. You went about this with far more precision than I did."

"You sleuth your way, I'll sleuth mine."

I continued reading, but recognized very few names. Being not such a swift sleuth, I hadn't bothered learning many names during my visit to the Command Center.

But at least I recognized the principal. Dr. Dempsey had a B next to his name, and the note, "Retiring—the sooner the better."

Jason the gym teacher merited a solid G. And lo and behold, there was Doris Carver with a B next to her name and the note, "Mess this morning."

"Ms. Carver was Miriam's department head," I said. "And she has a big fat B next to her name. What's the 'mess this morning' mean?"

"Remember, it's how she treats the janitors," Karen said. "Some kid threw up in her classroom, and Ms. Carver didn't even thank Jack for, you know, cleaning it up."

I wrinkled my nose. "Trevor Ploof must be quite a challenge."

"I don't remember that name. What's he teach?"

***

But we never did get around to analyzing Trevor's emotional or physical ailments. Because right then Karen turned onto Sullivan Street. Dare I say, the situation had heated up considerably while we were away?

As usual, Alistair Pritt and his ilk occupied center stage. Around and around the intersection of Sullivan and Vine they marched, stomped, and shouted.

Nothing new there, but Alistair's poster certainly was new and different. He had abandoned his 'Queen of Smut' poster for a new 'Cry for Rye' poster.

"The 'Queen of Smut' one was prettier," Karen said as she inched the van a bit closer.

Indeed, Alistair's old poster had been a work of art, what with its bright red lettering and the gold glitter crown embellishment. In comparison, his new 'Cry for Rye' specimen looked downright sinister. It sported black lettering and a big black teardrop in the upper left corner.

"He must be upset about Wilson staying with you last night," Karen said.

"Like it's any of his business? Like destroying my career isn't bad enough?" I waved an altogether indignant hand. "Now he's out to ruin my private life?"

I could have continued ranting about Alistair. But really, there were too many other things begging for my attention. For instance, Roslynn Mayweather.

Yes, you read that right. Roslynn Mayweather, decked out in a pink business suit, was leading a small group of—

"Is that a counter-demonstration?" Karen asked. She, too, had turned her attention to the Mayweather devotees, who rounded the street corner in the opposite direction from the Pritt crowd. Roslynn's bunch carried posters bearing such sentiments as 'Romance Rocks,' 'Romance Rules,' and 'Read Romance.'

"Now those are some attractive posters!" Karen was downright enthusiastic. "And would you look at those outfits? The romance people have the book-banning people beaten by a mile."

One had to agree. Roslynn's crew, all women, were a well-heeled bunch. Each wore a pastel-colored business suit, with matching pumps and matching corsage pinned to each earnest chest. The pastel theme even extended to their posters, an assortment of baby blue, mint green, sunny yellow, and pink placards.

"Our agent must have put her up to this," I said. "You've heard me mention Geez Louise?"

"Oh boy," was Karen's response as we reached our parking lot.

A shocking, but certainly a pleasant surprise, no one even noticed us. The two groups of opposing demonstrators were too busy concentrating on each other. And Jimmy Beak was too busy running back and forth between the protesters.

Karen parked without incident, and we were even able to get out of the van unnoticed. We hid around the corner of our building and watched the spectacle unfold as Candy Poppe and Puddles moved into the fray.

"Bless their brave, brave hearts," I whispered, and Karen tore her eyes from the scene to look at me.

"Say what?"

I pointed to Candy. "Remember I mentioned I had a task for her. Candy's on Jimmy Beak patrol."

"Say what?"

"She's to talk to Jimmy and ascertain his plans—how long he intends to follow this stupid story, et cetera, et cetera."

Karen raised an eyebrow.

"Come on, Karen. Just this morning you scolded me about keeping my enemies close." I again indicated the circus. "I should know what's lurking in Jimmy's mind. Because once he loses interest, Alistair and his groupies will be much less of a nuisance, no?"

"They couldn't be much more of a nuisance," she said, and we watched as Candy put her special skill set to use.

She may be an army of only one—two if you count her dog—but Candy Poppe is an expert at attracting attention. Her petite yet voluptuous figure is a proven show-stopper, as are her numerous mini-dress and stilettos outfits. While Roslynn's brigade was pretty in pastels, Candy's cheerful daisy-print ensemble also heralded spring.

First she talked to Alistair. The man actually stopped the protest line to speak to her. Or maybe the ilk, mostly male, stopped of their own accord.

Candy tilted her head and gave Alistair her rapt attention as he whispered who knows what in her upturned ear. Was the man actually smiling?

"Kiddo can charm anyone," Karen said.

As if to prove the point, Candy moved on to Jimmy Beak. He jumped back and pointed to Puddles, and Candy bent over—all male eyes fixated on that maneuver—and whispered something to her dog.

"Maybe he'll pee on Jimmy," Karen said hopefully.

Alas, no such luck. Puddles and Candy scurried off toward Roslynn and the pastel people, and I directed Karen's attention to the newest arrival. "One imagines Gabby Yates is why Candy ran off."

Superintendent Yates had indeed stepped out of her car and set a collision course with Jimmy Beak.

"Yikes!" Karen said. "That tote bag she's carrying looks heavy. Maybe she'll bonk Jimmy on the head with it."

***

Poor Karen was destined to be disappointed again. And clearly Alistair Pritt had no idea what Gabby had in mind, either. He marched over, perhaps under the impression he had found himself a new ally.

But Gabby had her own agenda. She paid Mr. Pritt no attention whatsoever, dropped her formidable bag at her feet, and addressed Jimmy.

Truly disappointing—we couldn't hear a thing.

Gabby soon realized she was mute and grabbed the microphone from Jimmy before he could even think to stop her. Still mute, or close to it, she examined the contraption and realized the problem. The mike worked well for Jimmy's TV broadcasts, but since no speakers were set up around the demonstration itself, no one other than those in her immediate vicinity could hear her.

She handed Jimmy back his instrument and an argument ensued. She kept pointing to the Channel 15 News van, he kept shaking his head, and Alistair kept waving his poster to no avail whatsoever.

She turned on her heel and set her sights on the cameraman, who had somehow gotten distracted over there with Candy and Roslynn.

"Young man!" Gabby's voice carried that time, and the cameraman hopped to.

He waved goodbye to the gals, jogged over to the news van, and emerged juggling his camera and a bullhorn. Gabby promptly relieved him of the bullhorn.

"Maybe she'll bonk Jimmy on the head with that," Karen suggested. But fun as that might have proven, Gabby stuck to her original plan. She reached down and pulled *Windswept Whispers* from her tote bag, and I grinned from ear to ear.

***

Gabby raised her bullhorn and got right to the point. "I, Dr. Gabriella Yates, Superintendent of the Clarence School District, read romance fiction."

Jimmy gasped oh so predictably. Also predictable, he had acquired his own bullhorn. "You actually admit it?" He aimed his bullhorn at the crowd. "Dr. Yikes admits that she reads pornography!"

"Pornography-schmornography!" Gabby handled that mouthful with aplomb and reminded the crowd that Adelé Nightingale is a bestselling author. "Adelé—that's Jessica Hewitt—has a national, nay international, audience." Even from my distance I could see her glare at Jimmy. "Can you say the same, Mr. Beak?"

"Oooo," Karen said. "Low blow."

"Far better than bonking him on the head," I agreed. For the record, Jimmy Beak has endeavored to attract the attention of a national news syndicate since he was in diapers.

He sputtered something else about pornography, and Alistair came to his rescue.

"Jessie Hewitt is the Queen of Smut!" he shouted. He, too, had found a bullhorn.

"Smut-schmut!" Gabby bullhorned back.

"Smut-schmut," Roslynn and her pastel people began chanting. Helping out the good guy, as it were.

"I always enjoy a good Adelé Nightingale romance," Gabby bullhorned over the din. "They are"—she hesitated—"fascinating stories."

"Fascinating," Karen murmured.

“No one reads these books for the sex scenes,” Gabby continued hallucinating out loud. “We read them for the intricate plots.”

I guffawed.

“The plots,” Gabby repeated as Alistair and Jimmy challenged her on that ridiculous notion. “*Windswept Whispers* is my personal favorite.” She held up the book, and for a moment I thought Alistair was going to bonk her on the head with his ‘Cry for Rye’ poster.

Instead he shouted “Pornography!” at the top of his considerable lungs and pointed his poster at Roslynn and the pastel people. “Look at them!” he bellowed into his bullhorn.

One had to agree the gals really were a sight to behold. They had replaced the “Smut-Schmut” chant to a “Pornography-Schmornography” ditty. And yes, apparently they could say that ten times fast. Even whilst jiggling their ‘Romance Rocks’ posters up and down at a frenetic tempo.

“Women writhing in the streets!” Alistair offered his interpretation of the situation. “This is where Jessie Hewitt leads our fair city! Degenerate! Degrading! Disgusting!”

“Oh!” Gabby said. “All those D-words remind me.” She dropped *Windswept Whispers* into her tote, and pulled out another of tome.

“A Deluge of Desire,” I told Karen.

Gabby held *Deluge* in front of Alistair’s nose. “I highly recommend *A Deluge of Desire* for Adelé Nightingale’s male audience,” she said. “You should try it.”

“I already have,” Alistair bragged. “I’ve highlighted my copy!”

“In yellow,” Karen reminded me.

Chapter 15

We were still laughing when Wilson's truck pulled into the parking lot, and all merriment came to a screeching halt.

"He's gonna kill you," Karen said, and I asked her to tell me something I didn't already know.

"Okay, how about, Jimmy sees us?" She pointed, and sure enough Jimmy was headed our way, followed closely by his cameraman and Alistair. "We're trapped!" Karen continued delivering the good news. "Wilson or Jimmy? Take your pick."

"Candy," I said and started moving. "She and Puddles can block us, and we'll make it to the door."

"You'll make it to the door, alright." Wilson was already at our backs. He grabbed each of us by the elbow and thrust us toward the stoop. "Get inside!" he ordered.

Candy and Puddles must have been following the action also. They skirted Jimmy Beak and landed on the doorstep with Karen and me.

"Inside!" Wilson shouted.

He turned to stave off the crowd, and for the first time ever, the four of us—Karen, Candy, Puddles, and I—followed a direct order simultaneously.

We made quite a ruckus as we rushed the lobby, but once inside, we quieted down and waited while Wilson locked the door behind him.

He leaned back on said door as if he were holding off an attack of the Huns and caught his breath. Then he folded his arms and frowned at the various residents of 607 Sullivan Street.

Candy broke the silence. "I'm not used to seeing you here in the middle of the day," she told him. "It's unusual."

His gaze landed squarely on me. "A lot of things about today have been."

***

My supposed friends somehow found pressing matters to attend to in their own homes, leaving me to face the wrath of Wilson Rye alone.

"What the hell are you doing?" he asked the moment we stepped into my condo.

"Making lunch." I headed for the kitchen. "Would you like something?"

"How about an explanation?"

I explained we would be having peanut butter and jelly.

"You know what I'm talking about. The stunt you pulled this morning." He pointed to my chest. "You're wearing the proof, Darlin.'"

I grabbed at my hall pass. Oops.

"I'll have you know, Superintendent Yates herself gave me this." I tossed my head. "I was perfectly within my rights to be at the school today."

"Rights-schmights." Wilson sat down at the counter and spoke to Snowflake. "Should I even ask how she knows Yikes?"

I explained how and why I knew Gabby, and Wilson groaned in all the appropriate places.

I looked up from spreading the peanut butter. "Come on, Wilson. Surely you knew I would get involved in this. Everyone and his brother thinks I should be involved."

Ignoring yet another groan, I explained the deal the superintendent and I had made. I waved my knife toward the windows. "That's why Gabby's down there right now."

"She lets you call her Gabby?"

"She does. I predict we're going to be good friends."

"You're a little scary. You know that?" Wilson didn't wait for an answer. "Who else have you been making these deals with? Who was in the elevator when I got here last night?"

I blinked twice. "Do you, or do you not, want lunch?"

"If you're sleuthing for those kids, I will wring your neck with that stupid hall pass."

For safety's sake, I removed my hall pass and returned it to my junk drawer. Then I assured Wilson I was not sleuthing for Frankie. "He merely asked me to talk to Rita."

"Rita? As in Sistina?"

"Correct."

While Wilson banged his head on the countertop, I explained my arrangement with Rita and assembled the sandwiches.

I pushed a plate and a glass of ice water in his direction. "You can thank me anytime," I said.

He did so and started eating, but I told him I wasn't talking about lunch. "I'm talking about Rita." I took a seat with my own plate. "We definitely got the better end of that bargain."

"We?"

"Yes, we. Rita agreed to stop accusing you of brutality, and she'll allow Frankie to see Lizzie." I sipped my water. "And all we have to do is solve this murder. Karen and Candy are helping, too. You should thank them also."

Wilson again spoke to the cat. "At least she didn't get Peter Harrison involved."

My eyes got wide at the mention of my other neighbor, but luckily Wilson didn't notice.

"Speaking of neighbors." I got up to fetch Karen's notes from my purse and handed them to Wilson. "G is for good guys, and B is for bad." I tapped the paper. "It's Karen's system. Mr. MacAdoo the janitor helped her, of course."

"Of course," Wilson said. But he lost the sarcasm as he reviewed Karen's list. "You agree with the G next to Jason Bell?"

I nodded. "How about you?"

"Other than he's a lousy baseball coach."

"You do know he overheard part of Miriam's last phone conversation?" I asked.

"I better know. I've talked to the guy three times." He made sure to catch my eye. "The last being right before you. Bruce Poleski called me as soon as you headed down to the Command Center."

"Figures," I said. "So who was fine?"

Bless his heart, not only did Wilson understand my question, he actually had an answer. And will wonders never cease? He actually told me what it was.

Apparently Jason Bell had overheard Miriam talking to her boyfriend. "Name's Eric Ashton. His daughter Paige was at the dance, and Jilton was telling Ashton his daughter was okay."

"He was worried?"

"He doesn't approve of his daughter's boyfriend—a kid named Cory Hanks."

I put my sandwich down. "Which explains why she was at that dance."

"How's that?"

"Miriam Jilton volunteered for cotillion duty, which I gather, is an unheard-of precedent."

"She must have volunteered to keep tabs on Ashton's daughter." Wilson was also connecting the dots.

I asked how he had learned about Eric Ashton. "Karen and I couldn't get a name out of anyone."

"Would you give us lowly cops some credit?" He pushed his plate away. "Believe it or not, Lieutenant Densmore is an even better sleuth than Karen Sembler."

"How?" I asked again.

"How about phone records? And Densmore even knew how to investigate further than that." Wilson raised an eyebrow. "Having a badge comes in handy."

"Sooo?" I said. "Is Mr. Ashton a married man?"

"Nooo." Wilson mocked my tone. "He's a widower. There was nothing sordid about him and Jilton, other than he's a parent of one of her students."

"Just as the janitor suspected." I stood up to clear the plates. "Is dating a parent allowed?"

"As long as neither party is married, the faculty handbook has no rule against it."

"But I can still see why she'd be so secretive," I said.

"And why everyone assumed she was having an illicit affair."

"And why she was left on my car."

"And why we can rule out Ashton as a suspect. He wouldn't purposely call attention to her love life." Wilson frowned. "Even if he didn't come forward on his own accord."

I glanced up from loading the dishwasher. "Oh?"

"Densmore had to track him down."

I was indignant, but my beau the cop—make that my fiancé the cop—insisted that innocent people don't always realize they're sitting on useful information. "Aston didn't even know he was the last person to speak to her until we told him."

Wilson took another look at Karen's list and asked if anyone in particular had caught my attention.

"Doris Carver," I said without a second thought.

Wilson agreed Miriam Jilton's department head didn't like her. "But Carver has a rock solid alibi."

"And being passed over to judge Focus on Fiction doesn't sound like much of a motive." "That's the trouble." Wilson continued studying Karen's list. "No one had a motive. Jilton was stellar."

"So I hear." I stood up and shut the dishwasher, and Wilson absently petted Snowflake, who had found a spot on his lap.

He tapped Karen's notes. "May I?" he asked. I nodded, and he put the notes in his lapel pocket. "This might have been a random act of violence," he said. "I'm beginning to think teachers get as much random hostility as cops."

Speaking of hostility, I asked about Dr. Dempsey.

"Hostile and uncooperative," Wilson said. "But what's his motive? All the principal wants is to finish his last month and retire with no mishaps."

"Does he have an alibi?"

"Claims he was home with his wife but can't remember what was on TV." Wilson shooed Snowflake from his lap and stood up to leave. "Dempsey's fishy. Every time I talk to him, the number of years he's worked for the schools changes."

Chapter 16

"Don't try to stop me," I told Snowflake as soon as we heard the door downstairs close.

The cat gave me a disapproving look.

"It was actually Wilson's idea," I said.

More feline disapproval.

"And besides," I tried again. "I'm only going downstairs. One can hardly call that sleuthing."

The phone rang.

"Don't try to stop me," I said again and headed out.

"Jessie!" Candy Poppe popped out of her apartment as I rounded the second floor stairwell. "I just called, but you didn't answer. I've been listening for Wilson to leave to tell you."

"Tell me what, Sweetie? Can it wait?"

"It's about Jimmy Beak."

"Jimmy can wait." I pointed down the stairs. "I need to catch Peter before his after-school piano students start arriving."

"But, Jessie."

"Later." I started moving again. "I'll stop by on my way back up."

"But, Jessie," she repeated, but I had already made it to the first floor landing.

***

And to Peter Harrison's door. Wasn't it clever of Wilson to put such an excellent idea into my head?

My elderly neighbor taught music at the high school for decades. Which meant he had spent countless hours in the Command Center of Bitch, Moan, and Gossip.

I stared at Peter's door. But he retired years ago, which meant he likely had never met the young Ms. Jilton.

But, I reminded myself as I knocked, Peter was still Lizzie's piano teacher.

I frowned. But I wasn't allowed to mention Lizzie.

"Don't fret, Jessie. We'll figure it out."

I glanced up at Peter's benevolent face. "Excuse me?"

"This murder you're trying to solve."

I scowled. "You know I'm sleuthing?"

"You always do. I've been waiting for you."

"You have?"

He giggled and waved me inside.

"I confess I've been quite jealous of Miss Sembler and Miss Poppe," he said as we found seats on his couch. "They always get to help you. But this time." He wiggled his hoary eyebrows and pointed to himself. "This time I'm an excellent source of information."

I smiled broadly. "That is exactly why Wilson suggested I talk to you."

Peter blinked twice. "What can I tell you?" he asked. "Lizzie's one of my students, you know?"

I glanced at the baby grand piano that presided over the room and bit my lip.

"Oh dear," he said. "You're wondering how I know Lizzie's involved in this."

"Her name's been kept out of the media, Peter."

He had two explanations for his knowledge. One, he overheard Rita Sistina arguing with her daughter as they left the building the night of the murder. And two, Lizzie had called to tell him what had happened.

He offered a mischievous grin. "We're, like, friends. Lizzie's been taking lessons with me since she was, like, five."

"She's, like, not a suspect," I said.

Peter got serious. "Of course she isn't. But she mentioned your bargain with her mother. I understand you know her young man?"

"His entire life. Frankie's a good kid."

"Lizzie is also. She's far more mature than her speech-patterns imply, and she's a brilliant musician. Her mother wants her to be a concert pianist."

"Excuse me? She keeps insisting Lizzie will go into law."

"If Rita has her say, Lizzie will do both."

"But that's impossible."

"Try telling Rita that."

I rolled my eyes and changed the subject to Miriam Jilton. As predicted, my neighbor had never met her.

"She was probably still in school herself when I retired," he said. "But I do know some of the older faculty."

I summarized the visit Karen and I had made to the school, and the list Karen had created. Peter agreed that Jason Bell and Jack MacAdoo were good guys, and that Doris Carver was not. But to my surprise, he refused to label Richard Dempsey a bad guy.

"Richard and I go way back," he said. "He taught chemistry for years before getting promoted. He was a good principal."

"He was very rude to me. He seemed like a bad guy."

Peter insisted some things aren't as straightforward as Adelé Nightingale's stories would suggest. "For most of his career, Richard was highly dedicated. I'd bet he was to chemistry what Miss Jilton was to English."

"Stellar," I said, and he nodded.

"But unfortunately some teachers lose their enthusiasm over the years. I'm afraid Richard grew weary." Peter shrugged. "Some would say wearisome."

I agreed Dr. Dempsey certainly was wearisome. "I think he was hiding something about the murder."

"Well then, let's try again." The old guy almost bounced out of his seat.

I tapped my watch. "Don't you have piano lessons to give?"

"Not on Mondays. Sleuthing, here I come!" he said, and I cringed at the baby grand.

***

"That's right, Richard." Peter winked at me but spoke into the phone. "I've been meaning to see those roses you used to tell me about. It's a beautiful afternoon, and I have no piano students scheduled."

He allowed his voice to drop off and listened to the other end.

"Yes, it has been a long time," he said. And then he politely, yet firmly, asked Richard Dempsey for his address.

He hung up the phone and smiled. “I’ll just get my keys.”

“Peter!” I finally stood up. “Are we really going there right now?” I watched my neighbor wander around the room searching for his keys. “I’m not sure I have the stamina to face Dr. Dempsey twice in one day.”

“Richard’s more bark than bite. Here they are!” He lifted his keys from an untidy stack of sheet music. “Hiding under Chopin!”

I gazed at the keys and tried not to frown. The only elderly person I had driven with recently was my mother. Don’t ask.

Peter must have read my mind. “Everyone knows the police have your car, Jessie. Come on now. Time’s a-wastin!’”

“But Jimmy Beak’s out there. And his cameraman. And Alistair.”

“Well then, we’ll leave through the basement.” He headed for his door. “We can pretend it’s a secret passageway. Like Nancy Drew!”

“Secret passageway?” I mouthed to the baby grand.

***

“I’ve never been in the basement,” I said as Peter led me down the proverbial dimly-lit stairway. “Are there spiders down here?”

“Oh, absolutely.” He hit the bottom tread and gave me a hand.

“Umm,” I said as I looked around. “I’m rather prone to the heebie-jeebies.”

“Come now, Jessie. Sleuths don’t let a few little spiders deter them.” He wandered off, and for fear of facing heebie-jeebies all alone, I followed.

My imagination kicked into overdrive as I tiptoed along avoiding the cobwebs. This place, far below my bright sunny condo, would make an excellent dungeon in one of Adelé Nightingale’s books. Here we had the requisite dirt floor, damp walls, and sound of water dripping in a distant corner. And when we walked below what must have been Karen’s living room, the sounds of power tools buzzing above could have just as easily been coming from a torture chamber.

Leave it to Mr. Harrison to know our building inside and out. Once upon a time the Merrikans, Peter's maternal ancestors, had run a textile mill in our building. Peter inherited the building long after the textile industry collapsed and had divided it into condos.

"There are definitely spiders down here," I said, quietly so as not to wake them.

But my companion had no such qualms. The man was gaily reminiscing about his childhood memories of the place. Apparently he and his brothers had spent hours in this hell-hole. "Playing pirates, telling ghost stories. At Halloween Uncle Curtis would come down here with us. He had the best ghost stories. Scared the dickens out of us!"

Proof that there is a God in heaven, we finally made it to the other side of the expansive space. But then Peter pointed to some steps even more dubious than those we had descended and started to climb. He kept pointing, this time upward, to what for all practical purposes was a trapdoor over our heads. "It may be stuck," he said. "It hasn't been used in years."

I sighed dramatically and followed.

We made it to the top, and it's a good thing we're fond of each other, because we had to squeeze together and push as one to loosen the door.

"Whew!" I exclaimed when I finally glimpsed daylight above. But Peter told me we weren't out of the woods yet.

"Oh?" I gave one last mighty heave, pushed the door all the way open, climbed to the last step, and took a look.

Lord help me, we were in the alley at the far end of our building—a place so unpleasant we don't even keep the garbage dumpster out there. It's no wonder I had never noticed the trapdoor I was now popping out of, puppet-style. No one in their right mind ventured willingly into that alley.

Until then.

"The city sends someone out once a year to clear it of poison ivy," Peter informed me as we crawled out and got to our feet.

***

I stared at the ancient Cadillac and scolded myself for having such an unjust prejudice against elderly drivers. I mean, Peter had to be better at it than my mother? Didn't he?

"I'm a very good driver." He must have noticed my frown. "I drive to the grocery store every week, and I drive to all my doctor appointments." He opened the passenger door for me. "I am not your mother."

"You know about my mother's driving?"

"Jessie, honey, everyone knows about your mother's driving."

And every normal person would have taken the passenger seat. But let's face it—I am not normal. And the situation at Sullivan and Vine was anything but.

I scrunched down in the area where my feet should have been. From that vantage point I could admire how roomy Peter's car was. I could not, however, witness whatever mayhem he was driving past on Sullivan Street.

It seemed to take an inordinate amount of time to get past that mayhem. But at the risk of slowing him down even further, I poked my head around the glove compartment and asked about the Sistina divorce.

"Very unpleasant business, that." Peter glanced in the rear view mirror and told me the coast was clear. And while I situated myself into the passenger seat, he explained the custody battle for Lizzie.

"She was fourteen," he said. "I understand the courts usually let a child that age have a say in matters. But the dear girl didn't want to hurt either parent. In the end, both father and daughter gave in to Rita."

"They got sick of the arguing with her?"

Peter stopped for a yellow light. "What do you think?"

I wondered if the divorce might have a bearing on the murder, but he couldn't see how. I also asked about Ray Sistina, and Peter told me what I already knew—Mr. Sistina was a hot-shot lawyer in Atlanta.

"Something you might not know." The light finally changed, and he slowly eased forward. "Ray's engaged.

Lizzie's very excited about it. She's been asked to be maid of honor."

"What was Rita's reaction?"

"What do you think?"

Chapter 17

"What's the plan?" Peter asked as we strolled up the driveway.

"You tell me. You're the one who worked with him."

"Yes, but you're the expert sleuth."

I reminded him expert was a relative term, and soon we were exchanging pleasantries with Richard Dempsey.

Of course pleasantries is also a relative term. I rattled off some nonsense about my great fascination with roses, and how jealous I was when Peter mentioned the tour of the rose garden. "We're neighbors, and I'm a gardener, and so we decided I should tag along, and—"

"Save it," the principal told me. "What's the meaning of this intrusion? I invite an old friend to visit and get you? I took the afternoon off to recover from you. I deserve better than this. I've sacrificed thirty-eight years to the schoo—"

"Are you done?" Peter asked, and the principal actually shut up. "You and I both know twenty-eight years is a little more accurate, Richard."

"Umm," Richard said quietly.

Peter turned to me. "And that's the best you could do?"

"Umm," I said quietly.

He rolled his eyes. "Let's start with the roses, shall we?" He gestured to Dr. Dempsey. "Lead the way."

Dare I say, the garden really was charming? Richard and I may have even bonded as we discussed his roses and my rooftop garden. As we admired a particularly lovely yellow specimen, I was even inspired to invite him up to the roof to see my yellow flowers.

"Perhaps sometime after the murder is solved," I suggested, and he literally collapsed.

"It's my fault," he told the rose in front of him. "Miriam's dead because of me!"

***

"Why, why, why?" the principal cried as Peter and I helped him to his feet.

"Why what?" we asked.

"Why did I ever let her volunteer for cotillion duty?"

Peter dropped the arm he was steadying. "Excuse me?"

"That's right," Richard said. "She volunteered. Miriam Jilton had cotillion duty two years in a row."

Now Peter looked like he might collapse also. "I need to sit down," he said in no uncertain terms and staggered over to the patio.

I stumbled along behind, more or less carrying the principal. "Ms. Jilton had her reasons for volunteering," I told him. "You are not to blame."

"Oh yeah?" he said as I got him into a chair. "What about Focus on Fiction?"

I whimpered slightly and decided I should sit down also. Then I reminded Peter what he likely already knew from watching Jimmy Beak. "Richard had to choose my replacement." I tilted my head toward the principal, and Peter's eye got wide.

"Miriam Jilton?" he asked.

"They gave her such a hard time." Dr. Dempsey spoke so softly I had to struggle to hear.

"Who did?" I asked.

He shrugged. "The sore losers, the parents of the losers, the distant uncles of the losers. You name it."

"You think one of the losers killed her?"

"Or a parent, or a family member." The principal closed his eyes. "I gave the killer motive."

"A thousand-dollar scholarship isn't motive for murder," I said firmly.

"How would you know? You write romance. But I read crime fiction." He thumbed his chest. "I know what your fiancé's looking for—motive, means, and opportunity."

"And?" Peter asked.

"And don't you see? I'm responsible for two of the three." Richard counted off on his fingers. "Motive—a sore loser from Focus on Fiction—a task I assigned to Miriam." He counted another finger. "Opportunity—she was only at that dance because I let her volunteer."

He shook his head in disgust. "The only thing I didn't give the killer was the means. He had to find his own damn gun."

I cleared my throat. "Miriam Jilton was shot?" I asked.

"Didn't you just talk to my faculty? Why are you still playing dumb?"

Luckily, he didn't wait for an answer but addressed Peter. "Speaking of dumb. Why didn't I assign the writing contest to Doris Carver? You remember her?"

Peter groaned in answer.

"I think she was jealous of Miriam," I said.

"The old bat," Richard muttered. "Does Doris have an alibi?"

I nodded, and he curled his lip.

"Too bad," he said. "Doris would make a great murderer."

***

"Is he our man?" Peter asked the minute we pulled out of the driveway

"No," I said. "He has some of the basics wrong."

"Motive, means and opportunity." Peter stopped at a stop sign and glanced over. "Richard's confused about something?"

I nodded vaguely and looked at the scenery as we wended our way through the suburb. Eventually I remembered to thank my driver. "I couldn't have done that without you," I said. "It was very helpful."

"But we're not done, are we? There must be some other sleuthing that needs doing?"

I thought about it. "I have an idea. But I warn you, my beau the cop would not approve."

"Fiancé," Peter corrected as he slowed for yet another yellow light. "And don't let Wilson fool you, Jessie. He loves your sleuthing."

An arguable point if ever there was one. But I chose not to argue.

I sat up and rearranged my seat belt. "Let's try the Sistinas," I said. "I have some questions for Lizzie. And maybe you can keep Rita occupied." I looked at my driver. "Are you up to that?"

"A sleuth's gotta do what a sleuth's gotta do."

"Maybe, but a sleuth's gotta plan ahead better than I do." I explained that I had left my purse, and thus my cell phone, at home. "I thought I was just going downstairs for a chat with you."

Peter smiled and pointed to his glove compartment, and I found his phone. I was impressed with his foresight, but he took no credit. Apparently his niece had given him "the contraption" for his last birthday.

"Natalie said I shouldn't be driving without it."

I told him to thank Natalie for me and clicked the number that Natalie had also had the foresight to pre-program in.

Meanwhile Peter made a careful and precise U-turn. "Sleuthing here we come!"

***

"Ms. Hewitt?" Lizzie said as I identified myself. "Like, I can't believe it!"

"Well, I'm with Peter Harrison, and he had your phone number."

"Like, not that! That you talked to my mother! Frankie told me you're, like, good at talking to people, but I had no idea you're that good. Like, thank you!"

"You're welco—"

"Here's Frankie."

"You're with Frank—"

"Miss Jessie! Thanks for talking to Ms. Sistina. I think she really likes me now. That's why I'm here. We're studying for our algebra test, and Ms. Sistina invited me to stay for dinner. At Lizzie's house!"

I congratulated Frankie and explained the purpose of my call.

"You're on your way over?" Frankie held his hand to the phone, but I could still hear every word he said. "She wants our opinion. She wants our help."

“Like, wow!” Lizzie was, like, on the line again. “This is, like, so cool. And my mother will be so happy. She says I should try to help!”

I blinked twice. “Your mother actually wants you to help me?”

“She says we have to find the killer, like, really fast to get my name out of the news.”

“Your name isn’t in the news, Lizzie.”

“Like, try telling my mother that.”

Chapter 18

I wasn't surprised when the teenagers came outside to greet us. But I was taken aback when Rita rushed out and gave me a great big hug. She held me at arm's length and positively beamed. "The kids just told me!"

"I'm glad you don't mind me talking with them."

"Jessie Hewitt, you can do whatever you want! So who was it?"

"Who was what?"

"The murderer!" She shook me in a manner meant to be friendly. "Lizzie tells me you've solved the case!"

"Excuse me?"

"Mom!" Lizzie made it a four-syllable word. "You, like, weren't listening. Ms. Hewitt wants our help because she, like, has not—not—solved the case."

"Not!?" Rita shoved me away.

"Not yet," I said. I brushed off my shoulders and rearranged my blouse. "But Peter and I have learned a lot of useful information."

"What!?" Rita screeched. "We had a deal, Jessie! It's been over twenty-four hours, and I've held up my end of the bargain." She jerked a thumb at the teenagers, who promptly stopped holding hands. "What is wrong with you?" she asked me. "Elizabeth's future hangs in the balance!"

"Why don't you invite us inside?" Peter asked in a calm, but loud voice.

Rita did better than that. She invited us for dinner. "Maybe some nourishment will light a fire under your butt," she told me, and I thanked her for her hospitality.

***

"Something smells delicious," Peter said as everyone converged on the kitchen. "I've worked up quite an appetite sleuthing."

"With no results," Rita muttered. She poked her head into the oven and informed us the chicken tetrazzini needed ten more minutes.

"I love chicken!" Frankie said.

Rita slowly lifted her head from checking on dinner, and Frankie lost his smile. "Algebra!" she snapped, and the kids dashed out.

She redirected her glare at me.

I glared back. "Frankie was only trying to be polite, Rita. He's thrilled you invited him to dinner."

"That better be the only thing that thrills him."

I silently appealed to Peter. He nodded, and I excused myself to go talk to the teenagers.

"I will not tolerate these incessant delays," Rita called out as I made my escape. "I know police brutality when I see it!"

I heard Peter remind her I am not a cop as an arm reached out from what must have been the den and yanked me inside.

***

I was immediately engulfed in the three-way hug, with much jumping up and down.

Eventually I was released, and Frankie and I watched as Lizzie hopped, skipped, and jumped across the room.

"I, like, can't thank you enough!" she said as she recovered from bouncing mode. "My mother is in, like, such a good mood about Frankie and me!"

"That's a good mood?"

"She's being really nice!"

I mumbled something about needing to sit down, and the teenagers escorted me to the couch.

Lizzie must have seen me glance at the piano. "Would you like, like, me to play something?" she asked. "I know some Beatles songs, and Frankie told me you, like, like The Beatles, and I'm trying to get Mom to buy me an electric piano, so I can, like, join a girl group. Kristi St. Clair asked me, and she's, like, this great singer and plays guitar, and Judy Tobler plays the drums, and—"

"Lizzie." Frankie tapped her knee. "Miss Jessie isn't here to talk about music."

"Sleuthing! This is, like, great practice for me!" Lizzie deftly changed course. "Learning how to prove who's, like, innocent, and who's, like, guilty, since I want to be a lawyer like my father and Darcy. They have all these interesting cases. Like, right now Darcy's defending a guy accused of murder, and she's investigating just like we are!"

"Darcy is your father's fiancée?"

"That's right. Darcy Kovacs. She's, like, why I want to be a lawyer."

"Mr. Harrison thinks you want to be a pianist."

Lizzie shrugged. "I, like, change my mind all the time. Do you think that's okay, Ms. Hewitt?"

I said it seemed perfectly reasonable to me. "You're only sixteen."

"How about you?" she asked. "Did you always know you wanted to be a writer? Like, when you were young?"

Bless her heart, Lizzie seemed truly interested in my response, so I told her I had been interested in three things as a teenager. "English literature, shooting pool, and basketball. Somehow I knew I'd never earn a living at basketball."

"So you became a novelist? Because, like, you knew you couldn't make a living playing pool either?"

Frankie and I exchanged a meaningful look, and he reminded his girlfriend I was there to discuss Ms. Jilton. "What can we do to help?" he asked me.

"You can tell me why people think she was shot."

"Because that's what we told everyone," he said.

"For Lord's sake, why?"

"Because she was, wasn't she?"

"Frankie," I said. "Did you see any blood?"

"No." He scowled. "But isn't that how everyone gets killed?"

I thought about it and decided what he didn't know couldn't hurt him. "Stick to that same story if the subject comes up again," I said, and they promised they would.

"Is that it?" Lizzie asked. "Like, can't we help more than that?"

"Actually, you can answer some questions for me." I assumed my most authoritative adult look. "But I'm depending on your discretion. Do you understand?"

They rolled their eyes. "We know what discretion means," Frankie said.

I took a deep breath. "Okay, so tell me about Focus on Fiction."

"Oh, yeah! Ms. Jilton was the judge for that." He slumped. "I didn't win."

"Don't tell me you were you a finalist?"

"No, but I entered. I wanted to do well so you'd be proud of me."

"But I am proud of you!" I smiled. "And I absolutely must read your story."

"You'll love it!" Lizzie bounced forward. "It's, like, a horror story, science fiction, and mystery all in one. There's these lake monsters—the Septosauruses, or Septosauri—that come back to life after, like, millions of years, and they terrorize this little town, Lake Looksee, because Frankie wanted it to be like Lake Lookadoo, but, like, fictional, and, the Septosauri are, like, octopuses—octopi—but with only seven tentacles, and they get into everyone's plumbing. Do you get it? Septo-Septic? They pop out of people's sinks and stuff and, like, strangle people!" She squealed in delight. "Doesn't that sound good!?"

"I can't wait to read it!"

***

Believe it or not, we somehow managed to forget about the Septosauri and focus our attention on the Focus on Fiction finalists.

I point-blank asked the kids if any of the sore losers could have committed murder.

They pursed their lips and gave it some thought. "No" was the mutual conclusion.

"Good," I said. I again mentioned the discretion thing and asked about Paige Ashton and Cory Hanks. "Anything interesting there?"

"Paige's father was seeing Ms. Jilton," Frankie said.

I groaned out loud. "Let me guess. You knew about this all along."

"Like, everyone knew," Lizzie said.

"I have news for you, Lizzie! Captain Rye spent a lot of time figuring out that little detail."

"Like, really?"

I closed my eyes and prayed for strength. "Was Paige okay with her father dating her teacher?"

"She was embarrassed," Lizzie said. "That's why she started seeing Cory. To, like, embarrass her father back."

I asked why dating Cory Hanks would be an issue and learned he was a bit of a trouble-maker. But he was also a bit of a clown, and Frankie and Lizzie liked him.

"Paige broke up with him today," Frankie said.

"Oh?"

"I have biology class with Mary Alice Meyer, who's, like, Paige's best friend," Lizzie said. "Mary Alice told me Paige got, like, really sad for her father yesterday, because he was crying all day, and so she broke up with Cory to, like, make her father feel better."

"How did Cory feel about that?" I asked. "Was he upset?"

"He was relieved," Frankie said. "He joked around about it during gym. He said if Paige had broken up with him before the cotillion, he wouldn't have had to wear a penguin suit on Saturday. Isn't that a great name for a tuxedo, Miss Jessie? Penguin suit?"

"Cory comes up with funny stuff like that, like, all the time," Lizzie told me, and I had to agree Cory Hanks sounded like quite the card.

Chapter 19

The good news? Sullivan Street was demonstration-free by the time Peter and I arrived home.

The bad news? Everyone and his brother had called, at least once, while I was away from home and without my cell phone. Candy held the record, with three messages on my land line and four on my cell. The poor woman. If memory served, I promised her I'd run right back upstairs to hear her urgent news when I had gone downstairs—I checked the time—six hours earlier.

I saved her and Karen for last, told Snowflake life is short, and set about hitting delete.

Needless to say, Jimmy Beak's three messages were the first to go.

Also deleted with nary a second thought were the various messages from my ex-husband. Like I said, life is short. And after months of angst and anger after our divorce, I do believe I had finally learned to ignore Mr. Ian Crawcheck.

"He must be upset about the hullabaloo with Alistair," I told Snowflake as my index finger worked the delete key. "And isn't it a pleasant bonus he has a bird's-eye view, just like us?"

I reminded the cat that Ian's office is just a hop, skip and jump from the corner of Sullivan and Vine as I deleted the last of the his messages. "Zip!" I said and moved on to Rita Sistina's numerous messages.

With a zip here, and a zap there, those disappeared also. After all, Rita had apprised me of her litany of complaints whilst serving me dinner.

I asked Snowflake for advice on the one message from Roslynn Mayweather. We agreed she had likely called to brag about her sales figures now that she was leading the Romance Rocks counter-demonstration.

"Zip," I said and hit delete.

"Zip, zap," I said again as I rid my machines of the four messages from Geez Louise Urko. No doubt, my hyperactive literary agent also wanted to talk sales figures, since no doubt, Roslynn was keeping her posted on the whole book-banning debacle.

"If I know Louise, she's happy about this latest publicity," I said, and Snowflake yawned.

"But what about Gabby?" I asked. Remembering that Superintendent Yates is not accustomed to waiting, I hit the play button.

"Did I do okay with Jimmy?" Her voice sounded almost breathless. "If I didn't, I can try again tomorrow." She skipped a beat. "But perhaps we should wait and see about this new stunt he's threatening."

I hit re-dial.

***

"What stunt?" I asked.

"Jessie?" Gabby answered. "I've been waiting for your call. How did it go today? What did you learn?"

"Not much." I summarized the basics of my sleuthing efforts and concluded Miriam Jilton was stellar. "But how about you?" I asked. "What have you learned?"

"Nothing." Gabby sighed. "I called a faculty staff meeting after school this afternoon. But as you know, Dr. Dempsey wasn't even there, and everyone else was tight-lipped. I was reduced to begging. 'Can't anyone tell me anything?' I asked, and some clown in the back of the auditorium called out 'Anything-schmenything!'"

The superintendent huffed and puffed. "I'll give them anything-schmenything!" she said and hung up.

"But, Gabby!" I said to the dial tone. "What about Jimmy's stunt?"

***

"Where are you!?" the frantic voice of Candy Poppe asked. Remembering life is short, I had skipped her earlier messages and gone straight to the last. "I have something to tell you," she continued. "I've been waiting and waiting, and calling and calling. Why don't you answer? Did you even watch TV tonight? Do you even know about Jimmy Beak's stunt?"

She took a deep breath. “Meet me at the bar,” she said. “Karen and I need a drink.”

The lone phone message from Karen was equally disconcerting. “Didn’t I warn you to keep your friends close and your enemies even closer?” she asked. “Kiddo and I are headed to the bar. We need a drink.”

I turned off both phones and told Snowflake I’d be at the bar. “Apparently I need a drink.”

***

My friends rushed over the moment they saw me, took me by the elbows, and escorted me through The Stone Fountain to our regular spot at the bar.

“Champagne!” Candy ordered, and Charlie handed me a glass before my bottom even hit the bar stool.

Karen gestured to Matthew. “We need The Beatles over here!”

“Already on it.” Matthew looked up from fumbling with the stereo and pointed to the speakers. “This fits,” he said, and I listened to the first line of “Help!”

Everyone watched while I took a slow sip of bubbly. “Okay, I’m ready.” I braced myself. “Exactly why do I need help?”

Matthew and Charlie went back to busying themselves with bartending tasks, Karen became exceedingly interested in her Corona, and Candy started chewing her knuckle—never a good sign.

Nevertheless, I remained calm and apologized for not getting back to her sooner. “Things with Peter took longer than expected,” I said. I turned to Karen and explained my afternoon sleuthing expedition. “Peter graciously agreed to be my chauffeur for that round.”

“Wilson’s gonna kill you.”

“Well then, he’ll happy to know I’m getting nowhere. There are far too many good guys in this case, and zero bad. And speaking of bad guys.” I faced Candy. “What’s Jimmy Beak up to? What’s this stunt everyone’s alluding to?”

She removed her fist from her mouth. “He’s going after your past, Jessie.”

***

"Surprise interview! Surprise interview!" Candy flapped her arms, imitating Jimmy Beak, and I pulled myself out of shock.

"Who?" I asked.

"It's a surprise. Don't you know what surprise means?"

"Whoever it is, you won't have to wonder for long," Karen said. "Jimmy's promising to broadcast this stunt tomorrow morning."

"A 'mystery guest' from your past." Candy made air quotes with her fingers. "I think he's trying to embarrass you."

"You think?"

"Yes," they said in unison, and I rolled my eyes.

"Maybe it's Ian," Karen suggested, and I groaned accordingly.

Had Ian called to gloat in all those phone messages I had erased so recklessly? Had he actually spoken to Jimmy? About me?

I blinked twice.

My ex did know a few things about my past that Jimmy could twist and distort. More specifically, Ian knew about my glory days sharking in pool halls.

"No," I said firmly. Perhaps a bit too firmly. "Ian wouldn't risk ruining his own reputation by mentioning anything even remotely embarrassing about me."

"Well then, you're safe," Karen said. "It's not like you have a sordid past anyway."

"Karen." I pulled her close and whispered. "I have a minor arrest record, remember? From my pool-hustling days."

"Yeah, but I wasn't even born yet." That was Candy. "No one can hold something that ancient against you."

Karen agreed. She argued, quietly, that some might even consider me pool-sharking my way through college as proof of my glowing character. "It shows you're resourceful."

"And that arrest was way back in the sixties," Candy added.

I folded my arms and glared. "Try 1982. I was in college, for Lord's sake. Not grade school."

"Even so, a misdemeanor at age twenty is no big deal."

I asked if she thought Alistair Pritt would be quite so open-minded.

***

Even so, it was too late to alter the course of history. Jimmy would pull his stunt, Alistair would work himself into a reinvigorated, self-righteous tizzy, and yours truly would be suitably embarrassed. Yadda, yadda, yadda.

I moved on and asked Candy what else she had learned during her excursion into the circus. "For instance, what about Roslynn?" I held up a hand. "No. Let me guess. Jimmy interviewed her on this evening's news. And let me guess some more. She read an excerpt from her latest book."

"How did you know?" Candy asked. "Roslynn read from *The Debutante's Destiny*. She told Jimmy she wanted to support you. That's why she's started her Romance Rocks demonstration."

"With friends like this," I said. But on second thought, I decided I needed all the friends I could get. "It took courage to stand up to Jimmy and Alistair like Roslynn did."

Karen nodded. "She gave you lots of compliments, Jess. She said you're an expert at the art of romance writing."

Okay, so I might have guffawed. "She actually called it an art form? Alistair must have loved that."

"He hated it." Candy sipped her champagne. "But mostly he hated how Roslynn and her romance people were distracting Jimmy. Alistair told him to focus."

"Let me guess. To focus on destroying me."

"That's right." She smiled brightly. "You're a good guesser."

***

"She's a better pool player," Kirby said. He and Gus came up from behind and lifted me from my bar stool. Gus reached out his free hand, and Charlie handed him my cue stick from behind the bar.

"I haven't won a game in ages," I said as the guys set me down.

"Well then, there's no time like the present." Gus challenged me to a game, which I proceeded to lose in record time.

While Camille complained I shouldn't get another chance, and while Gus racked for Kirby and me, I tuned in to John Lennon singing "You Make Me Dizzy Miss Lizzy."

The thought of Lizzie Sistina must have inspired me, because my break was actually good. I double-checked. "Did the three ball just fall?"

Kirby, a former Marine, saluted in answer. And Gus suggested I clear the solids. "Don't even give Kirby a chance."

I reassured Kirby he needn't worry much and took aim at the one. Lo and behold, it disappeared.

That time I double-double checked, as did everyone else.

"Jessie!" Candy clapped in glee. "You haven't made a shot that good in months."

Karen shushed her. "Don't jinx it, Kiddo."

The crowd fell silent, and John Lennon stopped telling Lizzy how dizzy she was making him, as I took aim at the seven ball.

Talk about feeling dizzy—it fell also.

But apparently the shock of making three shots in a row was too much for me. I missed the six and stepped back for Kirby as Gina Stone wandered by with some pitchers of beer.

"At least this book-banning nonsense has a silver lining," she told me. "You're so angry, you got your game back."

"Maybe," I said as we watched Kirby pocket the fourteen. "I hope all the nonsense right outside the door isn't harming your business."

"Just the opposite." She started gathering empty mugs scattered on tables near the pool game. "We're doing a booming business at lunch. They eat a lot."

"Alistair or Jimmy?"

"Both. Everyone. Those two, Jimmy's crew, Alistair's demonstrators. They have to eat somewhere, right?" Gina stopped what she was doing to catch my eye. "Are you okay with this? That we're feeding the enemy?"

I shrugged. "At least it's proving positive for someone."

"How about you?" she asked. "This won't sound right, but has all this Queen of Smut stuff helped your book sales?"

"Maybe. But I haven't checked my latest sales figures."

"Yeah, right." Camille, the ever-cordial, elbowed her way into the conversation. "I bet you're keeping a running tally on all the extra books you're selling. You love this Queen of Smut stuff."

Her stance suggested she wanted to argue, but luckily Kirby missed the thirteen, and I was able to step away without a word in my defense.

"That teacher who died is the one who deserves attention," Camille kept at it while I surveyed the table. "But Channel 15's too busy with you to bother with any real news."

"Be nice, Camie," her husband Bernie said quietly.

"Get real, Bernard." She raised her voice even further. "I just heard her bragging to Gina. Jessie loves all this attention."

"Jessie hates all this attention," Kirby argued for me as I bent forward to take aim at the four ball.

But I stopped mid-swing and stood up.

I hated all the attention.

***

The rest of that game is a blur. I know I missed the four, I know Kirby won, and I hope I was coherent enough to shake his hand and congratulate him properly.

I vaguely recall stumbling over to Candy and Karen afterwards. "I'm a good guesser," I told them.

"Say what?" Karen patted my bar stool.

I spoke to Candy. "You said I'm a good guesser. And guess what?"

She gasped. “You’ve guessed something!” She reached over to Karen. “Look at her, Karen. Jessie’s got that look.”

Karen glanced up and flinched. “We’re out of here,” she said, but Candy was already propelling me toward the door.

Chapter 20

"I've got to get to Wilson," I said as we crossed Sullivan Street. I looked at my watch. "I need to borrow a car for the night. I need to get to the lake"

"Are you okay to drive, girlfriend?"

"I had all of three sips of my drink tonight, Karen."

"Not that. But Kiddo and I know that look. You're in one of your I've-solved-the-murder stupors."

I told her I hadn't solved the murder, and I promised to snap out of my stupor. "But I've got to see Wilson."

"You hardly ever stay at his cottage," Candy reminded me as we entered our building.

"It's a shack," I said impatiently. "I need a car, ladies."

Karen shook her head and apologized. "I need my van first thing in the morning. I'm going to the lumber yard, and then I'm starting on a huge kitchen cabinet project."

I tried not to cringe when Candy offered her car.

"As long as I have it back by eleven," she said. "I have the afternoon shift at Tate's. We're stocking up for Mrs. Marachini's next shopping spree. Remember her?"

How could anyone forget the polka-dot bra lady? Candy Poppe is a bra and lingerie saleswoman at our local department store. She's the best there is. And Mrs. Marachini is her best, albeit most eccentric, customer.

I promised I'd have her car home before eleven and said a little prayer the old clunker would get me out to Lake Lookadoo and back again.

I would have started for the stairwell, but Karen grabbed my arm and held me back. "What!?" I tried pulling away.

She held her grip. "Anytime you've acted this weird, a killer was on the loose and after you. You need to be safe, Jess."

"Please," Candy added.

I took a deep breath. "If my guess is correct, the killer is done killing. The last thing he wants is to see me dead."

"Now you're really scaring me." Candy was struggling to pull her car key off her key chain. I took the stupid thing from her and separated the keys.

"I'll explain tomorrow." I kept the car key and handed her the remaining. "In the meantime you guys need to stay safe also. Keep your doors and windows locked." I looked back and forth between them. "And call Lieutenant Densmore if anything unusual happens. Promise me?"

Karen said I was scaring her, too, and I ran upstairs to get my cat.

***

"Road trip!" I called out. I rushed over to the closet, pulled down the cat carrier, and got Snowflake inside before she could even think of protesting.

"Don't worry," I told her when she thought of protesting. "We'll be with Wilson shortly."

I took the yowl as a sign of approval and turned in circles as I tried to remember what clothes and other necessities I had at the shack. Not nearly as much stuff as Wilson kept at my place. I threw a pair of clean underwear in my purse, grabbed my laptop, and headed for the door.

Luckily, I also remembered my cell phone. I called Wilson as soon as I had Candy's car up and running.

"Are you home?" I said by way of greeting. "Snowflake and I are on our way."

"Out here? Now? Are you feeling well?"

"I feel sick actually." I turned out of the parking lot and made it through a yellow light at the corner. "But yes, I'm coming over. Meanwhile you need to assign some extra patrols to Sullivan and Vine. I doubt it's an issue, but I want my friends to be safe."

Dead silence.

"Wake up, Wilson!" I said, and Snowflake meowed from her cat carrier. "Will you, or will you not, put an extra patrol on my building tonight?"

"I have news for you, Darlin.' I've had extra patrols on your building since Saturday."

I had to stop for a red light. "You have?"

"The body was found on your car, Jessie. Until I know why, I'm taking precautions."

I stared at the light and blinked back tears. "I know why."

"Why what?"

"Why Miriam Jilton was left on my car." I took a deep breath and said it. "This was all about me."

Chapter 21

Wilson stood in his driveway, two glasses of champagne in hand, when I pulled up.

"You need this," he said. He handed me a glass and went to retrieve Snowflake. "What about dinner?" he asked. "Have you eaten?"

"Of course I have." I tried holding the glass steady as I stumbled along the dirt path to the shack. "It is after midnight."

"Yeah, but I know you, Jessie. You don't eat enough. Especially when you're thinking about murder."

I held the door to the porch for him and Snowflake and then collapsed into the yellow Adirondack chair. Meanwhile Wilson got Snowflake settled. Perhaps settled isn't exactly it. He opened her cat carrier, and she and his cats spent the next few minutes racing gleefully around the porch.

Wilson took the red chair next to me. "What did you have to eat?" he stayed on topic. "Your usual bowl of lettuce?"

"It's called a salad. But tonight I had chicken tetrazzini."

He skipped a beat. "Don't tell me you actually cooked?"

"Rita cooked," I said, and he almost dropped his glass.

"Rita? As in Sistina?"

"Yes, Rita. She invited me to dinner. Frankie was there, and Lizzie of course. And Peter Harrison, and me. Rita's a good cook. Not as good as you, but the casserole was delicious."

"What the hell were you doing at Rita's? And if you tell me you were asking those kids about the murder, I'll kill you."

I reminded Wilson he had already mentioned that option earlier in the day and watched as Bernice, the oldest and fattest of the three cats, stopped the chase and climbed into his lap.

"But there's absolutely no reason to kill me." I reached out to pet Bernice. "The high school angle is a moot point now. This wasn't about Miriam Jilton."

"Because it was all about you." Wilson and the cat both seemed skeptical.

"It came to me while I was shooting pool."

"I assume you lost?"

"To Kirby, thank goodness."

"You're happy you lost? To Kirby? Are you feeling well?"

"No! I most decidedly am not feeling well. But I needed to end the stupid pool game so I could get out here to you. You've got to hear me out, Wilson."

"Have I ever not heard you out?'

Good point.

I took a deep breath and looked into the baby blues. It was dark on the porch, but apparently not that dark.

"You've been crying," he said.

"Unusual, huh?"

He kept staring. "What's going on, Jessie?"

I took another deep breath. "I don't know who the killer is, but I do know why he killed Ms. Jilton. And I warn you. It is really, really sick."

He kept staring. "Keep going."

"Someone killed her to make me look bad. Pure and simple."

He raised an eyebrow, and I agreed it sounded outrageous and egotistical.

"But you said it yourself, Wilson. This was all about the million-dollar question. This was all about putting a body—any body—on my car."

"Why? Just to get Jimmy Beak's attention?"

"Exactly." I sipped, or maybe gulped, my drink. "Everyone in town knows he has it in for me. The man's been dying to accuse me of murder ever since the Stanley Sweetzer fiasco backfired on him."

"So the killer assumed Jimmy would latch onto this murder and accuse you?" Wilson asked.

"Correct."

"But Jimmy hasn't accused you of murder."

"But who could have predicted that? Jimmy was all set to accuse me until I threatened him with a lawsuit." I paused. "And why exactly did you suggest that, Captain Rye?"

His face dropped. "To shut him up."

"Exactly. We put a damper on the murderer's plan." I shook my head. "But he's still getting what he wanted, because of Alistair and his stupid Queen of Smut campaign." I clicked Wilson's glass with mine. "Here's to dumb luck," I said sarcastically.

Wilson rested his glass on Bernice's ample tummy. "If the murderer wanted to make you look guilty, he did a terrible job of it, Jessie. It's been clear all along you weren't the culprit."

"But he didn't care if I actually got arrested. He just wanted to make me look bad." I curled my lip. "And who better to handle that job than Jimmy Beak?"

Wilson blinked twice. "If you're right about this, it really is sick."

"Oh, I'm right alright." I squinted at the crescent moon hanging over the lake. "Miriam Jilton was simply in the wrong place at the wrong time. No one had any reason to kill her." I turned to Wilson. "You agree, don't you?"

He hesitated before answering. And then admitted he and Lieutenant Densmore had ruled out virtually every suspect.

"I rest my case," I said.

"Not so fast. I'm still trying to figure out the principal."

"It's not Dr. Dempsey. I talked to him twice today."

"Excuse me?"

"Peter Harrison wanted to see his rose garden."

Wilson spoke to Bernice. "Should I even ask?"

"Of course you should." I explained how dissatisfied I had been with Dr. Dempsey's uncooperative behavior earlier in the day. "So Peter and I went to his house this afternoon to try again. Peter knew a secret passageway out of our building and everything."

"I knew I shouldn't ask."

"I don't know why you're so surprised," I said. "You're the one who gave me the idea. You told me not to get Peter involved." I shrugged. "So of course I got Peter involved."

"You're a little scary. You know that?"

"He thinks she was shot."

"Peter?"

"No, Richard Dempsey. He thinks Miriam Jilton was shot," I said as Snowflake and Wally finally decided to join us. They took one look at the overabundance of cat on Wilson's lap and chose me. While I wrestled the two of them for space on my Adirondack chair, I summarized the guilt trip Dr. Dempsey had gone through over Ms. Jilton's death.

"He's wrong about everything. Motive, opportunity, and definitely means," I concluded. "He didn't do it."

Wilson reluctantly agreed. "Dempsey's a pain in the neck, but I can't come up with any motive for him to kill Jilton."

"Which brings us back to the million-dollar question—why she was left on my car." I continued struggling for space on my chair. "She wasn't having any kind of illicit affair, so the killer wasn't making a statement about Miriam." I finally got Snowflake settled onto my lap, with Wally squished in next to us, his chin resting on my knee. "The killer was calling attention to me."

Wilson looked at the moon. "Maybe so," he said quietly, and I groaned.

"What's wrong, Jessie? I'm agreeing with you. You've come up with a plausible answer to the million-dollar question."

"But I hate the answer." I sunk my hand into the fur at Snowflake's neck. "I'm responsible for that poor woman's death."

"No, Jessie." He took my hand away from Snowflake and made sure I was paying attention. "You are not responsible. The murderer is responsible." He gave me his sternest cop-like look. "We straight on that?"

I bit my lip and fought back another wave of tears.

***

"Who knew where your car was that night?" Wilson asked eventually, and I let out that sob I'd been holding back.

He squeezed my hand. "If we want to find this guy, we have to think about this. Everyone and his brother knows about your license plate. But."

"But only a finite number knew where it would be on Saturday."

"Yep." Wilson tried to sound encouraging. "For instance, I didn't know you'd loaned your car out. Not until I was looking at the body on it."

"Well then, I guess we can rule you out."

He squeezed my hand again. "Work with me. Who knew the Smythe kid had your car."

"The Smythe kid himself, obviously. And Frankie was so excited, I know he told all his friends." I thought back. "He called me on Thursday and picked up the Porsche Friday after school. Which means he had all day Friday, and Saturday, to tell who knows how many people."

"Where was it parked on Saturday? During the day, that is."

"At the Smythes' house on Maple Street, I imagine." I bolted upright, and Snowflake and Wally both scolded me.

"Yep." Wilson nodded. "Ian knew."

Yep, he did. My ex-husband got the house in our divorce settlement, I got the car and the cat. This means, of course, that Ian and his new wife live next door to the Smythes and could have easily noticed my car in the Smythe driveway.

"Ian might have asked the Smythes what the Porsche was doing back in the old neighborhood," I said. "Or Amanda could have asked. Or any of my old neighbors, for that matter. Alistair Pritt, even."

"Start with the people who hate you," Wilson said. "The Crawchecks."

I told Wilson to brace himself. "You're not going to believe this, but."

"But let me guess. You've been talking to Ian again."

"He left three messages on my answering machine today."

"Saying what?"

I shook my head. "Believe it or not, I didn't listen. I was so proud of myself for ignoring him, Wilson. I deleted them without a second thought." I snapped my fingers. "Zip!"

Wilson frowned at Snowflake. "She had to choose today to get mature about her ex?"

"Convenient, no?" I thought about my stupid ex and his even stupider new wife. "Ian did not kill Miriam," I concluded. "Neither did Amanda."

"Let me guess. Because they hate it when you get attention."

"Just think what Amanda's country club friends would say if Jimmy Beak accused me of murder again." I feigned a gasp. "Just think of the humiliation to dear, innocent, sweet Amanda."

"I get it," Wilson said. "No on the Crawchecks. But I'll still have Densmore check."

"Tell Russell to do me a favor and put the fear of God in them."

"I'll do just the opposite."

I was indignant, but Wilson insisted we needed to keep the true motive for the murder to ourselves. "Densmore needs to be discreet. We want the rest of the world to continue thinking this was about Jilton. Not you."

"Thus keeping the murderer complacent?"

"Very good."

I asked permission to explain the new theory to Candy and Karen. "They know something's up, and they're very concerned."

Wilson told me to remind them about the discretion thing. "But focus on your old neighborhood for now," he said. "Who else could have seen your car at the Smythes? You mentioned Pritt? He hates you, and the Hava Java is right there." He raised an eyebrow. "And his protest started right after the murder."

"And Captain Rye does not like coincidences," I told the cats.

I complained that I had wasted enough time fretting about Alistair Pritt, and recommenced fretting about Alistair Pritt.

"No," I said eventually and shook my head. "You're just going to have to accept the coincidence. Alistair didn't need to kill anyone to start his book-banning crusade. Jimmy Beak's given him ample ammunition against me without a murder."

I counted off Jimmy's ammunition on my fingers. "The Stanley Sweetzer fiasco, the Focus on Fiction fiasco, and the Romance Writers Hall of Fame-slash-Shame fiasco."

"What about Beak?" Wilson asked, and my mouth dropped open.

What about Beak?

"He hates you," Wilson reminded me, quite unnecessarily, and I got up to pace.

"All those other attempts to tarnish my character didn't work, did they?" I didn't wait for an answer. "So Jimmy decided to kill someone. And then blame me! For murder!"

"Keep going."

"And!" I rounded the small porch for the fifth or sixth time. "And Jimmy knew exactly what the media would do with this story! For Lord's sake, he is the media!"

"Your threat of a lawsuit would have upset the plan."

"Which explains why he's latched onto Alistair with such abandon. He's ignoring every other story under the sun in order to concentrate on the Queen of Smut campaign."

Wilson watched while I paced back and forth at a frantic speed, huffing and puffing in righteous indignation.

"What!?" I snapped.

"You think Beak's capable of murder?"

I stopped short. "Do you?"

"No."

I stamped my foot.

"Sorry, Jessie, but Beak doesn't have the brains for something this sinister. And there's another problem with this theory."

Unfortunately, I knew what it was. I plopped back into the Adirondack chair. "Jimmy had no idea where my car was that night."

"The Junior Cotillion wasn't real newsworthy until the murder." Wilson reached for his cell. "But we'll check anyway."

He called Russell Densmore, apologized for the late hour, and gave him some instructions.

Meanwhile the cats and I got comfortable again. We listened to the night sounds of Lake Lookadoo—the water lapping against the dock, the occasional quack from a duck in the distance, a bullfrog somewhere closer, the wind rustling in the trees. Snowflake looked up at me and clicked contentedly.

I closed my eyes.

***

A phone rang, and I awoke with a start. "How long have I been asleep?" I asked into the darkness.

"Ten minutes." Wilson tapped his phone. "Densmore."

"Wow. That was fast." I sat up and tried to focus while Wilson listened to whatever Lieutenant Densmore was saying. Even in the dark I could see his face drop. And drop some more.

"What?" I said as soon as he clicked off.

"Let's go to bed." He shooed all the cats away and pulled me to my feet.

"Wilson! Did Russell find out where Jimmy was on Saturday? Where?"

"You're tired. We need some sleep." He held the door to the shack open, and the cats and I paraded in.

Wilson and I brushed our teeth in the rusty old sink of his supposed bathroom and climbed the rickety stairs to his supposed bedroom. But the rustic amenities dissuaded me not at all, and I remained on topic.

"Where was Jimmy on Saturday?" I asked for the umpteenth time.

"We don't know yet. Densmore didn't want to ask him over the phone."

I watched my beau—make that my fiancé—as we undressed for bed. Now bed, of course, is a relative term. Wilson's bedroom is a low-ceilinged loft with a mattress on the floor. Yes, it's a comfortable mattress. And yes, the sheets and linens are quite cozy, and yes, the floor is clean, and yes, there's a lovely view of the lake.

But still.

He got into bed—or onto mattress—and patted the one clear space the cats had yet to steal. "Join me?"

I folded my arms and glared from a kneeling position. "What is going on, Wilson? What did Russell say?"

"Beak wasn't home tonight, but Densmore tracked him down."

"And?" I prompted as I plopped onto the mattress.

"Jimmy and his cameraman are on the road. They've also been busy tracking someone down."

Why was my heart starting to race? "Where?" I sang.

He cleared his throat but still managed to mumble. "Umm. Columbia."

I blinked at the ceiling a mere four feet above my head. "Please tell me you're referring to Colombia, South America."

"No." He took me in his arms, perhaps to keep me from exploding through said ceiling. "Columbia, South Carolina." He held me tighter. "Jimmy Beak paid a visit to your mother tonight."

Chapter 22

"LaSwann," Kipp Jupiter muttered to his horse Rex. "What kind of name is that? LeSwine is more like it." Kipp realized he was talking to his horse and snarled in the general direction of the LeSwine ranch.

You would think his new neighbor, a man with practically no ranching experience, would appreciate some advice. But no.

Here Kipp had taken an hour away from his midday chores to ride over there and explain the basics of well-water management. And what did he get for his efforts? A gruff "Thanks, but if you don't mind, I have chores to do."

"Chores, my foot." Kipp told Rex. "I saw LeSwine. Right after I left, he saddled up and rode off toward town."

Kipp squinted at the sun. Four more hours of daylight, but five more hours of work that needed doing. He cursed his new neighbor once more for the hell of it and hastened off toward his lower forty.

***

I smacked my computer and glanced at the three cats. "Do ranchers even have lower forties?" I asked them. "Or does that only apply to farmers? And what about the 'for the hell of it?' Will Adelé's readers tolerate such language?"

Snowflake, who was used to assisting me with such details, looked up from watching the ducks and meowed. But Wally and Bernice ignored me completely.

Who could blame them? The morning sun glistening off Lake Lookadoo was downright mesmerizing. And the duck swimming by with her brood of eight ducklings was also distracting—worthy of all the feline tail twitching happening on the porch.

Snowflake meowed again.

"Yep," I agreed. "The 'hell' has to go."

I was making the minor revision when Wilson came out carrying two plates heaping with scrambled eggs, bacon, and biscuits. Talk about distracting.

“What’s the occasion?” I asked and set aside my computer. “On a Tuesday morning, no less.”

He handed me a plate and sat down with his own. “Watching you write out here inspired me to cook. We’ll go back to Cheerios tomorrow.”

“I wish I was inspired to do something this useful,” I said as I dug in with gusto.

Wilson pointed to my laptop. “No luck?”

“I’m more exasperated with myself than Kipp is with Will-slash-Willow.” I waved a slice of bacon at the lake. “And the beauty of this place isn’t helping matters.”

Wilson looked at the cats. “Did she just call Lake Lookadoo beautiful?”

I pursed my lips and insisted I was referring to our breakfast. I finished my biscuit and indulged in a rather large forkful of eggs while Wilson regaled me with some nonsense about how Lake Lookadoo could actually inspire Adelé Nightingale’s creative powers. “If she allowed herself to get used to it.”

Yadda, yadda, yadda. I ignored him and ate a second biscuit.

***

“You can stop ignoring me now. I’ve stopped talking about the lake.”

“Excuse me?”

“I said.” Wilson waited until he caught my eye. “Who else knew where your car was?”

He got up to clear the plates, and I followed him inside with the coffee cups. He filled the old porcelain sink with soapy water while I poured more coffee and found a dishtowel.

“Have you ever considered getting a dishwasher?” I asked.

“The plumbing couldn’t handle it.” He handed me a wet plate.

“Supposed plumbing,” I said. “What about Septosauruses? Do you have any trouble with them?”

“Huh?”

"The Septosauri. They're ancient monsters who thrive in ancient plumbing such as this." I pointed my dish towel at the faucet. "Lake Looksee is having serious issues with the varmints. They pop out of sinks and stuff, and strangle people."

Wilson dropped the plate he was washing back into the abyss and considered his faucet. "Since when do you write science fiction?"

I credited Frankie Smythe for the brilliant Septosauri premise. "But maybe Adelé should try sci-fi."

"Maybe we should focus on your car," Wilson said, and I reminded him I had spoken to very few people the previous week.

I pulled the next dish from the drainer. "I was quite the recluse, since I was desperately trying to make headway on *A Singular Seduction*. You called a few times. And Frankie called."

I stacked the plates on the open shelf above my head and took a handful of silverware. "Geez Louise called about a dozen times between Friday and Saturday," I continued. "She kept suggesting I get together with Roslynn for a brainstorming session about *Seduction*. She insisted Roslynn could help me get some sex on the page."

"Either of them know about your car?"

The silverware fell to the floor.

"No!" I said. "As Louise would say, no, no, no!" I huffed and puffed, and we bent down to gather what I had dropped.

"No, they didn't know about your car?" Wilson stood up. "Or, no, you refuse to consider the possibility?"

I folded my arms and glared.

"Well?" he asked and dropped the silverware back into the soapy water.

"Of course they knew about my car." I grabbed a handful of cooking utensils. "I specifically told Louise I couldn't meet with Roslynn because I had no car. And so Roslynn volunteered to come to my place. Remember she was at the condo when you called on Sunday?"

"Either Louise or Roslynn have it in for you?"

"Of course not! You know Louise, yourself! She may be excitable, but she's an absolute sweetheart, and she adores me. The same goes for Roslynn. They want nothing but the best for me."

He waited.

"Oh, come on!" I stamped my foot and the floorboards squeaked. "Neither of these women would want to harm my career, or me. Louise gets paid on commission from my royalties, for Lord's sake. And the better my books do, the better Roslynn's do. We write for the same publisher."

"How about the opposite? How have your sales been this week?"

I stared aghast as his logic dawned on me. Louise and Roslynn were both very interested in boosting my sales. And like it or not, negative publicity is quite effective in doing just that. I blinked twice and silently lamented all those phone messages I had deleted so haphazardly the day before.

"Ludicrous," I said and starting hanging the utensils onto the little pegboard next to the stove. "Louise may be crazy-interested in my bestseller status, but she's not that crazy. Geez!" I reminded Wilson that I have known Louise for over two decades, and that she lives and works way up in Manhattan. "She did not fly down here to commit a murder."

"Well then, how about Roslynn?"

What about Roslynn?

I tried to ignore it, for some reason her words rushed back to me. What had she called the murder that morning at my condo? Inconsequential nonsense? Or maybe she was referring to Jimmy Beak?

Even so, Roslynn was certainly enjoying the fruits of Jimmy's attention. Her behavior was a bit—I scowled at the spatulas—a bit what? Inconsistent? Confusing?

"She's devious," Wilson interrupted my thoughts. "She lied to me during the Stanley Sweetzer investigation."

"But that was only to protect Billy Joe Dent."

Wilson handed me a wet frying pan. "My point, exactly."

I pursed my lips and considered a few more disconcerting facts about my friend and colleague. Once upon a time Roslynn Mayweather had been involved with Billy Joe Dent, a married man. And yes, she had lied about it during a murder investigation. So yes, perhaps her character was a few shades shy of stellar.

"She's ambitious," Wilson kept going. "And you just admitted her sales figures reflect your sales figures. And why'd she start that counter-demonstration? Did you see her with her Romance Rockettes on the news last night?"

I confessed I had missed that particular piece of fun. "But I didn't need to watch her on TV. I saw her for myself—live, out on Sullivan Street."

"She read from *Debutante's Delight* for Jimmy."

"*The Debutante's Destiny*," I corrected. "But this is ludicrous. Roslynn Mayweather is not a murderer."

"You never know." Wilson pulled the old-fashioned stopper out of the drain, and the water made a very loud gushing noise as it entered the realm of the Septosauri. "Sometimes people surprise you." He kept his eyes on the drain. "Not always in a good way."

I put down the frying pan. "You're referring to Dianne Calloway?"

He took a deep breath, and when he looked up, he was back to his normal cop-like demeanor.

"You're going to investigate Roslynn, aren't you?" I asked.

"And Louise."

I sighed dramatically. "I have to work with these people, Wilson. And they're my friends. Please don't harass them."

"I don't harass people. I talk to people." He turned on the baby blues. "And I can be charming."

I folded my arms and glared with full force. "The baby blues don't work over the phone, Captain Rye. And exactly how often do you call Louise Urko? Like, never? She's not an idiot. She'll put two and two together and realize why you're calling. I can't take that, Wilson. My career is in enough jeopardy right now."

"Okay, so I won't call Louise," he said. "But I will look into Ms. Mayweather."

"You and me both," I said.

"Jessie! Think, will you? We're talking about a murder suspect here. Murder. You've got to be more careful."

"Wilson!" I shot back. "Think, will you? I'll talk to Roslynn out on Sullivan Street. No one's going to attack me in the middle of that three-ring circus."

Before he could argue the point, I tossed him the dishtowel and pointed to the clock. "On that happy note, let's watch Jimmy Beak harass my mother."

Chapter 23

The cats came inside for the show, and the five of us settled on the couch to watch anchorwoman Belinda Bing go through her usual gyrations about the exciting and shocking stories that were all "Coming up!"

Needless to say, Ms. Bing emphasized the morning's top story—Jimmy Beak's exciting and shocking interview with my mother.

"Russell is going to check on Jimmy today?" I asked as Channel 15 cut to commercial.

"Yep, but he'll be discrete."

I reached out and put the TV on mute. "Just like you'll be discrete when talking to Roslynn?"

Wilson reminded me he knew how to do his job. "Everyone, other than you, me, and Densmore, will still think this was about Miriam Jilton." He gave me a meaningful look. "That okay with you, Ms. Hewitt?"

I ignored the sarcasm. "What should I be working on?" I asked.

"How about your own job? Concentrate on *Singular Sensation* and the Septosauruses."

"*Seduction*," I corrected. "And the Septosauri are one of the few problems Willow doesn't have to worry about. I don't write science fiction."

Wilson shushed me and clicked the sound back on as Jimmy Beak's face illuminated the TV screen.

"Jimmy Beak, here!" he said. "Reporting from The Live Oaks Center for Retirement Living in Columbia, South Carolina!"

I recognized the door to my mother's assisted living apartment—number 204—and groaned accordingly.

"Let's see what Jessica Hewitt's mother has to say about her daughter's nefarious career."

"Jimmy knows what nefarious means?" I asked.

But before Wilson or the cats could consider my question, Jimmy knocked, and my mother answered.

"Is that you, Vivian?" she called out. And there she was, on Wilson's TV screen, blinking at Jimmy Beak. "Oh, but you're not Vivian," she stated the obvious.

Jimmy didn't even bother asking about her best friend. Instead, he took advantage of Mother's surprise, age, and size, and was inside her apartment in a flash.

"May I help you," she asked as the camera got a close up of her beautiful old face. "My heavens!" she exclaimed. "Am I being filmed?"

With what had to be his sneeriest of sneers, Jimmy told her she was on camera.

I spat a four-letter word, and Wilson and the cats scattered to the outermost edges of the couch.

But bless her elderly heart, Mother took Jimmy and his stupid cameraman in her stride. First of all, Tessie Hewitt possesses far more gracious southern hospitality than her daughter. And second of all, she's a ham. Dare I say, she seemed rather flattered by the attention?

"She looks good," Wilson said as Jimmy explained his purpose.

He spoke in ominous and threatening tones, but Mother didn't get it.

"You mean, you want to interview me?" she asked. "About Jessie? For your news show up in Clarence?" She clapped in glee. "I've never been on TV before! Hello-o, Honeybunch!" She waved at the lens. "It's me, your mother." More fluttering of arthritic fingers. "Mr. Beak is going to interview me! About you!"

She winked as if only I could see her and turned back to Jimmy. "Is this about Jessie—I mean, Adelé Nightingale's—induction into the Romance Writers Hall of Fame? I bet she's the talk of the town, isn't she? Especially since the *Clarence Courier* did such a nice feature about her! Look here. It's two whole pages!"

Mother patted Jimmy's astonished arm and invited him and the cameraman farther into her apartment. While he, and one assumes the cameraman, stared aghast, Mother bent over her coffee table and came up holding one of the five copies of the *Courier* I had sent her. Needless to say, she was displaying the "Living" section with a large color photograph of yours truly adorning much of the page.

"It's Jessie! I mean Adelé Nightingale!" She jiggled the newspaper and peeked around the edge to smile for the camera. "Isn't it marvelous?"

Wilson laughed out loud, and I do believe the cats joined him. But I myself tried concentrating on Jimmy as he informed Tessie of the book-banning campaign. I shushed my couch-mates as Mother spoke again.

"Book-banning is such a silly notion, isn't it?" she asked, but she didn't wait for an answer. Instead she again held my photograph for the camera. "This is Adelé Nightingale, the bestselling author of the best romance fiction ever. So all you people out there in TV Land should go right out and buy her books. That's Adelé Nightingale. A-D-E—"

"Stop!" Jimmy shouted, but I barely heard him since Wilson was busy chanting something like, "Go, Tessie, go! Go, Tessie, go!"

"Stop!" Jimmy repeated, and one could see him in the background trying fruitlessly to get the camera to turn its lens away from Tessie.

But evidently the cameraman was enthralled by my mother. I mean, who wouldn't be?

"She looks wonderful, doesn't she?" I asked.

"Peachy." Wilson stopped chanting to reply.

"That's a nice color on her," I agreed. "I gave her that blouse for her birthday."

Mother had listened to Jimmy, by the way. She settled down after the final E in Nightingale and put the newspaper back on her coffee table. "Where are my manners?" she asked her guests. "Would you care for some tea, Mr. Beak? Or how about you?" She turned toward the cameraman. "I'm sorry, young man, I don't believe I know your name."

"Joe," the cameraman spoke from off camera. "Do you have green tea, Mrs. Hewitt."

"Green, black, herbal. Whatever you heart desires, Joe!"

Oh, but there was Jimmy again. Snarling again. "Don't you dare try to bribe us, Ms. Tessie Hewitt. Everyone knows your daughter is a pornographer!"

"It's just tea," Joe the cameraman could be heard saying.

Mother pretended not to get Jimmy's drift. She tilted her head and did some more demure smiling. "What can I tell you about my daughter, the world-famous author, Mr. Beak?"

Jimmy let out a string of unflattering adjectives to describe yours truly and tried in vain to prompt Tessie to call my work pornography, or smut, or at least to attest to its X-rated tendencies.

Mother listened politely. In fact, I do believe she was purposely utilizing her most serene, pleasant, and angelic smile.

Jimmy finally begged. "Don't you have anything to say in response, Ms. Hewitt?"

Mother continued smiling, but something in her gaze must have changed, and I am happy to report Jimmy Beak squirmed.

"Those are some ugly words," she said in a tone that used to make my big brother and me run for cover. "People call Jessie those ugly names because they're jealous."

"Huh?"

"Of Jessie. Of Adelé Nightingale!" Tessie gained momentum. "My daughter is not a pornographer," she continued loud and clear. "She writes romance fiction. She can't help it," Wilson and I finished her favorite saying with her, "—if she's just better at it than everyone else."

While Wilson and I dissolved into cathartic fits of laughter, Jimmy tried desperately to gain control of the situation.

"Ms. Hewitt!" he snapped. "Your daughter is the Queen of Smut! What do you to say to that!?"

"The Queen of Smut?" Mother giggled. "Oh, but that tickles me."

***

"Remind me why I was worried?" I asked as Channel 15 cut to a commercial.

"Because Jimmy isn't done." Wilson pointed the remote at the TV, and my smile disappeared. "No way would they have shown that segment unless there's more to come."

He reached over and held my hand as the commercial break came to an end, and we were once again subjected to Jimmy Beak. He now stood in front of the camera all by himself.

"That's the front entrance to The Live Oaks," I explained as Jimmy launched into his diatribe.

"There you have it, Belinda!" Jimmy said. "Our Channel 15 viewers heard it for themselves. The Queen of Smut's mother has as little modesty as the Queen of Smut herself! Tessie Hewitt is proud—proud!—of what her daughter does for a living!"

Jimmy tut-tutted with relish. "I am frankly shocked at the old lady's audacity! The good citizens of Clarence must stand united against the mother-daughter duo of destruction! Women like this are out to destroy the moral fabric of society! The public has a right to know!"

I squinted at the TV. "Did he just call Mother and me a duo of destruction?" I asked, but Wilson didn't have time to respond before Jimmy raised his voice a full decibel level.

"And this is not just a local issue!" Jimmy shouted into his mike. "I've been working with a special source to get this vital information out to the entire nation!" He pointed a jagged index finger at the camera. "Be sure to tune in to our national affiliate for tonight's evening news. National anchorwoman Dee Dee Larkin can't wait to sink her teeth into this top story!"

"Say what?" Wilson asked.

"You heard me!" Jimmy answered and thumped his chest proudly. "Stay tuned tonight, when this reporter and Dee Dee Larkin take book-banning to the national level!"

National this. National that. "National, my foot." Wilson clicked off the TV. "Beak really thinks the entire nation will get behind him and Pritt over your stupid books?" He caught himself. "I didn't mean stupid."

I continued staring at the blank screen.

"Come on, Jessie." Wilson snapped his fingers in front of my face. "You know Beak and Pritt will go nowhere nationally."

I looked up. "Jimmy mentioned his special source."

Wilson's face dropped. "Geez Louise?"

I cringed. "She keeps Dee Dee Larkin on speed dial. They do lunch together at least once a week."

Truth be told, Geez Louise considers it her number one professional priority to get me national news coverage as often as humanly possible. And unfortunately, she has a pretty good track record. In fact, she and Jimmy Beak have a track record together. The previous year they had conspired to get Adelé Nightingale nation-wide exposure about Stanley Sweetzer.

Positive or negative attention? Louise doesn't care. According to her, all publicity is good publicity. Or to quote my insane agent herself, "All publicity is fantastical, fantastical, fantastical!"

"There's no way I'm gonna stop you from calling her?" Wilson asked.

"None whatsoever."

***

"On that happy note." Wilson stood up. "I've got to get to work."

"Me, too," I said. "I need to get back to town."

"You can stay here, you know?" He tilted his head toward the porch. "I like watching you write out there."

"Yeah, right." I tried turning away.

"No, really." Wilson had hold of me. "Bernice and Wally want to help with your stories. Like Snowflake does."

We looked at the cats. Bernice and Wally yawned in unison and then scooted back out to the porch. Snowflake gave me a feline shrug and followed. And by the time Wilson and I got out there, Bernice had settled her ample self on top of my computer.

"See?" Wilson said. "Everyone wants you to stay. What do you say, Jessie?"

I said no thank you and reminded him I had to return Candy's car. "She has a busy afternoon at Tate's, restocking lingerie for Mrs. Marachini's next visit."

"Excuse me?"

"The polka-dot bra lady. She's Candy's best customer."

Wilson shook his head. "If you're going back downtown anyway, I have a job for you."

"Oh?"

He took a deep breath. "I know I'll regret this, but spend part of the afternoon out on Sullivan Street. Make a point of talking to Pritt and Beak."

"You're kidding, right?"

"Get on camera and get interviewed," he continued hallucinating. "Get indignant, get angry, jump up and down. The whole nine yards of crazy."

I asked if he were feeling well, and Wilson explained his logic—he wanted the murderer to see me having a breakdown on TV.

"Let him think your life's falling apart." He grinned. "Play it up, Jessie. Let's use Beak to our advantage."

It did make sense. If the murderer thought his plan to make me look bad was somehow working, he might get cocky.

"The killer might end up bragging to someone, correct?" I asked. "About how crazy he's made me?"

"Very good. Act crazy, Jessie. You're good at that."

I thanked him for the vote of confidence and spoke to Snowflake. "It seems we have another exciting day ahead of us."

"Talk about exciting." Wilson was still smiling. "I hope you noticed all the hot water we had this morning. Enough for my shower, and to do the dishes."

"Will wonders never cease?" I asked. "Dare I expect hot water for my own shower?"

"Oh, heck no. Just the opposite."

Chapter 24

Call me finicky, but I decided my shower could wait until I got home.

My mother, however, could not. I stuck around the shack after Wilson went off to work, settled into the yellow Adirondack chair, and dialed.

"Are you okay?" I asked the moment she answered.

"Jessie?" she asked. "Did you see me? Was I really on the news show? I've never been on TV before."

I rolled my eyes. "I take it you survived the ordeal?"

"Ordeal?"

"Of Jimmy Beak and his cameraman."

"Such nice boys."

"Excuse me?"

"Well, maybe not Mr. Beak. But Joe is an especially nice young man."

I shook my head and decided I hadn't had nearly enough coffee. "You're talking about the cameraman, correct?"

"Mm-hmm. Joe showed me how to use his camera. I've never seen such a fancy contraption. It's digital, of all things. But Joe was very patient with me, and I learned a lot." Mother giggled. "They did, too."

"Oh?" I braced myself and asked my mother exactly how long she had entertained Jimmy and Joe.

"Goodness, it must have been at least two hours. We had tea after my official interview was finished and chatted about any old thing."

Any old thing?

I braced myself some more and asked what "any old thing" might have entailed.

"Well now, let's see." Mother stopped to think. "Mr. Beak wanted to continue discussing the book-banning foolishness, but I put a swift end to that. There's no sense giving it any more credence by fretting over it, is there?"

"Good point," I agreed. "So what did you talk about?"

"I showed them my drawings. Joe was fascinated I keep drawings of my family instead of photographs." She hesitated. "He told me I'm quite talented."

"Because you are."

"Jimmy was mostly interested in my sketches of you, Honeybunch."

"What a surprise," I said. "You didn't show him the ones of Daddy and me, did you?"

"Of course I did."

"What!?" I sat up even straighter and shooed Snowflake from my lap. "Jimmy Beak knows I play pool? Oh, Mother. Please say no."

"No," she said, and I breathed a sigh of relief. "I wasn't born yesterday, Jessie. I could tell Mr. Beak doesn't like you very much. Therefore, I was cautious. I didn't show him anything he might misconstrue."

"You're a savvy old lady, Tessie Hewitt."

"Like mother, like daughter. And those drawings of you and your father shooting pool are my favorites. I keep them in my bedroom. I certainly didn't invite the boys in there, did I?"

"Did Jimmy ask about Daddy?"

"Oh yes. I told him your father was a small businessman who happened to travel a lot."

I smiled at Lake Lookadoo. My father, better known as Leon Cue-It Hewitt, had enjoyed the esteem and regard of his peers. But somehow I doubted Jimmy Beak would consider Daddy's career as a pool shark a positive reflection on my own character.

Mother switched topics. "But what about your work, Jessie? I hope this book-banning mischief hasn't distracted you from *A Singular Seduction*?"

I scowled at my laptop, or what little I could see of it beneath Bernice. "I'm thinking of trying science fiction," I said. "Or maybe I'll try writing children's books."

"What!?" Mother veritably screeched. "Jessie, honey, don't startle me like that. My heart isn't as strong as it used to be."

I apologized for the shock and explained Adelé Nightingale's sex-scene dearth. "A pornographer who can't write a decent sex scene." I whimpered. "Who would have thunk it?"

"You are not a pornographer," she scolded. "You write romance fiction. And speaking of romance."

I waited for it.

"When's the wedding? I hope you and Wilson have finally set a date? I can't wait."

"Well, you're going to have to wait," I said. "I don't even have hot water for a shower this morning."

"You mean, you're at Wilson's cottage right now? Isn't that nice."

"It's a shack, Mother. And trust me, there's nothing nice about the water situation."

"How is the water, Honeybunch? Lake Lookadoo must be beautiful this time of year."

I frowned at the lake, which was indeed lovely. Darn it.

I stood up and went inside.

"And you stayed there last night?" Mother was asking. "That must have been so cozy and charming."

I looked around and frowned some more. Okay, so maybe Wilson had taken a stab at improving the décor over the past few months. Bright and cheerful throw covers and cushions now adorned the less-than-new furnishings. And I stood barefoot on a pleasantly soft rag rug his mother had sewn and assembled. Wilson had even hung some Fiestaware plates on the kitchen walls.

"The cottage could use some new curtains," I said.

"Did you just say cottage?" Mother asked, and I told her to check her hearing aids.

***

"How did it go?" Candy asked as she gestured me into her condo.

"Surprisingly well." I dropped the car keys into her hand and thanked her again for the use of her vehicle. "No one noticed when I filled your gas tank at the corner. And for some reason Alistair isn't even out there this morning. But his groupies are still there. And Roslynn and the pastel people. And Jimmy."

I bent down to open Snowflake's door. "So once I parked, I took Peter Harrison's secret staircase. It wasn't easy with the cat carrier, but we managed with only a minor bout of the heebie jeebies."

"Secret staircase?" Candy asked but then held up both hands. "Forget about the staircase," she said. "Puddles and me want to know what you figured out last night. What about the murderer?"

Actually, Puddles couldn't care less about the murderer. He was far more interested in getting Snowflake to venture out of her cat carrier. We left them to negotiate on their own and walked over to the windows.

"And what about your mother?" Candy pointed to Jimmy Beak, who was getting in his morning aerobics, running back and forth between the various demonstrators. "Did you see the news this morning?"

My snarl answered that question. But I told Candy that Tessie seemed no worse for wear, and then explained my new theory about the murder. "Believe it or not, Wilson agrees it was all about me," I said. "But he wants to keep the murderer guessing. So keep this latest a secret, Sweetie?"

"Karen will want to know," she said. "But otherwise you know I'm good at keeping secrets."

I did.

I continued watching the circus on Sullivan Street. "Don't these people ever work?" I asked, and Candy reminded me Jimmy Beak actually was working.

"Lucky me." I sighed. "And apparently Alistair has a whole slew of relatives running the Hava Java for him."

"And Roslynn's like you," Candy said. "She's a writer, so she works weird hours."

Speaking of weird. Roslynn and her pastel people had begun some sort of synchronized dance routine, twirling and whirling their posters to the beat of what was clearly their own drum.

"I wonder what makes Roslynn Mayweather tick," I asked.

"She loves romance fiction," Candy said. "And she loves you, Jessie. When I was out there yesterday, she told me how worried she is. About you, and about *A Singular Seduction*."

"I wrote a whole scene on Wilson's porch this morning." I turned from the window. "Kipp Jupiter is mad at Will-slash-Willow because she won't listen to him about the water issues on the ranch. He's taken to calling him-slash-her Will LeSwine. Do you get it?" I smiled. "LeSwine instead of LaSwann?"

Candy tilted her head. "You have your hero calling your heroine a pig?" she asked, and I agreed that the scene might need some work.

"But what about your work?" I asked as I gathered up Snowflake. "You have a big day ahead at Tate's, correct?"

"Mm-hmm." Candy held onto Puddles while I once again maneuvered my poor cat into her carrier. "Every department is gearing up for Mrs. Marachini's visit tomorrow. It's an emergency shopping spree."

I stood up after putting Snowflake away. "A polka-dot bra emergency?"

Candy rolled her eyes. "Don't be silly. The emergency is Mrs. Marachini's niece is getting married on Saturday, but something happened to all the gifts from her bridal shower. There was a fire or something. Anyway, Trisha Fister—she's the niece—was really upset, so Mrs. Marachini promised her a store-wide shopping-spree extravaganza before the wedding. Have you heard about this wedding, Jessie? It's gonna be huge."

Candy stopped and gave me that look.

I folded my arms and glared. "Don't you dare ask me about my own wedding."

"Okay, I'll ask about the water issues instead. How was Wilson's plumbing last night?"

"At least the Septosauri didn't show up."

"Huh?"

"I haven't showered yet, if that answers your question. The cottage ran out of hot water."

Candy raised an eyebrow. "Did you just say cottage?"

***

"Cottage, shack. What difference does it make?" I asked once Snowflake and I got back to our condo. I released her from her carrier, headed to my ultra-modern and altogether luxurious bathroom, and took a long and altogether relaxing shower.

As I got dressed I mentioned it was time to call Geez Louise, and the cat scooted under the bed. "So much for relaxing," I agreed and picked up the phone.

"Jessica!" Louise screamed like no one else on planet earth can scream.

"How are you, Louise?"

"Perfect! Stupendous! Fantastical!"

I waited.

"Fantastical! Fantastical!" she completed her thought. "Did you get my messages?"

"Umm," I said as Snowflake poked her whiskers out. "I think I might have accidently erased them."

"Accidently erased!? This kind of mishap occurs far too often, Jessica. It's a good thing I have Roslynn down there to keep me posted."

"Ah, yes." I sat down cross-legged on the bed, and Snowflake bravely came out to join me. "What exactly has Ms. Mayweather been telling you?"

"Hello-o! She's been telling about your book-banning scheme! An absolutely, fantastically brilliant publicity stunt! Brilliant, brilliant, brilliant! How do you comes up with these things? You always have such brilliant ideas!"

I rolled my eyes. "It was Alistair Pritt's idea, not mine."

"Excellent! Roslynn told me all about this Alistair Fitt guy. I must, must, must call to thank him! Your sales are going to skyrocket because of his brilliant plan! Brilliant, brilliant, brillia—"

"Louise!" I spoke loudly enough that she actually shut up. "The name is Pritt. And don't you dare call him."

"Pritt has a fit!" What a surprise—Louise wasn't listening to me. "That is just too, too, too perfect! Better yet, you should thank him yourself, Jessica! And Roslynn! She says he owns a coffee shop?" Louise gasped. "I just had the most fantastical idea!"

I waited.

"Fantastical! Fantastical! You can schedule a book signing there! With Roslynn, too! Adelé's fans would love, love, love that! What a goldmine!"

"Louise!" I shouted, and Snowflake again disappeared under the bed. "The man who owns this supposed goldmine wants to ban my books. Ban books!" I repeated the phrase three times, Geez-Louise style. "This is bad," I said. "Bad, bad, bad."

"As if!" she said, and I got up in search of an Advil. "The book-banning scheme is brilliant," she insisted. "Your local sales are proof positive."

I filled a glass at the bathroom sink. "You put Roslynn up to this, didn't you?"

Louise was silent—a silence that spoke the proverbial volumes.

I stared at my reflection in the mirror. "You told her—you ordered her—to start that ridiculous counter-demonstration outside my front door, didn't you?"

More uncharacteristic silence.

"Answer me!" I said. "Whose idea was it?"

Louise hesitated yet again. "It wasn't like she wasn't willing," she mumbled.

"Louise!"

"Okay, okay, okay," she said. "You need to calm down, Jessica. You are so excitable!"

I swallowed two Advils and endeavored to remain un-excitable while Louise explained. Apparently Roslynn had reported in with her after leaving my place on Sunday. And apparently this counter-demonstration idea had come to Louise at the spur of the moment.

"You know what I always say, Jessica! Let's make lemonade out of lemons? And soooo."

"And so, I think I need to sit down." I went back to my bed while Louise spouted off about the lemonade.

"And so," she said, "I told Roslynn to gather up some friends and start the pro-romance demonstration. We spent some time discussing the color scheme, slogans, dance steps, et cetera, et cetera. And you can see for yourself how fantastically it's working! Both of you are cleaning up with your local sales. And, and, and!" Louise began hyperventilating. "It's not just local! Because, guess what?"

"Earth to Louise," I said. "I don't have to guess. Jimmy Beak announced it on the morning news."

"Fantastical! I love, love, love Timmy Beaky! That man is the best thing to ever happen to your career! We worked together just like we did when you were accused of murder last summer. Remember that?"

"Who could forget?" I asked, but Louise was still talking—something about Dee Dee Larkin.

"Dee Dee promised me she'd include this latest story tonight! Adelé Nightingale receives national coverage once again! Is that not perfectly fantastical!?"

"What if Adelé doesn't want national coverage?"

"As if! And besides, it's three against one—Timmy Beaky, Roslynn, and I all want this for you! You can't argue with that logic, Jessica!"

No, actually. I really couldn't.

I gave up and did some deep breathing while Louise shouted "national coverage" a few thousand times.

"And you know," she sang in a completely different tone.

"What do I know?"

"I don't see how 3P can fire you now."

I sat up straight. "Speaking of which. Why haven't you mentioned what's going on with Perpetual Pleasures Press before now? Why did I have to hear this news of my impending unemployment from Roslynn? It was humiliating!"

"Calm, Jessica. Stay calm."

I considered taking another pill as my agent admonished me not to worry. "All is well," she said in what I think was meant to be a soothing tone. "Or all will be well once 3P sees your latest sales figures!"

"You should have warned me they're thinking of dumping me."

"No," she said firmly. "That's what you pay me for—to worry about 3P. You do the writing, I do the business. Remember?"

I did. And as much as I complain about her, Geez Louise Urko is the best literary agent a romance author could ask for. She is, in a word, fantastical.

"But I still want to know what's happening with my contract," I said.

"Nothing! No changes! Just get me *A Singular Seduction* filled, filled, filled with sex scenes and all will be well. Weller than well! Now then," she said. "What's the latest with Kipp Jupiter and Willow LaSwann?"

I told her the latest. I expected some input, but the other end of the phone offered only silence. Something akin to dead silence.

"Well?" I prompted. "What do you think?"

More dead silence.

"Louise?"

"Don't worry," she said eventually. "I won't tell the folks at 3P about this."

"About what?" I asked indignantly. "This is good news. *A Singular Seduction* is finally moving forward."

"But Jessica! You have your hero calling your heroine a pig!"

Chapter 25

Snowflake emerged from her hiding place and glared.

"Okay, okay," I said. "Maybe the LeSwine thing isn't Adelé's best idea ever."

The cat glared some more.

"But let's keep things in perspective, shall we? The good news of that conversation?" I pointed to the phone I had thrown across room. "Clearly, Louise is not the murderer. She's insane." I went to pick up the phone. "But she's not violent."

I frowned at the phone, but bless her heart, Snowflake forgave me for my outburst. She sauntered over, and we sat down at the desk to assess the damage. I checked for a dial tone.

"It still works." I frowned some more. "Unlike yours truly."

Snowflake nudged my hand, and I petted her absently while I studied the crowd below. Was anyone down there violent, I asked myself.

By then Roslynn Mayweather and the pastel people had perfected their Romance-Rockettes routine and were dancing up a synchronized storm. The book-banning gang also seemed reinvigorated, perhaps because their leader had returned. Alistair Amesworth Pritt was back from who knows where and was waving his poster around with more vehemence than ever. And the ubiquitous Jimmy Beak flitted from one group to the other, his energy level making everyone else look positively lethargic.

I recollected Wilson's parting request that morning. I was to march down there and act crazy. And if my behavior toward my poor telephone was any indication, I was in a crazy mood.

I stepped away from the window in search of my key to Candy's condo.

"Believe it or not, I actually have a plan," I told Snowflake as I rummaged through my junk drawer.

"Puddles is going to help me orchestrate this little showdown."

Snowflake scowled.

"No, really," I said. "Puddles is just the ticket."

***

"We'll tackle Roslynn first," I told the dog as I grabbed his leash.

Puddles yipped enthusiastically and licked my nose while I got the leash on him. Whether or not Snowflake approved, clearly the little poodle was game to assist me. And I was sure Candy wouldn't mind me borrowing her dog. Puddles is always in need of an extra walk. Indeed, some might consider the amount of piddle in Puddles downright legendary.

"Hold it until I say when," I told him, and we rushed down the stairs and out the front door.

Never one to disappoint, Jimmy Beak saw us immediately. He sprang directly into our path, but I was ready.

"Back off, Beak." I used my nastiest, angriest, craziest voice, curled my lip, and added a snarl for good measure. Wilson would have been proud of me. And of Puddles. The little dog remembered his end of the bargain, lifted his leg, and aimed. Lo and behold, Jimmy backed off.

I praised Puddles for his perfect timing, and we headed over to Roslynn.

"Jessie!" She seemed genuinely pleased to see me. "And Puddles! I'm so happy you guys are joining us." Roslynn waved to one of her cronies. "Go get Jessie a poster from my car, Nora."

"No, no." I held up a hand and told Nora to never mind. Then I turned back to Roslynn and asked her to take a break. "We need to talk."

"No can do! But you're welcome to march with me. We can talk and walk." She got back into formation with the pastel people, and for want of a better solution, Puddles and I joined her.

"What did you think?" Roslynn asked as we stepped in time. "How did I look? More importantly, how did my book look?"

"Excuse me?"

"On TV last night." She tilted her poster toward the cameraman, who hovered back near Jimmy. "I'm so happy he got a few more close ups of *The Sultan's Secret*. How did the sultan look? Oh! And I read an excerpt from *The Debutante's Destiny*. Did you hear? How did the debutante sound?"

"Whatever happened to Jimmy Beak being inconsequential nonsense?" I asked.

"Inconsequential? Are you kidding?" She jiggled her poster up and down. "Have you talked to Geez Louise lately?"

I groaned in answer and made an effort to twirl in time with the rest of the Rockettes. Even attached to his leash, Puddles was better at it than I was.

"Think about our sales figures," Roslynn was saying. "Lemonade out of lemons!"

She stopped and held a hand up, and the pastel people stopped to listen to their leader. Needless to say, Puddles and I stopped, too.

Roslynn reached over and gave my shoulder an affectionate squeeze. "Let's show her majesty the Queen of Smut how much we appreciate her, ladies!"

And I kid you not, the pastel people paraded past and bowed, one by one, in honor of yours truly. Meanwhile Roslynn regaled me with our latest sales figures, spouting off phrases like "Skyrocketing sales!" and "National attention!"

Somewhere in there I lost my patience. I looked down at Puddles and asked if he wouldn't like to piddle on the closest pink pump, and Roslynn finally got the hint. She handed her poster to Nora and allowed me to guide her a few steps away from the other demonstrators.

"What is it you wanted to talk to me about?" She kept a wary eye on the dog. "I mean, if it isn't our book sales?"

I, too, focused on Puddles and wondered how exactly I should broach the subject of Miriam Jilton's murder.

It’s not like I could point blank ask Roslynn if she had murdered a completely random person, so that Jimmy Beak would accuse me of murder, so as to draw negative attention to me, so that Geez Louise would have adequate reason to get me on Dee Dee Larkin’s program, so that my book sales would skyrocket, so that Roslynn’s book sales would skyrocket, so that—

“Jessie?” Roslynn waited until I looked up. “What’s the matter?”

I took a deep breath. “If I ask you a question, will you promise not to hold it against me? Even after you’ve figured out why I asked it?”

“You can ask me anything,” she said sincerely. “You’re my hero, Jessie.”

I asked her not to make me feel any worse than I already did and then blurted it out. “Where were you Saturday night?”

Roslynn grimaced. “Candy told you, didn’t she? I know I shouldn’t have done it, okay? And I know I should have broken it off long before now. But he needed to talk, and I figured it wouldn’t hurt to meet him in a public place. So we met at a little diner on the outskirts of town. This dump called Hastie’s Diner. And I swear, it really is over and done with now. Completely and totally.”

“What are you talking about?”

“Billy Joe.”

“Bill Joe Dent!?” I shouted. I looked around, hoping Jimmy and Alistair hadn’t heard me.

Luckily, they had not, since the two of them were in some sort of heated debate. Alistair kept pointing to me and saying something to Jimmy. And Jimmy kept pointing to Puddles and saying something to Alistair.

Roslynn was saying something to me. “I was with Billy Joe on Saturday. I mentioned it to Candy yesterday. And don’t worry—she’s already scolded me for being so stupid. So you don’t need to bother, okay?”

I told Roslynn her love life was none of my business. “Although seeing a married man is bound to end badly for everyone.” I shrugged. “If you’re looking for any sort of happily ever after, you need to look elsewhere.”

"I'm working on it. But what about you?"

"Don't you dare ask me about my wedding."

"No." She waved a dismissive hand. "I'm wondering about Willow and Kipp. Have you gotten them to the happily ever after?"

"Not hardly." I summarized my latest effort, and Roslynn gasped accordingly.

"Yep," I said. "I now have my hero calling my heroine a pig. Brilliant, no?"

And speaking of swine. Jimmy and Alistair were on the move and headed our way, with Joe the cameraman and several of the book-banning brigade in close pursuit. A veritable herd of swine. Some with bullhorns attached.

I pointed Roslynn back to the pastel people, adopted a demeanor which I hoped conveyed crazy, and stood my ground.

Puddles looked up at me for instruction, and I told him to pee whenever the mood struck.

***

I yanked the bullhorn from of Jimmy's startled hands and plunged on into my performance. "I'm trying to write up there!" I pointed my free hand to my third floor windows. "I have a job to do! I can't concentrate! You're ruining my career! You're destroying Adelé Nightinga—"

I put the megaphone down and blinked at the camera. The crazy-lady act was, perhaps, a bit too easy?

Speaking of crazy. Jimmy procured another bullhorn and launched into his own act, spouting off the typical nonsense about the public having a right to know.

I ignored him and leveled my bullhorn at Alistair. "I haven't written a decent sex scene in days! Days, I tell you!" I may have exaggerated my distress, but at the same time, I neglected to admit it had actually been months since Adelé Nightingale added a decent sex scene to her repertoire.

Alistair jabbed his poster upward. "Well then!" he snapped at me. "Get back up there and get to work, Miss Queen of Smut! You have sex scenes to write!"

"Huh?"

I looked at Jimmy, but he seemed as confused as I. Was Alistair actually encouraging me to write sex scenes? The man might as well have been channeling Geez Louise herself.

A slow smile made its way across my face as I suddenly understood the logic of Alistair Amesworth Pritt. He'd be having no fun at all if it weren't for Adelé Nightingale.

"Look at her, Jimmy!" he bellowed. "She's thinking about sex!"

I raised my megaphone. "I'm not thinking about sex," I announced to the crowd. "I'm thinking about writing children's books."

Well, that certainly got a reaction.

Alistair dropped his poster, Jimmy dropped his bullhorn, Joe fumbled his camera, the synchronized step Roslynn and her cronies were executing ended in an all-out collision, and Puddles shook himself all over and snorted.

While Alistair recovered his poster and the pile of pastel people untangled themselves, I explained. "Alistair would be mighty disappointed if I switched genres." I turned the bullhorn in his direction. "If I stopped writing romance, you'd have nothing to harass me about, would you? This should be illegal!"

"Your books should be illegal!" he bullhorned back.

"Book banning is illegal, Alistair! Read the Bill of Rights. Get out your yellow marker and try highlighting the First Amendment!"

Oooo. That was good.

Also encouraging—Puddles remembered his task and was staring at Jimmy's pant leg with renewed interest. Jimmy kept his distance and even seemed reluctant to raise his bullhorn at me. The thing drooped forlornly at his side.

"Mission accomplished," I told the dog. I was about to surrender my bullhorn and go inside when Alistair spoke again.

"Speaking of the law," he shouted. "Tell Captain Rye to get back to work!"

I re-raised my bullhorn. "Excuse me?"

"The taxpayers of this fine city aren't paying your boyfriend to protect you. We're not paying him to be your hero! He is not a character in one of your books!"

I brandished my bullhorn one more time and told Alistair to take a look around. "Wilson isn't even here." I pointed to Puddles. "It's this little dog who's protecting me."

Another valid point, if I do say so myself.

Alistair must have realized this also. He switched gears to something a bit less objective. "Evil!" he shouted and pointed his poster. And the ilk, who had been rather complacent, chimed on in. "Evil, evil, evil!"

I rolled my eyes and again made as if to go inside, but Jimmy braved Puddles and blocked my path. Apparently Channel 15's finest had not been getting nearly enough attention.

"Like mother, like daughter," he bullhorned at me. "Evil!"

"Evil, evil, evil!" the ilk reiterated.

I abandoned the crazy act and opted for truly sincerely berserk. "Did you just call my mother evil?" I screamed. I forgot to use my bullhorn, but I doubt anyone missed it.

Jimmy sneered. "The public has a right to know about the woman who spawned the Queen of Smut. For anyone who missed my special report, I travelled all the way down to Columbia, South Carolina—"

"Forget about the mother!" Believe it or not, that was Alistair, not me. "No one cares what's happening in Columbia."

Jimmy skipped a beat but quickly recovered himself with his old stand-by. "But the public has a right to know. That's why this reporter travelled all the way—"

"One thing at a time," Alistair scolded. "Let's clean up our own backyard before worrying about someone else's."

"But the public," Jimmy sputtered.

"The public needs to worry about the evil lurking here at home!" Alistair again waved his poster at me. "Beware, all ye citizens of Clarence!" he bullhorned.

All ye citizens?

"Beware the influence of this creature on our fair hamlet!"

Our fair hamlet?

Poor Alistair. Clearly the man had spent far too much time studying my books. I glanced down at Puddles. "He's starting to sound like Adelé."

Chapter 26

Willow LaSwann stared into the abyss and blinked back tears. But alas, her tears fell, not into a pool of water, but onto a dry floor far, far below.

Kipp Jupiter told her this would happen. Only yesterday he had warned her the well would run dry. Pointing yonder, into the thicket of sagebrush, he suggested a more suitable location for a well, and had even offered to assist with the digging.

Why, oh why, had she not listened to him? Why, oh why, had she sent him away?

Lamenting her rude behavior, Willow wept even more, her bosom straining beneath its bonds. Eventually she brushed the tears from her sapphire blue eyes and gazed across her land toward Mr. Jupiter's ranch.

God rest his soul, Uncle Hazard had been wrong about Kipp. Why, everyone in Hogan's Hollow had only positive things to say about Mr. Jupiter. He had not acquired the largest ranch in Wilcox County because of greed. Heavens, no! Kipp Jupiter was the most successful rancher because he was the most informed. Kipp understood the water issues better than anyone. And he managed his land with all due skill, preserving it for future generations!

But where was he now? Now, when she so desperately needed his help?

But hark! There he was! Willow caught a glimpse of her handsome neighbor as he rounded the corner of his barn. She would go to him! Yes! She would go over there, and she would apologize for being rude the day before, and she would ask his forgiveness, and she would ask him to please come over to help her locate the exact place for her new well!

Her determination recovered, Willow LaSwann started toward her own barn to retrieve her horse, but suddenly stopped short. She lifted her delicate, if somewhat sunburned, hands to her face and touched her tear-stained cheeks.

Oh, misery and despair! She could not visit Mr. Jupiter after all. For she had been crying. And the rugged ranchers of Wilcox County simply did not cry.

Willow plopped her most unmanly bottom down on the nearest haystack and cried even more. At this rate she wouldn't be able to visit her neighbor for hours.

***

"Oh, misery and despair?" I slapped my laptop for the umpteenth time and warned Snowflake that I, too, was close to tears. "Willow LaSwann's well is dry, and so is this insipid story." I waved my arms. "Where's the water? And more importantly, where is the sex?"

While I stood up to pace, Snowflake hopped down from her windowsill and strolled over to her water bowl.

"Showoff," I muttered.

I watched the cat lap up her water, and tried picturing the prairie where Willow LaSwann and Kipp Jupiter lived. It would be nice to know something—anything—about ranching, wells and water rights in the Nineteenth-Century American west. Was Adelé Nightingale going to be reduced into doing some actual research?

"Research instead of sex scenes," I said, and Snowflake deigned to glance up from her dish. "The situation has become altogether depressing."

***

Luckily my cell phone rang so I could avoid further contemplation of my rapidly deteriorating creative output.

"Superintendent Yates here," Gabby greeted me. "I understand you did not utilize your hall pass today, Jessie."

"No," I said. "Will I be punished with after-school detention?"

She skipped a beat. "I did it again, didn't I?"

"Somehow I seem to inspire your scolding-a-truant-teenager voice."

She groaned and apologized. "It's not just you. I use that tone far too often. Why do I do that?"

"Probably because you've scolded a lot of truant teenagers. What can I do for you?"

"You can tell me who killed Miriam Jilton. I've just finished another faculty staff meeting at the school."

"It didn't help," I said.

"Nothing." She might have actually whined. "I'm getting nowhere with these people."

"Because you won't get anywhere with those people."

"Pardon me?"

I told Gabby I had some crucial news to report. "But we shouldn't discuss it over the phone."

"I'll be right there. Don't move." She hung up but called back before I could even look askance at Snowflake.

"I did it again!" she said when I answered. "I'm so bossy!"

I grinned at Snowflake. "Would you care to stop by for a visit, Gabby?"

"That would be lovely, thank you. But I don't want to interrupt your work."

I told the superintendent she'd be doing me a favor. "Adelé Nightingale is trying to tackle Willow LaSwann's plumbing issues. Which, believe it or not, are even more bewildering than Wilson Rye's."

"Pardon me?"

"Willow's my new heroine," I said. "And she is positively desperate. Her well has gone dry, and she has no idea what to do about it."

"Isn't that what your hero is for?

A thought occurred to me, and I crossed my fingers. "Maybe you can help Willow, Gabby. Once upon a time you were a teacher, correct?"

"I was in the classroom for twenty years. Why?"

"What subject?"

"Is Willow a teacher? I'm sorry, Jessie. I'm not following you."

"What subject did you teach, Dr. Yates."

"History. Why?"

I gave Snowflake a thumbs up and told Gabby to hurry on over.

***

"Get me out of here!" Gabby pleaded.

"Will do," I said into the intercom and assured her I was on my way downstairs. "In the meantime, be sure Jimmy Beak knows you're here to see me."

"Pardon me?"

"Tell him we're in cahoots to catch the killer. Oh, and be sure to mention my hall pass. And for Lord's sake, get on camera."

"Pardon me? I don't understand."

"Just do it, Gabby."

Bless her authoritarian heart, she just did it. "I am here to see Jessica Hewitt," she said. She had turned away from the intercom, however she was using her scolding-a-truant-teenager voice, and I heard her loud and clear. "We are in cahoots to catch Miriam Jilton's killer."

One assumes she was speaking to Jimmy Beak and had her gaze firmly affixed on Joe's camera lens. And one assumes she also mentioned the hall pass. But by that point I was racing down the stairs.

I reached the front door and stepped out to the stoop to give my visitor the hug she so richly deserved. "Dr. Yates!" I exclaimed. I whispered in her ear, "Go along with this."

"Jessie Hewitt!" she exclaimed.

We swung around and smiled for the camera, and Jimmy observed that I was in a much better mood than earlier.

"Oh, yes," I said. "I feel much better now that Dr. Yates is here."

Jimmy squinted. "Why's that?" he asked, and from the look on Gabby's face, she wondered the same thing.

"Because Superintendent Yates and I are going to clear things up." I redirected my gaze toward Alistair. "Superintendent Yates and I are concentrating on the real issue."

"What's that?" Jimmy asked.

"The murder, of course. Surely you haven't forgotten about the murder at the high school?" I fluttered my eyelashes for the camera. "Superintendent Yates and I are in cahoots to catch Miriam Jilton's killer."

"Cahoots!" Gabby squeezed the dickens out of my left shoulder, and I tried not to wince.

"The two of us and Captain Rye," I said. "Three heads are better than one! Isn't that right, Dr. Yates?"

"Three heads!" she enthused to the camera.

"We'll solve the murder. And then!" I directed an index finger skyward.

Jimmy looked alarmed. "And then what?"

"And then the three of us will be local heroes! I'll be a local hero, Jimmy. My reputation will be restored, Alistair will stop his book-banning demonstration, and I'll be able to concentrate on my writing again!"

"That will be good," Gabby said with another shoulder squeeze.

"I can't wait until I can get back to work," I said and squeezed back. "That should do it," I whispered, and we worked together to get ourselves on one side of the door, and Jimmy and Joe on the other.

Mission accomplished, we leaned back against said door and breathed a few sighs of relief.

"I'm growing quite fond of you," Gabby told me. She stood up and brushed off her shoulders. "But what in the world was that performance all about?"

"That performance," I said, "was for the benefit of the killer."

***

"All about you?" Gabby stumbled out of the elevator and toward my condo. "I don't understand."

I got her inside and closed the door. "Miriam Jilton was simply in the wrong place at the wrong time," I told her. "The only purpose of her murder was to put her body on top of my car."

Gabby plopped herself down on the couch. "You're sure you don't have any bourbon in this place?"

Time flies when you're having fun. It had indeed gotten to be happy hour. And even though we didn't have much to be happy about, Gabby again accepted a glass of Korbel.

As I poured the bubbly, I explained the details of my new theory. "I'm really sorry," I said in conclusion. "I feel responsible."

"But it wasn't your fault." Gabby waited until I was seated and made sure to catch my eye. "I know that. And so do you." She was using her scolding-a-truant-teenager voice again, but this time it didn't bother me.

"But Ms. Jilton was so stellar," I said.

"All the more reason I'm grateful you figured this out. You and your fiancé have to catch this guy, Jessie." She caught my eye. "Captain Rye agrees with your theory?"

"Believe it or not, yes."

"Because your intuition is perfect." She watched Snowflake, who sat on the coffee table cleaning her front paws. "Now I understand why you didn't use your hall pass today."

I nodded. "If I'm correct, there's no point in sleuthing at the school. However, we still want the killer to think, that we think, that this was all about Miriam Jilton. This must be kept top secret."

"Absolutely," she agreed. "I won't even tell Gordon, and I usually tell my husband everything." She sipped her beverage and thought about things. "This theory explains our performance out on your stoop." Gabby was starting to catch on. "Keep the superintendent of schools involved, and you throw the killer off guard."

"You did great, by the way."

She curled her lip. "I have a lot of experience handling Mr. Beak."

"We also want the killer to think he's succeeded in ruining my life." I pointed toward my windows and described the other ridiculous scene I had made a bit earlier. "Wilson asked me to act crazy."

"You're good at that."

I thanked her for noticing and got up to rummage around in my junk drawer. I came back carrying my hall pass. "I'll keep you posted on what we find," I said. "But I won't be needing this anymore."

She pushed my hand away and told me to hold onto the ID. "You'll need it next fall."

"Oh?" Something told me I had better sit back down.

"Clarence High is offering a creative writing course for our upper classmen next year."

Oh, yes. Sitting was an excellent idea.

"And guess who's going to teach it, Adelé?"

I blinked twice and thought fast. "Gee-ee," I said. "Umm," I added. "Umm, I'm sorry I can't help you out. But, umm." I blinked again. "But I have no teaching certificate." I threw my hands up. "I'm not qualified!"

"Nonsense." The smile on Gabby's face was most disconcerting. "It's only for one course, for one school term," she informed me. "As superintendent I have the authority to make an exception."

"But, umm. But what about the school board?" That sounded good. "They didn't even want me to judge a writing contest, correct? So they definitely won't want me to teach in the public schools."

I shook my head and tut-tutted. But much to my chagrin, Gabby's smile faded not at all. If possible, she smiled even more enthusiastically and told me she had learned her lesson about bowing to the whims of the school board.

"School board-schmool board," she said to prove her point. "Never again will I let those fools intimidate me when it comes to what's best for our students."

"But," I sputtered. "But."

"But nothing." She was back to her speaking-to-a-truant-teenager voice. "You'll be an exceptional teacher. The students will listen to you."

"Oh? And why is that?"

"Because of your notorious reputation! You're the Queen of Smut, herself!"

The Queen of Smut appealed to the royal cat for help. But Snowflake was otherwise occupied, merrily playing with what was fast morphing into my permanent hall pass.

"You have an opportunity to do our young people some good," Gabby continued. "Therefore, you will."

She informed me I would start after Labor Day, which would, evidently, give me plenty of time for something called "prep." She scowled at the stack of *Sensual and Scintillating* collecting dust on my coffee table. "I'll provide you with a suitable textbook," she promised.

"Now I see why they call you Dr. Yikes," I said.

***

Call it determination. Call it desperation. But somehow I steered Gabby off the topic of what I would be teaching in the near future, and onto the topic of what she had taught in the distant past.

She was arguing her subject had been European history, and I was arguing that she still had to know something about the ins and outs of ranching in the Wild West, when Wilson walked through the door.

He immediately noticed Superintendent Yates, and the bag of groceries he held would have slipped to the floor had I not rescued it.

"Wilson!" I said brightly. "What are you doing here?"

"I promised you dinner tonight, remember?" He pointed to the groceries I had set on the kitchen counter, but kept his gaze fixed on Gabby.

"I think you know Gabby?" I said. "I mean Dr. Yates." I gestured to Gabby. "And Gabby, you know Wilson."

Gabby stood up and waved her empty champagne glass Wilson-ward.

"Uh," he said, and then remembered his manners. "You're welcome to join us, Superintendent." He again pointed to groceries. "I'm making risotto."

"It sounds delicious," she said as she walked over. "But I was just leaving. You have a lovely fiancée, by the way. Jessie is beautiful, smart, and intuitive. I approve."

Wilson looked back and forth between the two of us. "Umm," he said.

"Say thank you, Captain Rye," Gabby told him.

"Thank you Captain Rye."

She patted his hand, winked, and was gone.

He frowned at me. "You sure you don't have any bourbon in this place?"

Chapter 27

I peeked in the grocery bag and counted at least six different vegetables. "Captain Rye must have a lot on his mind," I told Snowflake.

"What do you mean?" Wilson asked.

"I mean, your cooking." I shooed the cat off the counter and started unloading the veggies into the sink. "Whenever a case is causing you trouble, you plan a meal that involves much, much chopping."

He denied it, but I insisted it was true. "I play pool to solve problems, you chop celery."

"Risotto doesn't have celery. And besides, you like vegetables."

I set the cutting board in front of him and handed him the onion. "Enjoy!" I stepped away to work on the champagne, and Wilson started chopping.

"Is Dr. Yikes making a habit of visiting you every day?" he asked.

"Every other day." I set a glass in front of him and took a seat at the counter. Snowflake hopped on my lap, and we watched him chop asparagus. "She's anxious we find the killer."

"You tell her your theory?"

"I hope that's okay?"

Wilson agreed the superintendent of schools probably needed to know.

"She promised to keep it to herself," I said. "And she really helped me with Jimmy Beak. We put on quite a performance for the killer."

"You mean live performance."

"Excuse me?"

Wilson pointed his paring knife at the kitchen clock. "She timed her visit here just right for the five o'clock news. Don't you think Beak included it live?"

"Good point," I agreed and watched as Wilson laid into a whole plethora of mushrooms. There had to be at least four varieties. "I imagine my showdown with Alistair earlier also made the news," I said. "You'll be happy to know I over-acted that performance also. The killer must think I'm a complete lunatic."

Wilson stopped chopping and spoke to Snowflake. "Whereas some of us know for sure."

"Yeah, yeah." I pointed back to the clock. "Should we at least watch Dee Dee's report?"

Wilson slid the last of the mushrooms into the sauté pan and found a towel to wipe his hands. "You're on, Jessie."

"Literally," I grumbled.

***

"Coming up!" Dee Dee Larkin's photogenic face filled my little TV screen as the three of us settled ourselves on the edge of my bed, and the screen shot changed to the Capitol building.

Jimmy Beak likely disagreed with their priorities, but evidently Channel 15's national affiliate considered the latest Congressional budget impasse more newsworthy than the trials and tribulations of Adelé Nightingale. Wilson had plenty of opportunity to run back and forth to the kitchen to stir the risotto before the segment on yours truly aired. In fact, he was in the kitchen for the beginning of what ended up being a very brief report.

"What's going on?" he asked as he came back to the bedroom.

"Same old, same old." I pointed to the screen, where Alistair Pritt was performing one of his usual rants about the Queen of Smut and borderline pornography.

"At least they're showing both sides," Wilson said as the image shifted to Roslynn Mayweather expounding the cause of free speech and freedom of expression.

"Louise will love it," I said. "I mean, who would you listen to? Roslynn or Alistair?"

"Roslynn," Wilson stated the obvious.

As always, Ms. Mayweather was well-turned out. Trim, fit, properly lipsticked, and dressed to the nines in her pink ensemble, she was coherent and articulate. As compared to Alistair, in all his corpulent glory.

Dee Dee Larkin seemed rather unimpressed and impatient with everyone. Indeed, we only got a chance to hear Roslynn read the briefest of excerpts from *The Debutante's Destiny* before Dee Dee interrupted. The anchorwoman allowed us one more glimpse of Alistair as he raised a fist and repeated some nonsense about my undue influence on society, then she closed the segment without further ado.

"My undue influence on society?" I said as Wilson turned off the TV. "Don't I wish."

***

"I wonder what they did with Jimmy?" I asked as we sat down to dinner. I was thrilled Dee Dee Larkin hadn't included him in her national report, but one had to imagine Jimmy was mighty disappointed.

Wilson agreed. "I have no idea where he was when that was shot." He raised an eyebrow. "But I do know where he was Saturday."

From the look on my beau—make that my fiancé's—face, I surmised Jimmy had an alibi. "What earth-shaking event did he and Joe cover that night? Do tell."

"Joe?" Wilson asked, and I reminded him how my mother had deftly uncovered the cameraman's name.

"She charmed him with a cup of green tea, remember?"

"Leave it to Tessie. Speaking of tea parties—that's Jimmy's alibi for Saturday. He was covering a tea party.

"Excuse me?"

"Things got a little out of hand. Violent, even."

"At a tea party? Jimmy was at a raucous Saturday night tea party?" Needless to say, I was incredulous, but Wilson explained.

It seems the tea party—an early evening bridal shower—had started out innocently enough. "But then two of the bride's aunts gave her the same set of stemware, and all hell broke loose about who was going to return what." He shook his head. "Have you heard about this wedding, Jessie? Fister and Bickerson?"

It was my turn to shake my head. "It's a small world," I said. "Or at least Clarence is small. Believe it or not, there's a Mrs. Marachini connection." Wilson looked puzzled, and I reminded him of Candy's polka-dot bra lady.

"A lot of kooky families are connected with this wedding," he said. "Someone at the shower dosed up everyone's tea with bourbon. And the booze made all the gift-givers—" he searched for the right word, "—passionate about their stemware."

I put down my fork and had a good laugh.

"Don't laugh," he stopped laughing to tell me. "The department had to send out Leary and Romero to break it up. There was glass everywhere. Piles of broken coffee pots, blenders. Torn sheets and towels. Unbelievable."

"What's unbelievable is that Jimmy Beak was called out."

Wilson reminded me the Fisters were a prominent family in town. And evidently Saturday had been a slow news day. "The bridal shower was the best story Beak could find, but then he had stories coming out his ears."

I got serious. "First the bridal shower brawl, then the murder."

"The timing's clear," Wilson said. "Beak went straight from the tea party to the school. Dozens of witnesses saw him at both places." He took a deep breath. "Which brings us to the alibis of two other people who might have it in for you."

I rolled my eyes. "Let me guess. The Crawchecks were at the tea party."

"Amanda's the bride's second cousin."

"Leave it to Amanda to be related to kooks."

"You'll be happy to know your ex has an alibi also."

"Let me guess again. Ian was out with the bride's kooky uncles, drinking bourbon or something."

"Close. The men were downstairs in the den watching the Braves game. Had the TV on so loud, they didn't even hear the commotion from above."

I recollected how often I had watched TV over the past few days and asked why none of the bridal shower brouhaha had been on the news. "For instance, Candy assumes all those shower gifts were lost in a fire."

"Money," Wilson said. "The Fister family paid our good friends at Channel 15 to sit on this story." He grinned. "Seems you weren't the only one to get in touch with Cal Ransom that night."

We agreed Jimmy Beak must have been exceedingly frustrated. First he was kept from reporting on the bridal shower of the century. Then he was forbidden from accusing me of murder. All on the same night.

"Yet another reason he's latched onto Alistair with such gusto," I said.

***

"What about you?" Wilson asked as we got up to clear the table.

"Oh, I'm frustrated, too," I said. "I know it wasn't my fault, but I still feel guilty about Ms. Jilton."

"No, Jessie. I meant what did you find out today. Who'd you talk to?"

"Only everyone and his brother." I loaded the dishwasher and tried not to forget anyone. "Mother, Candy, and Louise." I rinsed some silverware before sticking it in the basket. "Then Roslynn, Alistair, and Jimmy out on Sullivan Street this afternoon."

"Dr. Yates," Wilson added, and I nodded.

"I think that's it. Karen's busy building who knows what, so she wasn't available." I shrugged. "And I'm rather surprised Rita Sistina hasn't called again."

Wilson suggested I count my blessings. "What did Alistair and Roslynn have to say for themselves."

"Alistair hates me. Roslynn loves me."

"Let's start with Alistair."

"I thought we ruled him out? He didn't need a dead body to begin his protest."

"Maybe."

I stood up from the dishwasher and squinted. "What are you saying?"

"I'm saying the timing still bothers me. I brought him down to the station for questioning."

"This morning!? Then that explains his newest kick, claiming I have undue influence over you." I winked. "I do believe he called you my hero, Captain Rye. What did you say to him?"

"I asked him his whereabouts on Saturday. But Pritt must have taken a lesson from Rita. He claimed police brutality. Claimed I was trying to shut him up to protect you. He claimed all kinds of garbage." Wilson groaned. "The interview took forever."

"But you persevered."

"Yep, and Pritt has no alibi. Says he was home alone reading."

"Was he?"

"I have no idea. But you're right, Jessie."

I went back to the dishes. "He didn't need a dead body to start calling me the Queen of Smut."

Wilson worked around me to run water into the tea kettle. "What did Roslynn Mayweather have to say?"

"Now there's someone who appreciates the Queen of Smut." I giggled. "I'm Roslynn's hero. Or at least Adelé Nightingale is."

"That's what I heard, too."

I closed the dishwasher and stood up. "Please tell me you didn't drag Roslynn down to the police station."

"I didn't." Wilson informed me he sent Sergeant Tiffany Sass out to do his dirty work. "Sass is a good sport," he said. "She even agreed to wear a light blue skirt suit to fit in with the Romance Rockettes."

"That's perfect," I said, and I meant it. Sergeant Sass and Roslynn are about the same age, and both are beautiful and ambitious young women. And apparently they had an informal, no-stress sort of chat—right there at the corner of Sullivan and Vine—while doing the "Rockettes Routine" as Wilson called it.

We took our tea over to the couch and sat down on either side of Snowflake. I asked what Tiffany Sass had learned, but Wilson wanted to hear about my encounter first.

"For instance," he said. "Did Roslynn mention where she was Saturday night?"

“She was with Billy Joe Dent. They met at Hastie’s Diner of all places”

“That’s what Sass heard, too.” Wilson frowned until I frowned also.

“I admit it’s not the most wholesome of alibis,” I said. “But at least it’s an alibi.”

“No, it isn’t. You know they have a habit of lying for each other.”

I cringed at Snowflake. “True,” I said.

“And we checked at Hastie’s. They only stayed for one cup of coffee. Your friend Roslynn had plenty of time to go out to the school afterwards.”

“Okay, but what about size?” I asked. “Whether or not she really was with Billy Joe, and whether or not she had much of a motive, Roslynn is simply too small. She could not have carried Miriam Jilton’s body across that parking lot.”

Wilson conceded that I had a point. “And strangling someone would have ruined her manicure.”

I thought about other options—or rather, the suspects. “So who was it?” I asked.

“It’s your life, Darlin.’ You tell me.”

I like to think I have a good imagination and a healthy dose of intuition, but I truly had no idea.

“Last night it seemed so clear this was all about me. But now?” I shook my head, exasperated. “I am still sure of one thing, though. This was not about Miriam Jilton.”

“I agree.”

“Really?”

“You’re on to something, Jessie. We just have to figure out what.” He stood up and held out a hand.

“What?” I asked.

“Shoot a game of eight ball with me. I chop celery, you shoot pool. Remember?”

I allowed him to pull me to my feet.

“Beat the pants off me,” he whispered in my ear, and I pointed to my stack of *Sensual and Scintillating*.

“Maxine Carlisle devotes a whole chapter to that sort of thing.”

Chapter 28

"My game is off lately," I said as we made our way downstairs and outside.

"I know what would improve your game," Wilson said.

I rolled my eyes. "Let me guess. Our wedding would miraculously solve that problem, and all others."

"Happily ever after on the shores of Lake Lookadoo."

"Oh, yes," I said. "You, me, and the three cats. One big happy family, all cozy-like in a shack with supposed plumbing."

"Everyone else calls it a cottage."

"Everyone else has running water."

I pushed the button to cross Sullivan Street and pointed up at my windows. "How about happily ever after high above the streets of Clarence?" I asked. "You and your cats could just as easily move in with Snowflake and me."

Wilson waved to the traffic streaming by us. "I need peace and quiet when I'm not working."

I waved to the neon sign hanging above The Stone Fountain. "And I need a little life when I'm not writing."

"Snowflake likes my house," he argued as we crossed the street.

"Snowflake doesn't use your shower."

He opened the door to the bar. "Come on, Jessie. I almost always have running water."

"That's what Willow LaSwann told Kipp Jupiter just yesterday," I said. "And look at the mess she's in now."

***

It was Motown night at The Stone Fountain, and The Supremes were singing "Someday We'll Be Together" as we stepped inside.

Wilson made some silly comment about Diana Ross being on his side and sang along. I ignored him as best I could, found my way over to the bar, and told Charlie I hoped he appreciated the mess I was in.

"Trying to plan the perfect wedding?" he asked and high-fived Wilson.

I glared and reached out a hand. "Cue stick!"

He pretended to cower and handed it over, and Wilson and I stepped up to the pool table.

Bless their hearts, the pool table gang seemed to appreciate the mess I was in. And they know me. Or at least they know when I need to shoot some pool. Gus took one look at me, quickly won the game he was playing against Camille, and gave up his cue to Wilson. Kirby Cox started to rack.

Wilson thanked everyone for their cooperation, but Camille doesn't believe in cooperation. She sputtered something about waiting our turn like everyone else.

"Leave them alone," Gus scolded her. "Jessie needs to play."

Kirby agreed. He lifted the rack off the table and waved it back and forth between Wilson and me. "They need to unwind after tonight's news."

"Believe it or not, we didn't think it was that terrible," I said. "I mean, Dee Dee Larkin didn't even give Jimmy any air time." I stepped forward to break, but something about the hush that swept over the gang made me stand up without taking the shot.

My eyes darted back and forth among the mute and apparently stunned spectators and stopped at Wilson. "Did I miss something?" I asked.

"The local news." He took a deep breath. "We missed the local news, Jessie."

***

I braced myself and turned to my best buddy Kirby. "Okay, so what exactly did we miss?" I asked.

He bit his lip, begged Wilson not to shoot the messenger, and divulged the unpleasant details.

Jimmy Beak might not have gotten air time with Dee Dee Larkin, but never fear. He had made more than sufficient use of his own local report. He began with the scene of Gabby and I pretending to be bosom buddies, since he was able to cover that live. Then he skipped back to my showdown with Alistair earlier in the day.

"You looked crazy out there," Camille informed me, and I bit my lip to keep from smiling. Good old Jimmy was playing right into our hands—broadcasting my craziness for all the world, or at least all of Clarence, to see.

"All this attention is driving me crazy," I said loud and clear. I took aim and broke, and the four ball disappeared.

I stood up and assessed the table. The one ball looked like a fairly straightforward shot, at least for the old Jessie Hewitt.

I got into position while Wilson continued quizzing Kirby. "That's it?" he asked. "If so, Beak's losing his touch. He usually does more damage."

"Yeah, but you know Jimmy," Kirby said as the one ball sank. "He couldn't pass up the chance to give us his own opinion."

"Of me," I mumbled. Was the five ball a possibility?

"Jimmy kept harping on Jessie's undue influence," Gus said.

"Over people like Superintendent Yikes." That was Bernie Allen.

"Then he got all hot and bothered about her influence over you." Camille Allen smirked at Wilson and smirked. "They said she's corrupted you."

"They?" Wilson asked. "I take it Pritt gave his opinion, too?"

"You know Alistair," Kirby said. He pointed to the table. "Are you actually trying for the five?" he asked me.

"I am." I bent over and made the rather brilliant bank shot.

"Well that's just great," Camille sputtered. I doubted she was referring to the five ball, but I thanked her anyway.

"Not that. I'm talking about your boyfriend." She put her hands on her hips and challenged the various men standing around the table. "Isn't anyone gonna tell him? Or do I have to do it?"

"You have to do it." Wilson stepped directly in front of her. "Tell me what?"

"Jimmy Beak wants you stripped of your badge," she said. "Immediately, if not sooner."

Needless to say, all eyes landed on my beau—make that my fiancé—the cop.

But Wilson kept his focus on me. "What did Pritt say to that?" he asked Camille. I had no idea what the guy was thinking, but his voice sounded calm enough.

"Alistair agreed wholeheartedly." Camille tapped her chin. "How did he put it? Oh yeah. He said Jessie's destroyed your better judgment." She smiled at me. "Your shot," she chirped.

***

I stood frozen, trying to garner Wilson's reaction.

"Camille's right," he told me. He twirled an index finger over the pool table. "It's still your shot."

Perhaps Wilson Rye was calm enough, but trust me. I had had just about enough of the Beak-Pritt duo of destruction. And I would have taken my frustration out on the six ball, but Camille was in my way.

"Move!" I snapped, and she jumped aside.

I took aim at the poor unsuspecting six, it zipped across the table at record speed, and obediently dropped into the far corner pocket.

Everyone except Camille clapped, and at the risk of being scolded, Kirby sidled up next to me. "Stay angry," he told me. "You're doing great."

I assured him staying angry at Jimmy and Alistair was exactly what I intended to do and sunk the two. And while I was at it, the three.

Lo and behold, only the seven and the eight remained for me to handle. But what with all those sad stripes in the way, the seven ball was going to be tricky.

Stay angry, I told myself, and lo and behold I managed another bank shot.

"Genius!" Gus shouted, and dear Kirby stood at attention and saluted.

I offered a slight nod and chalked up for the eight ball. "Right corner," I said and bent down to take aim.

"The million-dollar question," Wilson announced from across the table.

I stood up. "Excuse me?"

"The million-dollar question," he repeated loudly. "Is whether you really can run this table."

Everyone scolded him for breaking my concentration, but Wilson kept staring at me. And I am happy to report, I got the hint.

I raised an eyebrow. "We'll answer that million-dollar question, Captain Rye. Never fear."

"I never do, Adelé." He grinned, and I returned to the task—or rather, the tasks—at hand.

"Right corner," I reminded everyone and shot in the eight ball.

The gang erupted in cheers. But while everyone was busy celebrating my success, I caught Wilson's eye.

I dropped my cue stick on the table, he handed his to Kirby, and we managed to meet somewhere in the middle of the crowd. I reached up and gave him a great big hug.

"It wasn't all about you," he whispered in my ear.

"No." I squeezed tighter and whispered in his ear. "It was all about you."

Chapter 29

"Look at her," Camille said. "She's all choked up."

I let go of Wilson and pretended she had found me out. "I am a bit overwhelmed," I said. "It's been months since I've played that well." I made a show of looking embarrassed before I swung back around. "Can we go home now—"

Wilson was already at the exit.

"Wait up!" I called out and raced to catch up.

"Wait!" I tried several more times on my way out the door.

"Would you watch where you're going!" Wilson shouted from the opposite side of Sullivan Street.

"Only if you wait up." I stopped to let a stream of cars pass by, and to his credit, he did wait for me to cross the street.

He took me by the shoulders and shook me. "Thank you," he said. He kissed my forehead, and started jogging away again. No, really.

I rolled my eyes and resumed running.

"Don't you dare leave without me!" I spoke loudly, but I have no idea if he heard me, since he was already on his cell phone.

But luckily Wilson's truck is so old it doesn't have automatic locks. He had to stop and fiddle with his keys, and I was able to catch up.

"Meet me at the station," he said and clicked off his phone.

"Russell?" I asked as I skidded to a stop.

"Stay out of this, Jessie." He reached out to keep me from stumbling. "It's gotten too dangerous."

"No. Way." I folded my arms and glared. "Absolutely, positively, no way."

"You're a little scary, you know that?"

"Oh, honey, you haven't seen scary. Just wait until we find this guy." I pointed to the passenger door, and Wilson stepped over to open it.

***

"Don't you want to hear why it was all about you?" I asked as he started the engine.

"I get it." He backed out of the parking space. "Same thing as before, with one more step.

"They killed Miriam Jilton and left her body on my car to hurt my reputation—"

"—to ruin mine. It's sick, Jessie."

I told him he needn't remind me.

Wilson continued the logic as we turned onto Sullivan Street. "The killer was sure Beak would accuse you of murder when we found a body hanging over your pornographic license plate."

"My license plate is not pornographic."

He stopped at a red light and glanced over.

I cleared my throat. "Perhaps it does attract a bit of attention." The light turned green, and we took off. "But the killer also knew you wouldn't arrest me on such flimsy evidence."

"Yep. And he knew Beak would make a big deal about it. Stripped of my badge. I'll give him stripped of my badge."

I reminded Wilson that Jimmy Beak never did clamor for my arrest, but we agreed he never had to.

"Not once Pritt got involved." Wilson hit the gas. "Me and the Queen of Smut."

"Maybe they're in cahoots," I said as the city whizzed by. "Maybe Jimmy planned this with Alistair when he realized he couldn't accuse me of murder."

"But think, Jessie. That was only after the murder. After. And Beak has an alibi, remember?"

I was still thinking when the police station came into view. "They really wouldn't fire you?" I asked. "Because of me?"

"No." Wilson spoke firmly. "Beak doesn't rule the police department. No matter what he, or the public, or the murderer might like to think."

"But Jimmy can still make your life miserable."

Wilson agreed I was the voice of experience on that one, and I frowned at all the patrol cars as we pulled into the parking lot.

"Maybe I should change careers," I suggested. "I could do something wholesome. I could write children's books."

Wilson drove over a curb.

"Jessie!" He pulled the truck to a complete stop. "Don't joke around like that. Not while I'm driving."

"But I'm serious."

"Well, don't be. You're in a slump, but the Queen of Smut will rise again." He pulled the keys from the ignition. "In the meantime, let's nail this bastard."

"Jimmy, Alistair, or the murderer?"

He raised an eyebrow. "How about all three."

***

Lieutenant Densmore was already in Wilson's office, poised in front of the computer, when we arrived. Without saying a word, he got up and rolled another chair behind the desk. Russell may be chivalrous, but I knew that chair wasn't for me. While I closed the door, the two cops sat down and got to work.

"Someone's out to get me," Wilson said as Russell booted up who knows what.

"It wasn't all about me." I squeezed in behind them to see the computer screen. "It was all about Wilson."

Russell scowled. "Really?"

"Think about it," Wilson said, and I could almost see the very sharp gears inside the lieutenant's head spinning.

It took him only a minute to understand. "If Jessie looks bad, you look bad," he told his boss. "So, like, when's the wedding?"

"Russell!" I shook the back of his chair. "Can we stick to the subject here? The murderer hates Wilson!" I shook the back of Wilson's chair. "Do you have any enemies?" I asked, and both cops snorted.

"Only hundreds," they more or less agreed, and I rolled my eyes at my own stupidity. Of course my fiancé the cop has enemies. He has enemies who kill people. Like, duh.

Wilson waved at the computer. “Let’s start with the ones I’ve put away for murder or manslaughter.”

“Who’ve been released,” Russell added. He began clicking at the keyboard, and an assortment of charts and lists popped up. But every time I could almost focus on a name, he clicked to a different screen.

Meanwhile, Wilson issued orders. “Start with the most obvious. Jessie and I got engaged at Christmas. Who’s left prison since then? And who’s in town?”

I blinked twice and gripped the back of both chairs to keep from falling over.

“Umm,” I squeaked in a very small voice.

Wilson swiveled his chair around. “What?” he said impatiently.

“Umm,” I said. “You might want to check on Dianne Calloway.”

***

You know that phrase ‘his face turned white as a sheet?’

Not an exaggeration.

And Russell? Who is African-American? He looked a bit peaked also.

“What did you just say?” Wilson snapped. He spoke to Russell. “What did she just say?”

The lieutenant held up both palms. “No way am I getting in the middle of this one.”

All eyes landed back on me.

“Umm,” I repeated brilliantly.

Wilson looked like he was about to pop an artery. “What,” he said slowly, “have you been up to?”

I tried stepping backward, but bumped into the wall. We really were rather tight in there—what with the three of us all squished behind his desk like that.

I braced myself and spit it out. “Dianne Calloway paid me a visit a couple of days ago.”

“What!?” he yelled, and Russell and I both jumped. “You let her into your home!?” he said. “Are you insane!?”

“I didn’t know it was her. I thought she was Jimmy Beak.”

"What!?" That time Russell joined in.

I took a deep breath, wondered if Wilson kept any Advil in his desk, and explained. "Gabby Yates promised if I let Jimmy into my condo, she would tell him how much she enjoys my books. And I thought maybe that would help my reputation, and maybe get Jimmy off my back, and maybe intimidate Alistair into giving up on the book-banning thing, and maybe—"

"Stop!" Wilson held up his hand, and I stopped.

"We did ask, Captain," Russell said quietly.

We waited until Wilson could speak again.

"Okay," he said in a mostly-calm voice. "Continue."

I cleared my throat. "As I was saying, I thought Dianne was Jimmy Beak, and so I buzzed her in. But when Gabby and I realized she was a she, and not a he, we knew it wasn't Jimmy, and so Gabby decided to leave. So it was only Snowflake and me when Dianne finally got upstairs to my condo." I shrugged. "I didn't know who she was until she introduced herself."

Russell actually gasped. "Then what did you do?"

"I fainted. I mean, what would you have done?"

Wilson had no answer, but Russell did. "I would have fainted, too," he said.

Chapter 30

Wilson started muttering incoherently. While Russell and I struggled to comprehend, he opened a desk drawer and pulled out a bottle of Advil. He slammed that onto the desk, stood up, and walked over to his filing cabinet.

Russell and I exchanged a meaningful look as a bottle of bourbon emerged from the bottom drawer.

Still muttering, Wilson found his seat and unscrewed the cap. He looked back and forth between the two of us. "Anyone care to join me?"

Well, what do you think?

We passed around the bottle, Russell divvied up the pills, and Wilson asked me to please continue.

"Believe it or not, Dianne wasn't all that scary," I said as the bourbon hit my stomach. "For instance, she wasn't carrying a broomstick."

"You're the one that's scary." That was Wilson of course.

"She wasn't scary, but she was rude." I pointed to the bottle sitting on the desk. "She demanded a bourbon on the rocks."

"You gave her a drink!?"

"Nooo! You know I don't stock hard liquor. I don't even have a filing cabinet, for Lord's sake." I huffed indignantly. "I didn't offer her any champagne, either."

Wilson had started mumbling to himself again, so I spoke to Russell. "Call me ungracious, but I refused to serve her anything."

"Way to be tough, Jessie."

"What did she want?" Wilson demanded.

"She seemed kind of interested in *Sensual and Scintillating*."

"What?" both cops asked.

"The book on my coffee table." I turned to Wilson. "I actually have two copies right now, remember? From when Roslynn came over to brainstorm?"

Wilson groaned and spoke to Russell. "This was on Sunday, you realize. The day after the murder."

Russell bit his lip and silently got up to return the bourbon to its filing cabinet.

Wilson took a deep breath. "What did Dianne want?" he asked again.

I thought about it. "She was trying to intimidate me. She told me not to trust you." I made sure I had his eye. "But I do trust you. So it didn't work, okay?"

"No. It is definitely not okay. Why was she even in town? She tell you that?"

"She was visiting her uncle," I said as Russell returned to his seat. "Apparently he's the only person in her family who's still speaking to her." I shrugged. "Since she was already in town, she decided to visit me."

Both the cops were shaking their heads.

"I'm sure she's gone back to Raleigh," I said. "She mentioned something about her parole."

I lost track of the expletives Wilson began spouting. Especially when Russell Densmore joined in.

"What's wrong?" I asked to interrupt the flow, and at least that stopped Russell.

He told me Dianne would have needed special permission from her parole officer to leave the Raleigh area at all.

"Well then, she must have gotten permission," I said.

"And pigs fly," Wilson said.

I again appealed to Russell, and he explained that no parole officer would have given Dianne permission to visit Clarence. "Captain Rye works here, Jessie." Russell tilted his head toward his boss. "He's her former fiancé, the guy she tried to set up for murder, and her arresting officer."

"Oh," I mumbled.

"What was the uncle's name?" Wilson asked.

"Dianne's?"

"No, Willow LaSwann's!" He threw his hands in the air. "Yes, Dianne's!"

I squinted. "You mean, you don't know?"

"Why would I know? I'm not the one who's been chatting with her."

"But you were engaged to the woman. Surely you met her family?"

"The name, Jessie," Russell said, quietly but firmly.

The name. I tried to think as Russell looked at a database of Clarence residents—under C for Calloway.

"Dave?" I said, and he clicked a D.

"No," I changed my mind. "But it was something simple like that. Something common—John!" I exclaimed. "Dianne's Uncle John."

"John Calloway." Wilson pointed at the computer and Russell resumed clicking.

"It's possible they don't have the same last name," I suggested as the three of us scanned the list.

Russell pointed. "Three John Calloways, Captain."

"What are you waiting for?" Wilson asked, and he shot up.

"Get Sass for back up," Wilson called after him. "And contact the parole officer."

***

I collapsed into the chair the lieutenant had vacated and sighed wearily. "Why, oh why, didn't you tell me she was out of prison?" I asked.

"I didn't want to scare you."

"Forewarned is forearmed, Wilson. I was completely unprepared when she showed up at my doorstep. And I'm sorry if I didn't do the right thing."

"And I'm sorry I didn't warn you. You're right."

"I am?" I shook my head. "I mean, I am. Married people shouldn't keep secrets from each other."

Wilson almost grinned. "Married people?"

"Almost-married people."

"Almost?"

I rolled my eyes. "Can we just concentrate on the fact that I was right, and you were wrong? You should have told me Dianne was out of prison."

"Yep. And you should have told me about her visit."

Darn if that wasn't a good point.

"Okay, so I'm sorry, too," I said.

"Great. Now move." He pointed to the computer behind me, and I actually laughed.

"Are you feeling well?" I asked. "You're not going to try to use this thing? Without Russell?"

"I do know how. It'll just take a little longer."

"A little?" While we switched chairs, I asked why he had sent Russell to check on Dianne. "Shouldn't you be doing that?"

"Nope. I need to sit this one out."

"Russell will lead?"

"He knows how."

I pointed to the computer screen. "What are we looking at?"

Wilson showed me the document he had pulled up and clicked to two others that looked about the same. "Parole records of the three people I'm most suspicious of."

"Other than Dianne?" I said, and his shoulders visibly stiffened. "Do you really think she'd commit murder again? Just to get back at you?"

"That woman is capable of anything, Jessie." He stopped what he was doing and twirled his chair around to look at me. "Take a guess what I would have done if she'd shown up unexpectedly on my doorstep."

"You would have fainted?"

"Bingo."

I took a long deep breath. Maybe several long deep breaths. At some point I asked how Dianne could have known where my car was that night.

Wilson admitted he had no idea, but he was also quick to point out that Dianne had plotted another murder quite successfully. "She only did time for manslaughter. But I know for a fact she planned it. It was first degree murder, Jessie."

I shuddered as he continued to enlighten me. "It's no great secret where you live, and your license plate is no secret at all."

I shuddered again. "She's been spying on me?"

Wilson reached out both hands. "I don't know, okay? And I don't want to scare you. But Dianne's dangerous. Trust me."

"I do trust you. But what about size?" I asked. "You told me no woman would have the strength to carry Miriam across that parking lot. Dianne didn't have the strength to do this, did she?"

He stared straight into me. "That's what everyone said last time."

***

Waiting.

I am not good at waiting. But unless I wanted to dive into the filing cabinet's stash of bourbon, I had absolutely nothing to do.

Wilson kept busy enough. First he called the police commissioner to report what was going on. Then he worked with those parole documents and made a few notes.

I sat around, twiddled my thumbs, and desperately tried to concentrate on Willow LaSwann's water and well issues. When the phone rang I jumped ten feet in the air.

Wilson picked up, and with much wild gesturing from me, he put the conversation on speaker.

Dianne's parole officer informed us she had last reported in the previous Wednesday, and that he was coordinating with Lieutenant Densmore and the Raleigh Police Department to verify her alibi for Saturday.

"You with her now?" Wilson asked.

"Oh, yeah," the parole officer said. "We're having ourselves a little tête-à-tête at the county jail. We're bonding, here. Waiting for a call from your lieutenant to decide what charges to book her on—breaking parole or murder."

Dianne Calloway let out a string of obscenities in the background.

I closed my eyes and prayed for strength.

***

"I don't know if this is good news, or bad news," Lieutenant Densmore said as he walked in.

"What?" Wilson and I asked in unison.

"She has an alibi, Captain. It's solid."

I ignored the ringing in my ears to listen to the particulars Russell was reporting.

Evidently Dianne had been seen—or at least heard—in Raleigh on Saturday night when she visited her mother. Ms. Calloway senior corroborated Dianne's claim, and several of her neighbors had heard the heated argument between the two women.

"They sure it was Dianne?" Wilson asked, and then corrected himself. "Never mind," he said. "There's no mistaking that voice when she's angry."

Russell told us the Raleigh police were certain. "Mother and daughter argued about a car. Dianne wanted to borrow her mother's car to come here. Mom said she wouldn't have any part in Dianne breaking her parole, no matter how misguided her Uncle John was. Daughter took the bus."

"You talked to the driver?" Wilson asked.

"We woke up everyone," Russell said. "The drivers, to and from, the desk clerk who sold her the round-trip ticket, and five of the passengers."

By all accounts, Dianne Calloway had arrived in Clarence late Sunday afternoon and left on Monday afternoon.

"She wasn't here at all on Saturday," Russell summarized the main point.

"That agrees with what she told me Sunday," I said. "She claimed she was only in town for the day." I felt relieved at this small bit of good news, but the two cops frowned.

"What?" I asked. "Isn't it good she has an alibi?"

"Think about it," Wilson said, and I shuddered from head to toe.

If Dianne Calloway wasn't the killer, who was?

Chapter 31

"You don't happen to know anything about water rights in the Wild West?" I asked Wilson as we finished our Cheerios.

At least that got a chuckle out of him. And Lord knows we needed some levity that morning. Wilson had spent the night with Snowflake and me. I told him I would sleep better that way. He told me the same. Neither of us had slept at all.

I yawned excessively and stood up to pour more coffee. "I thought maybe Gabby could get Willow out of this pickle," I said. "But no such luck."

Wilson gave me the same puzzled look he used every time I mentioned Gabby Yates.

"She has a degree in history," I said as I sat back down. "But in European history, not American. 99 percent of Adelé's books are set in Europe, so tell me why I chose now to try a western?"

"Because you were getting bored with medieval Europe," Wilson said. "What did you call them? Dreary dukes and dismal lords?"

I sipped my coffee. "Maybe. But now I may have to break down and do some actual research."

I curled my lip at that altogether unpleasant prospect, and Wilson chuckled again. "Adelé Nightingale never worries about facts," he reminded me. "Do what you usually do, Jessie. Twist the history to fit your story, and concentrate on sex scenes."

"But I can't write sex scenes anymore. So here I am. Reduced to obsessing about the facts."

"What is the world coming to?"

"You mean what's Adelé Nightingale coming to." I frowned at my cereal bowl. "Unemployment is what."

"What?"

"You heard me. Perpetual Pleasures Press is threatening to dump me."

"No way! You just made the Hall of Fame."

"But only for my past work." I studied my cat, who had finished eating her own breakfast and settled onto Wilson's lap. "Maybe I really should try writing children's books."

Wilson choked on his coffee. "Would you stop doing that?" he pleaded. "Warn me next time."

I told him to be thankful he wasn't driving and kept hallucinating out loud. "My pen name could be Auntie Abigail Nightingale. And Snowflake could be my protagonist." I reached over to pet my protagonist. "She could solve crimes or something equally ludicrous. Mother could do the illustrations."

Snowflake seemed to like the idea, but Wilson wasn't convinced. "Auntie Abigail?" he said. "You really do need to get some sleep."

I yawned in agreement, vowed to tackle a sex scene before the day was through, and asked Wilson about his own plans for the day. "I have a hard time imagining you sitting on the sidelines during any murder investigation."

"Unfortunately, I can say the same about you."

I smirked. "Your plans, Captain Rye?"

"Act irritated while Densmore and Sass track down the whereabouts of every perp who might have it in for me. Willow LaSwann has a better chance of finding water in her well than we have of finding the murderer this way."

"What about those three men you were looking at last night?" I asked, but he insisted they were only remote possibilities.

I remained positive and suggested that most of the "perps" were still in prison. "That should narrow down the possibilities, correct?"

"What about family and friends?" Wilson insisted prisoners often have connections on the outside, making the list of suspects almost infinite.

He shooed Snowflake down and got up to fill our cups again. "There is another possibility," he said. "What if my enemy isn't a criminal? Or wasn't a criminal until Saturday?" He set my cup in front of me and sat back down. "What if it's another cop?"

"You're kidding, right?"

"I hope so. But every cop in North Carolina knows the Dianne Calloway story. Maybe someone thinks I don't deserve my job. Maybe Jimmy Beak and Alistair Pritt aren't alone in their logic."

"That's impossible." I shook my indignant head. "You're a great cop. You absolutely deserve your job."

"You want to hear this or not?"

I shut up, and Wilson reminded me how he had become the chief homicide investigator on the Clarence force. He applied right after the Dianne Calloway fiasco because he'd become the subject of far too much gossip down in Raleigh.

I knew all that, but then he gave me a bit more history. "I was the only applicant not already on the force here," he said. "Some other people were hoping for the promotion."

I writhed uncomfortably. "Russell?"

"Didn't even apply."

I breathed a sigh of relief.

"Everyone knows Densmore will go far," Wilson said. "But he's young. Three years ago he wasn't even thirty yet."

"What about the people who did apply?"

"Any one of them could be mad at me. Especially the other two finalists."

"It's like the Focus on Fiction Contest," I said. "Maybe one of the finalists is bitter."

"Which is where this whole idea falls flat. Neither of them is bitter."

Apparently candidate number one, Gene Fagan, had left the police force, moved back to his hometown in Knoxville, and was doing very well for himself as a private investigator.

"Fagan's one of the best PIs in the whole southeast," Wilson said.

"And the other finalist?" I asked "Is he bitter?"

"She." Wilson took a deep breath. "Darla Notari is dead."

"Dead!? What!? Where? When? How?"

Oh, yes. I had lots of questions. But my infuriating fiancé chose that moment to inform me he needed get going.

Yeah, right.

Snowflake and I followed him toward the bathroom, and watched while he brushed his teeth. And then we watched while he rummaged around in the closet, looking for a tie.

I finally got the full story once he was standing in front of the mirror tying said tie.

"Lots of people were surprised Notari didn't get the job I now have." He looked at my reflection behind him in the mirror. "She was stellar."

"So are you."

"Maybe, but Darla Notari was a groundbreaker on the Clarence force. She was one of the first women to make sergeant, and the first woman to be promoted to lieutenant. And she was married with two kids. She was one of those super-women.

"But she died in the line of duty," I said quietly.

He turned around. "How do you do that?"

I chalked it up to intuition, but considering Wilson's behavior, it wasn't very difficult to figure out.

"Well, you're right, Jessie. When she didn't get the promotion, Darla moved her family and took a job as the sheriff of one of the counties outside Atlanta. It was a great job." He frowned. "Until she got killed."

I asked how, and he frowned some more. "During a routine traffic stop. Routine until the bullets started flying."

I let that tragedy sink in as Wilson donned his suit jacket. "Most everyone went down for her funeral. Densmore, Sass, a bunch of others."

"Not you?"

"I'd only known her for a year before she left Clarence, so I volunteered to stay here. Someone had to keep this city safe for democracy. Speaking of which." He gave me a peck on the cheek and headed toward the door.

But the stack of *Sensual and Scintillating* languishing on my coffee table caught his attention. He picked one up, and shoved it into my hands . "Sex scenes," he said and was gone. I clutched *S and S* to my chest and stalwartly marched over to my desk. While I booted up my laptop, Snowflake made herself comfortable on the windowsill.

"A sex scene if it kills me," I told her, and my muse yawned accordingly.

But who knows if it would have killed me? Because a sex scene, or any other scene for that matter, evaded me completely. I was actually relieved when the intercom buzzed and the less-than-dulcet voice of Rita Sistina wafted through my condo.

"Get me out of here!" she demanded.

Snowflake found her safety spot on top of the fridge, and I buzzed in our guest.

***

"Lunatics! Every last one of them!" Rita was saying—or rather shouting—as I opened the door. She marched over to the couch and sat down. "Can't you at least offer me coffee?"

I did so, and while I prepared a pot of decaf, Rita gave me a refresher course on the shenanigans at street level.

"It was bad enough the other day," she said. "But now it's a three-ring circus—Alistair Pritt and his clowns, Jimmy Beak and his, and now that romance woman and her group. They're the scariest of all, you know? They invited me to dance with them."

I swallowed a smile and served the coffee. "At least Roslynn Mayweather's on my side," I said as I sat down.

"And at least she's keeping busy." Rita glared at me over her coffee cup. "Which is more than I can say for some people."

I cleared my throat and insisted I was trying. "But sometimes the writing just doesn't flow as smoothly—"

"Writing!" Rita snapped forward. "I'm not here to talk about your writing! We had a deal, Jessie. In fact, why are you even here?" She waved an exceedingly agitated hand to indicate my condo. "You should be at the high school! Elizabeth tells me she hasn't seen you there since that one measly visit days, and days, and days ago!"

I reminded Rita I had visited the school on Monday. "And today is only Wednesday."

"And that's supposed to make me feel better? Elizabeth's future is at stake! We had a deal, you and me!"

"Yes, but the situation has changed." I explained, as vaguely as possible, that the murder investigation had taken a new direction. "I can't be more specific, but I really can't be sleuthing right now."

Rita put down her coffee cup. "Well then, let me be specific. You stop sleuthing, and Frankie stops seeing my daughter. A deal's a deal."

"Come on, Rita." I sat up and prepared to do battle. "You're the first person to insist Lizzie wasn't to blame for the murder, so why punish her?"

"Her name is Elizabeth. And the Smythe boy has got to go."

I studied my guest. "So tell me," I said. "How did Elizabeth do on that algebra test?"

Rita blinked twice.

"You know," I continued. "The one she and Frankie were studying for the other night?"

Rita took a deep breath. "The teacher's giving them back in class today. But she posted the grades on the school's internet grade book last night."

"And?"

"And Elizabeth got a 95. Your stupid friend Frankie called. He got a 98."

By the look on Rita's face I assumed she had hoped Lizzie would do even better. But with a bit more prompting, I learned that 95 was the best math grade Lizzie had seen all year.

"Then why do you seem so disappointed?" I asked, and to her credit, Rita answered honestly. Apparently my "stupid friend Frankie" was helping Lizzie in her hardest subject.

"He's always been a straight-A student," I said proudly.

"As has Elizabeth." Rita frowned. "Except in math. I made a deal with my daughter. I promised her an electric piano to join a band with her girlfriends. But only if she improved her math grades." Rita sighed dramatically and informed me Lizzie's math grades had been steadily improving all semester.

I smiled. "Since she started dating Frankie."

"Okay, yes," she snapped. "Since then."

I sat back and smiled some more.

***

Thus assured that Frankie's love life was safe and sound, I fortified Rita with another cup of coffee to face the circus on Sullivan Street, and sent her on her way.

Then I had a choice. I could tackle *A Singular Seduction* and Willow's well issues, or I could tackle the voice mail messages I'd been avoiding all morning. Geez Louise Urko had left numerous messages the previous night while Wilson and I were busy narrowing down murderer suspects. I deleted the first five, warned Snowflake to stay put in her safety spot, and hit play.

"Jessica! I'm so sorry! Sorry, sorry, sorry!"

"Sorry?" I asked as Louise continued.

"Dee Dee promised we'd get at least four minutes' airtime. Stupid, stupid, stupid Congressional budget impasse! But the short segment was fantastical enough! Lemonade out of lemons! Didn't Roslynn do fantastically?"

I nodded silent agreement.

"Oh!" Louise's voice continued. "And didn't the debutante look fantastical? *The Debutante's Destiny* is one of 3P's best, best, best covers! Don't you just love the fuchsia pink?"

I nodded again.

"And don't you just love Alistair Fitt?"

I most decidedly shook my head no to that one, but Louise continued anyway, "The Queen of Smut has a fantastical ring to it! It's a great new by-line for your next book! We'll put it right on the cover! Right under Adelé's name! Oh! And speaking of *A Singular Seduction*, how are the sex scenes coming along? Sex, sex, sex!"

I hit delete, and was apologizing to Snowflake for listening as long as I had when I noticed one final message.

"My mother called," I said. Snowflake meowed her approval and hopped down to listen. Instead, I hit delete and punched in Mother's number.

"Hello, Miss Queen of Smut," she chirped happily. "I so enjoy this caller ID system you suggested, Jessie."

"Mother! Please tell me you haven't programmed me in as the Queen of Smut."

"Don't be silly. But wasn't Dee Dee Larkin's report last night marvelous? You and Louise must be so pleased. Roslynn, too. She certainly held her own again that Alistair fellow, didn't she?"

I rolled my eyes. "Let me guess. You think it was good publicity."

"Don't you? I'm no expert on these things, but have you considered putting 'The Queen of Smut,' below Adelé's name on your next cover? I bet *A Singular Seduction* would sell like hotcakes if you did that!"

***

Somehow satisfied my mother wasn't traumatized by Dee Dee Larkin's report, I called my neighbors. Maybe if I begged, one of them would agree to come upstairs for a brainstorming session.

"I need your help," I told Karen. "Maybe you can convince Willow and Kipp to hop into a haystack together."

"Are you feeling well, girlfriend?" Karen reminded me she doesn't read romance, much less write it, and claimed she had a pressing appointment with some custom cabinetry.

"I'm finishing up a few pieces and then heading out to install them before the big wedding."

"These cabinets aren't for Trisha Fister, by any chance?" I asked.

"Well, yeah. The wedding of the century is this Saturday. So I better get a move on."

"Believe it or not, this same wedding is keeping Candy busy also. Mrs. Marachini's related to the bride."

"Kiddo told me," Karen said. "And this bride is something else, Jess. A fire destroyed all her shower gifts, and now everyone in town is hustling to keep her happy—aunts, uncles, cousins, godparents."

"You."

"Me," she agreed. "You should see the honeymoon mansion. The kitchen alone stretches a good half mile. The mother of the bride promised me I'll never work in this town again if I don't get these cabinets installed before the wedding." Karen hesitated. "Speaking of the W-word."

I groaned out loud, but she ignored me.

"I saw Wilson leaving this morning," she said. "He didn't look so good. The poor guy needs a wedding of his own."

"No," I said firmly. "The poor guy needs is to solve the Miriam Jilton case."

Karen asked if we had any theories.

"We do," I said. "But it's even more complicated than Willow's well issues."

"Say what?"

I started explaining, but Karen interrupted to mention that mile of kitchen cabinets. "We'll talk later," she said. "We'll cover all these W-issues—your writing, Willow's well." She skipped a beat. "Wilson's wedding."

I groaned again.

"Tell you what," she said. "Marry Wilson, and I'll build you guys some furniture as a wedding present. Anything you want for the little cottage."

"It's a shack," I said, but she had already hung up.

A call to Candy proved equally fruitless.

"I'd love to brainstorm about Willow and Kipp," she said. "But today's the big day."

"Mrs. Marachini's much-anticipated emergency shopping spree, correct?"

"The Fister-Bickerson wedding is right around the corner. Gosh, it's a small world. All that stuff Karen's building is also for Trisha." Candy hesitated. "Speaking of the W-word."

"W as in world?"

"Duh. W as in wedding. And speaking of your wedding—"

"We weren't speaking of my wedding."

“Speaking of your wedding, you need to come into Tate’s sometime soon. I’ll set you up with lingerie for your honeymoon. It’ll be my wedding gift.”

Chapter 32

Kipp Jupiter stood stock-still and watched Zachary Clark ride away. He had plenty of chores to get back to, but Kipp waited until Zachary disappeared beyond the horizon, and still he didn't move.

The man had come all the way out from Hogan's Hollow to warn him about his new neighbor. The lowdown, no-good Will LaSwann was out to get him—out to get Kipp's land, to be exact.

According to Zachary, LaSwann, or LeSwine, or whatever he wanted to call himself, had ventured into Hogan's Hollow that very morning and had spoken to everyone in town about Kipp. According to Zachary, LeSwine asked every question under the sun about Kipp's land and how he had come to own the largest ranch on the prairie.

"I'd watch my back if I were you," Zachary told him. "That new neighbor of yours is up to no good, or my name isn't Zachary Zebediah Clark."

Kipp Jupiter finally moved. Indeed, he turned in the direction of the LeSwine ranch and snarled accordingly. That varmint was after his ranch! That's why he hadn't paid any attention when Kipp tried explaining the water and well situation. Why bother? The greedy LeSwine had his eyes set on Kipp's land instead!

Kipp took off his cowboy hat and swatted at a fly. "The varmint!" he exclaimed to the fifty or so steer grazing in the field before him.

***

"Varmint, swine?" I tore my eyes from my computer and spoke to a sleeping Snowflake. "Is there no end to Kipp Jupiter's disdain?"

The cat opened one eye.

She was right of course. My stupid story wasn't worth waking up for.

"Stupid Uncle Hazard." I stood up and started pacing. "Why did he give his niece such stupid advice? Impersonating a man. Sheesh!"

Snowflake opened both eyes and stared at the nearest copy of *Sensual and Scintillating*.

I snatched it up and started rifling through the pages willy-nillly. "How are these people ever going to hop in a haystack together!?" I asked.

Snowflake gave up on her nap. She sat up and stretched, and made a point of ignoring my histrionics to watch the histrionics down at street-level.

I tossed the book aside and gave my long-suffering muse a few forehead-to-tail-tip strokes.

Varmints, swine. Whatever I wanted to call the fools outside, I needed some fresh air and exercise. I needed a walk.

I changed out of my sloppy writing attire, and into a pair of jeans and a summer cardigan, and was out the door before the thought of facing Jimmy and Alistair on limited sleep could deter me.

I hurried past the second floor landing and past Candy's empty apartment. Ms. Poppe was off selling bras and other unmentionables to Mrs. Marachini and company. And before I even made it to the first floor lobby, I could hear the power tools buzzing from behind Karen's door. She, too, was hard at work on those custom cabinets. I stopped short at Peter Harrison's door. Even in retirement, he kept busy. I listened to the piano music coming from within.

But something wasn't right.

I checked my watch. It was too early for afterschool piano lessons. And what about that music? Even I knew it wasn't Mozart.

I reached out and knocked loudly.

***

"What did you think?" Peter asked as he invited me in.

I told him it sounded good to me and pointed to his piano. "But that certainly wasn't Beethoven. It was Elton

John. "Crocodile Rock" to be specific." I tilted my head. "Are you feeling well?"

The old guy blushed and produced a stack of sheet music from beneath the piano bench. "All rock and roll," he said as he handed it to me.

"But I'm the rock and roll enthusiast, Peter." I shuffled through a stack of music I knew and loved. "You prefer classical music, remember?"

"Well," he sang. "Lizzy Sistina is broadening my horizons."

I looked up. "Her electric piano? Don't tell me you've given up Beethoven for Lizzy and her girl group?"

"Of course not. But the girls have big plans. They've named themselves Like, The Lyricals, and they plan on playing at weddings. They want to put some rock and roll oldies into their repertoire."

Peter swiped his thumb down the entire keyboard. "That move's called a glissando," he informed me. "Lizzie and I are embarking on a study of all the great rock pianists—Elton John, Billy Joel, Jerry Lee Lewis."

"Stevie Wonder, Carole King." I smiled. "I think I'm going to like The Lyricals."

"No, Jessie. You going to like Like, The Lyricals."

"I do like The Lyricals."

"No," Peter repeated. "The band's name isn't The Lyricals. It's Like, comma, The Lyricals. Like, Like is part of the name."

I shook my head and warned my neighbor I was functioning on very limited sleep.

"The murder investigation?" he asked. "Richard Dempsey continues to call me. He's still worried this will ruin his retirement plans."

I told him Principal Dempsey needn't be concerned, and rummaged through the sheet music while Peter asked a string of questions I couldn't answer.

"Here it is." I slipped "Your Song" onto the top of the stack and handed it back. "That's my favorite Elton John song. Perhaps because I'm a writer." I tapped the sheet music. "I always thought it'd be a nice song at a wedding."

Peter grinned. "Whose wedding are we talking about?"

***

“Stupid, stupid W-word,” I sputtered to myself as I stepped outside to face the usual jibes and insults from Jimmy, Alistair, and the like.

Oh, but what was this? Lord help me, they, too, had picked up on the wedding theme. Alistair and his gang sported new posters—about the ‘Wedding Bell Blues,’ and being ‘Engaged To The Enemy.’

A gleeful Jimmy Beak bullhorned the significance to me in case I wasn’t catching on. “Captain Wilson Rye,” he shouted. “Engaged to the enemy!”

Yadda, yadda, yadda. I raced down the stairs, pushed Jimmy aside before Joe the cameraman could come to his rescue, and headed down Sullivan Street as fast as my feet could carry me. I didn’t even take time to wave to Roslynn.

Why aren’t there laws against such harassment, I asked myself as I made it past the fray. But if I despised book banning because it impinged on my right to free speech, then I had to accept Alistair and the ilk’s right to assemble, correct?

I shook my head and decided my sleep-deprived brain was ill-equipped to tackle questions concerning the Bill of Rights. I’d do better concentrating on Willow and Kipp.

Alas, no ready solutions presented themselves on that front either. And by the time I wandered onto Hamilton Avenue, my baffled brain had wandered back to thinking about the murder and Wilson’s enemies.

Annoying but true, I knew very little about my fiancé’s work. The man made a point of telling me virtually nothing about the people he had arrested over the years. Dianne Calloway being the perfect example.

Of course, I did know many of the people Wilson worked with. Call me naïve, but intuition dictated that none of those cops was a cold-blooded murderer. I thought about the two I had never met, Gene Fagan and Darla Notari. Unlikely or downright impossible. I didn’t need a degree in criminology to tell me dead people don’t kill.

Willow’s well, or Wilson’s arch-enemy. Whatever the problem, I had no solution, and by the time I rounded the corner onto Vine Street to head home, I was thoroughly annoyed. And passing the building where my ex-husband had seen fit to set up business didn't help my mood any.

Whatever Wilson might say, Clarence really was a small city. I mean, how unlikely was it that my seriously irritating ex-husband's equally irritating wife Amanda had actually witnessed Trisha Fister's bridal-shower debacle? Leave it to Amanda Crawcheck to somehow be related to the kooky Marachini-Fister clan.

I stopped short.

A few passersby had to step around me as I focused my attention at the corner of Sullivan and Vine. A three-ring circus—Roslynn and the pastel people, Jimmy and Joe, Alistair and the ilk.

"They have different last names," I said out loud, and the next pedestrian crashed into me.

"He's her uncle!" I told him and ran for home.

Chapter 33

No car.

That altogether infuriating revelation hit me as I elbowed my way around this, that, and the other protester at the corner.

Candy was at Tate's, Karen was off installing custom cabinets, and Peter drove way too slowly.

I made it to the semi-safety of my stoop, and proof that there is a God in heaven, remembered I had my cell phone with me. I pulled it from my back pocket and tried finding a number for a taxi while the three-ring circus worked on distracting me. Alistair and his clowns screamed at me, Jimmy and Joe jeered at me, and Roslynn and the pastel people cheered at me.

Roslynn!

I clicked off my phone and made a beeline for my protégé.

***

"If you really want to help me," I yelled at her over the general commotion. "Put down that sign and take me to your car." I reached for her 'Romance Rocks' poster, but Roslynn refused to relinquish it.

"No can do!" she said. "I can't leave until Alistair does. Geez Louise's direct orders."

"I need a lift, Roslynn. It's an emergency."

"No can do!" She jiggled her stupid sign even more aggressively. "Geez Louise wants me to stay on Dee Dee Larkin's radar. If this lasts long enough, maybe I'll get another spot on the national news. That'll be good for both of us, Jessie."

"Oh, for Lord's sake!" I reached out and none too gently pulled her toward me. "I need to get to the police station," I whispered in her ear. "Now!" I said a lot louder.

While Roslynn looked me over, perhaps to see where I was bleeding, I yanked the poster from her hand and shoved it at the hapless demonstrator standing closest to us. She fumbled, trying to rearrange her own poster to accommodate carrying two. Meanwhile I wrestled with Roslynn, trying to move her unyielding person in any direction whatsoever.

"Cat fight!" Jimmy exclaimed, and he and Joe the cameraman came rushing.

"Please!" I shouted at her, and Roslynn finally got the hint. Or maybe the sight of Alistair and his groupies stampeding toward us stirred her to action. Whatever the reason, she grabbed my hand, and we raced down Sullivan Street toward her car.

Behind us Alistair was shouting some nonsense about the unbecoming behavior of women who write smut, and Jimmy kept asking where we were headed.

"The public has a right to know," he screamed, and it occurred to me I have a bad habit of making a scene whenever I figure out who a killer is.

"Stop!" I yanked poor Roslynn's arm, and we came to a screeching halt.

While Roslynn inspected the damaged heel of her lilac pump, I turned to head off Jimmy. He and the cameraman were so shocked we had stopped, they stopped, too. Alistair plowed smack into Joe, and down they went.

"Roslynn will be back shortly," I told Jimmy as he stepped over the two big guys. I tried to sound calm. "I just need a ride to the—" Nothing came to me. "I need a lift to the—" Again I stopped.

"To the library!" Roslynn helped me out. "Jessie's out of reading material!"

***

"The police station," I ordered as Roslynn started her car. "And would you please lock the doors," I said as Jimmy came running. Evidently he'd seen right through our ingenious library-excursion ruse.

Bless her heart, Roslynn followed orders. And as soon as we were safely ensconced in midday traffic, I called Wilson.

"I figured it out," I told him.

"Great. I can't wait to read it."

"What? Read what?"

"The solution to Willow's water rights."

I scowled at the dashboard. "We're not talking about Willow's well, Wilson. We're talking about the murder. I know who did it."

Dead silence. No pun intended.

"Did you hear me?" I asked. "Are you at the station? I'm on my way over. Roslynn's driving me."

"Who?"

"Is Russell there? If not, get him."

"Who?" Wilson asked.

"Lieutenant Russell Densmore!"

"No, Jessie. I mean, who's the killer?"

I glanced sideways at my driver. "Later," I said and hung up.

***

"Stick with the library story," I told Roslynn as I climbed out of her car.

"But what about the murderer, Jessie. Aren't you going to tell me?"

"Nooo. I am not going to tell you." I shook my head and started closing the passenger door, but remembered something. "Roslynn?" I bent down and peeked back in.

"Yes?"

"Thank you." I took the time to smile. "Thank you for your help with *A Singular Seduction*. Thank you for your protest march. And thank you for this." I pointed to her steering wheel. "Thank you."

She waved me away, and I noticed she had chipped a nail. "Anything for Adelé," she said and drove off.

I turned around and into Wilson.

"Who?" he asked, and I told him he'd been right all along.

"It wasn't a coincidence," I said. "It was Plan B."

Chapter 34

"Who?" Russell asked from behind Wilson's desk. He patted the empty chair beside him. "Come join me, Jessie."

I glanced at Wilson, and he also pointed me to the chair. "Motive, means, and opportunity," he said. "Start talking." He spoke to Russell. "Alistair Pritt," he said. "Start typing."

"Typing what?"

Both cops looked at me, and I confessed I didn't have all the pesky details worked out.

"Well then. Let's work them out." That was Wilson of course. My fiancé the cop is a stickler for pesky details. Motive, means, and opportunity? The man can't get enough.

"Motive." I gave it a go. "Alistair's her uncle. He's a bit like Dianne Calloway's misguided Uncle John. Or even better—he's like Willow's Uncle Hazard. Eccentric, over-protective, and misguided. Uncle Hazard is the reason Willow finds herself in such a pickle."

"Uncle Hazard?" Russell said. "Who is this Willow person?"

"Willow-slash-Will, LaSwann-slash-LeSwine, is the heroine of my latest book."

"Jessie!" Wilson scolded. "Can we get back to Pritt, please? The guy you're accusing of murder."

"Exactly," I said. "Alistair Pritt is her uncle. Or rather, he was her uncle. But they don't have the same last name. Just like Mrs. Marachini and her niece Trisha Fister." I slapped the desk. "Different last names!"

"Who?" the cops asked.

"Candy Poppe's polka-dot bra lady."

Russell glanced at Wilson."Permission to shoot her?"

"Granted."

"Okay, okay." I waved my hands and promised to do better, and began explaining what had occurred to me during my power walk. "I'd bet my daddy's cue stick Alistair Pritt is related to that poor woman who got killed."

"Miriam Jilton?" they asked.

"No! Alistair killed Miriam. But he was related to Darla Notari. He's her uncle, or cousin, or something."

"What?" the cops continued speaking in unison.

"Think about it, Wilson. If you hadn't gotten your current position, Darla Notari would have. She wouldn't have moved to Georgia, and she wouldn't have gotten killed."

Blank stares.

"I'm sorry," I said. "But Alistair, her misguided uncle, blames you for all that. And he killed an innocent person, and put her on my car to draw attention to me—your fiancée." I raised an eyebrow. "Because if I look bad, guess who looks bad?"

"Keep going," Wilson said.

"But Plan A failed miserably," I continued. "Because Jimmy Beak didn't play his part as expected. He never did accuse me of murder."

"Because of the lawsuit threat," Russell said.

I sat back. "So there you have it. Enter Plan B."

"Not yet." Wilson started pacing rapidly. "I think it gets worse."

"It does?" Russell and I asked.

"Yep." He made a U-turn at his office door. "What if Pritt expected Beak to go even further than accuse you of murder?"

"What could be worse than that?" Russell asked for me.

Wilson stopped and stared at me. "What if Pritt knows about Dianne Calloway? Lots of people do."

I shook my head in confusion, but clearly Russell was following the logic. His jaw dropped and he, too, stared at me.

"What?" I asked.

"Jessie," he said gently. "What if Alistair Pritt was hoping Jimmy Beak would compare you to Dianne?"

I let out a squeak and looked at Wilson.

"My other fiancée." He groaned. "The murderer."

***

Wilson resumed pacing, but I myself was happy to be sitting down at that point.

I took a deep breath. “Okay, so now we get to Plan B. Jimmy never accused me of murder, and therefore the comparison to Dianne wasn’t going to happen. And meanwhile Alistair has just killed Miriam Jilton. So what does he do?”

“He thinks of some other way to keep Beak focused on you. And eventually me,” Wilson said as he wore a hole in the carpet. “He starts the book-banning parade.”

“Exactly,” I said. “The timing is perfect.”

“Ah, so it wasn’t a coincidence,” Russell said. “Pritt started his protest right after the Sunday morning Weekly Wrap Up program.”

“Wherein Jimmy point-blank told his audience I did not kill Miriam Jilton.” I sat back and folded my arms. “So there you have it.”

Wilson stopped again. “No we don’t. Your theory has too many holes, Jessie.”

“Oh, come on! You yourself just filled the hole.” I threw my hands in the air. “The big huge Dianne Calloway-Jessie Hewitt comparison hole!”

“But you still haven’t given us motive,” Wilson argued while I huffed and puffed.

“How do you know Pritt cared about Darla Notari?” Russell asked me.

“How do you know he was her uncle?” Wilson said. “And don’t say intuition.”

“Intuition,” I said, and he started pacing again.

“Okay, then. What about the picture?” I tried. “Alistair keeps a family photograph behind the cash register at the Hava Java. He pointed it out to me.” I nodded at Wilson. “Remember the Missy incident?”

Wilson stopped and leaned over the desk. “You know for sure the picture’s still there?”

“No.”

“You know how many years ago it was taken?”

“No.”

“You know Darla Notari is in it?”

“No.” I pouted. “But I bet she is.”

"Maybe when she was ten," Wilson mumbled. "That is, if we're lucky." He frowned and started pacing again.

I turned to Russell and pointed him toward the computer. "Work with me, here. Do that magic that you do, and prove the connection."

"The Darla Notari-Uncle Alistair Pritt connection." Bless his cooperative and capable heart, Russell started tapping at the keyboard. "This may take a while," he said as various charts, graphs, and spreadsheets of what I assumed was Darla Notari's family tree flashed onto the screen.

"Her funeral," Wilson said. "You were there, Densmore. Was Pritt?"

I jumped. "That's right, Russell! Did you see Alistair?"

The good lieutenant looked up from the computer to roll his eyes at us. "It was a year ago, you guys. Hundreds of people attended that funeral to pay their respects—cops, politicians, friends."

"Family," I added.

"Check the obituary," Wilson said and hustled himself around the desk to see.

Russell returned to the computer and located the archives of several Atlanta newspapers.

"Look at that." I pointed at the screen. "It says Sheriff Notari left behind a large extended family of loved ones." I sat back. "And Alistair has a large extended family of loved ones. They've been marching with him, and they've been running the Hava Java all week."

"Yeah, so?" the cops said.

"And his large extended family is in that photograph I just mentioned."

"Yeah, so?"

I sighed dramatically and was busy getting discouraged, when Wilson reached over Russell's shoulder and pointed. "Date look familiar?" he asked.

"May fifth," I whispered.

"Darla Notari was killed exactly one year to the day before Miriam Jilton," Wilson said in case we didn't get it.

He shuffled around behind us. "Check the photos," he told Russell, and soon we were squinting at the pictures taken at Darla's funeral.

Wilson and I were complaining about our middle-aged eyesight when Russell started.

"Bingo," he said. He pointed at something—or more accurately—someone, and Wilson and I strained our eyes to focus.

Russell zoomed in on the person in question, and we took another look.

I glanced up at Wilson. "Motive."

***

All three of us jumped when someone knocked at the door.

Wilson recovered first and cleared his throat. "Come in," he hollered, and I was relieved to see Tiffany Sass poke her head in.

"Sass!" Wilson said. "Get in here and shut the door."

She did so, but didn't move very far into the room. She looked back and forth at the three of us huddled behind Wilson's desk. "Sorry to interrupt," she said. "But can I do anything to help, Captain?"

"You sure can." Wilson told her to go down to the corner of Sullivan and Vine. "Keep your eye on Alistair Pritt. Don't let him out of your sight until you hear from me."

"Got it. Am I to make my presence known?"

"No. Put on that blue outfit you wore yesterday and join the Romance Rockettes again. Fit in, if possible."

Tiffany nodded and reached for the doorknob, but I called over to stop her. "I'm still at the library if anyone asks."

"Pardon me?"

"It's the excuse Roslynn and I used to get me over here. We told Jimmy we were on an emergency library run." I glanced around at several pairs of perplexed eyes. "Apparently I'm out of reading material."

Chapter 35

"Motive, means, and opportunity," Wilson reminded us of the goal. "Means."

Russell patted my knee. "I've got this one, Jessie." He swiveled his chair around and again pointed to the computer screen. "The picture says it all."

That, it did. Alistair dwarfed everyone else in the photograph. "He's a big guy," Russell stated the obvious. "Strong enough to strangle Miriam Jilton and carry her to Jessie's car."

"What about opportunity?" Wilson asked. "That's not so easy."

"You mean, how did he know where my car would be?" I said.

"That, and why wait all this time? It's been a whole year since Darla died. Pritt could have found out where you live and dumped a body on your car anytime." Wilson scowled. "And, did he even know your car?"

Russell guffawed. "Come on, Captain. Of course he knew her car. Everyone in town knows the Add-a-lay car."

"And the Hava Java is in my old neighborhood," I said. "Alistair knew my car."

"So why'd he wait so long?" Wilson asked again.

"The date," I said. "That year-to-date thing you yourself just noticed."

"Not enough."

I threw my hands in the air. "Would you stop being so demanding? Who knows why he waited?"

"I know," Russell said. "Jessie's been on Jimmy Beak's radar lately. He got her fired from that writing contest, and he made fun of the Romance Hall of Fame."

"All in the last month or so," I said, and even Wilson had to agree Jimmy's shenanigans could have put this sick idea into Alistair's head.

"Alistair's likely been waiting for the right moment." I gave my fiancé a meaningful look. "He's been waiting for the right opportunity."

"The opportunity." Wilson caught my emphasis. "To use Beak against you, to get to me."

"And there you have it," I said.

"No we don't," Wilson the naysayer said.

I sighed dramatically. "And why, pray tell, not?"

"Opportunity." He remained on topic. "How did Pritt know where your car was Saturday? And another thing—"

"Oh, yes," I said. "Please do give me another thing."

"And another thing." He ignored the sarcasm. "Why didn't Pritt take someone out at Sullivan and Vine? He didn't need to wait for your car to be at the Junior Prom."

"Umm," I answered, but luckily Russell was still working with me.

"That corner where Jessie lives is way too busy, Captain. You're always complaining about it."

"Someone's always traipsing in and out of The Stone Fountain," I agreed. "And the gas station is open twenty-four-seven. It's right next to where I usually park."

"Pritt wouldn't do it down there," Russell said. "Too big a chance he'd be seen."

"But that still leaves one question," Wilson said. "How did Pritt know where the Porsche was on Saturday?"

I glared and pulled out my phone. "Give me a minute."

***

"Miss Jessie?" Frankie answered in a whisper. "I'm in algebra class. I'm not supposed to use my phone."

"Get a hall pass," I told him. "We need to talk."

He gasped. "You know who did it?" he whispered, and I again told him to work on the hall pass.

"Be discrete, Frankie."

I was entertained at both ends while I waited on the line. On my end I was able to watch Wilson and Russell go through all kinds of amusing gyrations. Apparently they considered it unwise to involve a "civilian," and a "minor at that," in our discussion. Russell swiveled his chair around and around, and Wilson paced up and down, continuing to wear out the carpeting.

On Frankie's end, I overheard the excruciating discussion between my young friend and his math teacher, who was reluctant to set her charge free during the middle of a lesson on quadratic equations.

I spoke into the phone. “Frankie!” I yelled until he heard me.

“Yes, Miss J—”

“Don’t!” I interrupted loudly. “Don’t say my name,” I whispered. “Let me talk to your teacher.”

“Hello,” the math teacher said, and I performed what I do believe was a brilliant impersonation of Gabriella Yates.

“I am no accustomed to waiting, Ms. –”

Shoot! I had no idea what this woman’s name was.

I tried again. “I am not accustomed to waiting, miss! I must discuss something of the utmost importance with Mr. Smythe! Kindly excuse him.”

“Dr. Ya—?” the hapless math teacher began.

“Don’t say my name! Do you not understand the delicacy of the situation! This is in regards to Miriam Jilton’s murder!”

The teacher gasped.

“Now then.” I pursed my lips and continued to channel Gabby. “Kindly release Mr. Smythe.”

Lo and behold, the next thing I knew, Mr. Smythe had his hall pass.

I gave the cops a thumbs up.

“She’s a little scary,” Wilson told Densmore.

“Everyone knows that, Captain.”

***

“What’s going on, Miss J—” Frankie caught himself. “Do you know who did it?” he whispered.

“We think so,” I said and then immediately shushed him when he started asking questions.

“I have a question for you,” I said. “And I don’t want you to repeat any part of this conversation to anyone until it’s all over. Even Lizzie. Do you understand?”

I swear I could hear him roll his eyes, and for the umpteenth time he reminded me he’s not a kid anymore. “I know how to keep a secret.”

“Okay,” I said. “So where were you when you called me last Thursday? When you asked to borrow my car.”

"Hanging with baseball team."

"Where?"

"At the coffee shop. A bunch of us went there after practice."

I squeaked. "The Hava Java?"

"I'm sorry," Frankie said. "But I didn't know Mr. Pritt was about to be so mean to you. I promise I don't go there anymore."

***

"No way," Wilson said.

"Way," I said. "The child is a caffeine fiend, and the Hava Java is in his neighborhood, and Frankie practically shouted the news from the rooftop when I said he could use my car."

I recollected the phone call. "He kept yelling 'The Porsche! The Porsche! Miss Jessie's Porsche!'" I shook my head. "The whole place must have heard him. Heck, the whole neighborhood likely heard him."

"Alistair Pritt heard him," Russell said.

"Absolutely. And in that same conversation Frankie promised me he'd be very careful. He promised to park way in the back of the school lot." I cringed. "To keep the car safe while he and Lizzie were at the dance."

"Alistair Pritt heard that, too," Russell said.

"And who knows what else got discussed after we hung up?" I asked.

Wilson raised an eyebrow. "Your vanity plates, is what."

"Excuse me?"

"Think about it, Jessie. Sixteen-year-old kids driving a car called Add-a-lay? Yep," he said. "That got discussed."

"Alistair Pritt heard that, too." Russell again.

I sat back and folded my arms. "And there you have it, gentlemen. Opportunity."

Chapter 36

"We need proof," Wilson said before I could enjoy even one self-satisfied smirk.

I told him that was his job. "I'm the intuition department. You're the proof department."

"The taxi driver," Russell suggested. "The guy who picked up Frankie and Lizzie Saturday night might have seen Pritt's car leaving the scene of the crime."

"Circumstantial," Wilson said. "Even if it were true."

"What about forensics?" Russell tried again. "The lab found a few hairs on Jilton that weren't her own."

Unfortunately, I had to say no to that. "Miriam was helping the girls with their hair-dos that night."

"Maybe," Wilson said. "But she was strangled and carried across that entire parking lot. There had to be something from Pritt on the victim or on the Porsche. I'd bet money forensics already has the evidence we need."

"They just don't know it," Russell said. "We don't have Pritt's DNA."

"Hello-o, you people in the proof department!" I waved my hands impatiently. "So go get Pritt's DNA. And then have forensics do the matching thing." I shook my head at Wilson. "Isn't that what they do on TV?"

"Maybe. But we need a warrant."

"Well then, go get one of those!"

Russell explained it wasn't quite that easy. Some pesky issue about "just cause."

"And let me guess," I said. "The motive, means, and opportunity we've covered ever so thoroughly isn't good enough?"

"Nope," the cops said, and Wilson reminded me I am rather enamored of a little thing called the Bill of Rights.

I whimpered slightly and asked him what exactly would warrant a warrant.

"We need Pritt to say something incriminating. In public."

Russell sat up. "How about on TV?"

"Oh, that's good!" I rubbed my palms together. "We'll get Alistair to spout off something incriminating in front of Jimmy Beak and Joe the cameraman."

Wilson grinned. "You read my mind," he said, and I was suddenly cognizant that grin was aimed directly at me.

***

"No!" I said. "No, no, no. Don't even think whatever it is you're thinking, Wilson Rye."

"What am I thinking?"

"I don't know. But stop it this instant."

"I know what I'm thinking." Russell seemed to miss my point. "Jessie can go on the air with Jimmy and Alistair," he said. "For an interview. Like, a showdown."

"Yep, Lieutenant," Wilson said. "That's what I'm thinking."

"Well it sure as hell isn't what I'm thinking!" I popped out of my chair and landed in front of him. I jabbed at my chest. "Intuition department!" I jabbed at his chest. "Proof department!"

That grin was downright relentless.

I folded my arms and tossed my head. "I cannot bother Jimmy Beak right now," I said defiantly. "He thinks I'm at the library."

***

Wilson checked his watch. "We need to act fast if we want it on tonight's news."

"We?"

He glanced around me and spoke to Russell. "I'm thinking a formal interview. In the newsroom."

"There'd be less commotion than out in the street," Russell agreed. "She'll concentrate better."

"She?" I stumbled back to my chair. "Concentrate?" I plopped down.

"She and Beak will need a clear plan," Wilson said.

"Beak?" I squeaked. "Plan?" I croaked.

"Good idea, Captain." That was Russell. Because it sure as heck wasn't me. "If they plan things out ahead, it's bound to work."

"Are you guys hallucinating!?" That was me. "You cannot possibly expect Jimmy and me to work together—together!—to get a confession out of Alistair Pritt. On the air, no less!"

"That would be perfect," Russell said.

"A confession isn't necessary." Wilson spoke over the strange squeaking noises emanating from yours truly. "We just need to him say to something incriminating. Make him mad, Jessie. Get Pritt to have a fit about how much he hates me."

"That would be just cause for a search warrant." Russell nodded encouragement. "And then we can go get the forensic evidence."

Squeak, squeak.

"One itty-bitty piece of evidence is all we need." Wilson offered a meaningful—a sincerely meaningful—look. "Miriam Jilton didn't deserve to die, Jessie. She deserves justice."

I closed my eyes and prayed for strength.

Russell reached over and shook me until I looked up. "You can do this, Jessie. You're good at making men mad. You make the Captain mad all the time!"

***

"Call Beak," Wilson said, and much to my chagrin, Russell was as efficient as ever.

He took out his cell phone, punched in some numbers, and handed me his phone. No—let me be clearer—he shoved the thing into my altogether unwilling hands.

And of course Jimmy answered his stupid phone.

"Is Alistair Pritt right there?" I asked before identifying myself.

"No, but I can get him? Who is this?"

I made sure to tell Jimmy to stay a good distance from Alistair, and then I identified myself.

He laughed out loud. "Getting bored at the library, are we?"

"Believe it or not, I'm not actually at the library."

I will spare you his response to that startling piece of news.

“I need your help,” I told him.

Okay, now that was a startling piece of news. Enough so, that Jimmy stopped laughing and/or cursing at me long enough hear my proposition.

“I’d be doing you and Rye a big favor,” he said as I finished explaining.

“But think about the drama of an on-air confession. Think about your ratings.”

Jimmy was thinking.

“Alistair killed Miriam Jilton in cold blood,” I said. “She deserves justice.” I cleared my throat and said it. “And the public has a right to know.”

“I’ll tell you what the public has a right to know,” Jimmy said. “Let’s you and me make a deal.”

I stared at Wilson and listened to Jimmy’s demands.

“What do you say?” he asked eventually. “We got a deal?”

I took a deep breath. “Deal.”

Chapter 37

I stared at the back door of the Channel 15 News station and recited a few hundred four-letter words.

Like it or not, I was all alone. Wilson had insisted he couldn't accompany me because his presence might "give it away."

"Coward," I took a break from some more colorful language to mutter into thin air.

Lieutenant Densmore had also deserted me. He drove me over, but then dropped me rather unceremoniously in the back alley. "If Alistair sees me out front, he'll get suspicious," Russell had explained ever so logically. "Good luck," he added and took off.

Luck would be nice, I told myself as I slogged around the building to the main entrance.

Three young women carrying clipboards, smart phones, and various gadgets I could not identify accosted me the moment I set foot inside.

"Jessica Hewitt!" Woman A said. I tried smiling, but clearly that little nicety was considered a waste of time. "We're wasting time!" she told me.

"We thought you'd never get here," Woman B scolded.

"Umm," I managed as Woman A took me firmly by the arm and hustled me over to the elevator. Presumably B and C were following. Being the expert amateur sleuth that I am, I could tell by the clickety-clacking of all those high heels on the polished floor.

Once the four of us were in the elevator and going up, I was shoved against the back wall and told to stand still while the three women assessed my person. By the way they were frowning and wrinkling their noses, I assumed the assessment was not all that positive.

The elevator dinged and now Woman C grabbed my elbow to whisk me away. "You didn't dress," she scolded as A and B clickety-clacked behind me.

"Well, I—" I stopped, and A and B bumped into me from behind.

I kept my footing and explained I had not planned on this interview when I left my house earlier. In fact, if Geez Louise ever found out I was wearing jeans and an old cardigan for a televised interview she might disown me.

As B and C scolded me for my lack of foresight, Woman A took off the scarf adorning her own neck and shoved it at B. “At least put this on her,” she said.

The scarf changed hands, and A and C scurried back to the elevator.

I smiled at Woman B, but of course there was no time for such niceties. She grabbed my elbow—an act I was starting to get used to—and shoved me into nearest room.

“Makeup!” she hollered. She gave me another push, and I stumbled into the one remaining seat in what I ascertained was the makeup room. “Jessica Hewitt!” she announced quite loudly. “And put this on her when you’re done.”

The scarf landed on my head and blocked my vision. That was probably a good thing. Because a moment earlier I had caught a glimpse of the people in the other two chairs.

You guessed it.

***

Unfortunately the makeup man assigned to Jessica-Hewitt duty decided his job would be easier if he could see my face. He removed the scarf, and I double-checked. Yep. I was indeed sitting smack dab between Alistair and Jimmy.

But apparently the odd and uncomfortable circumstances were lost on everyone but me. My makeup man began dabbing, brushing, puffing, and combing yours truly, while he chattered away about blush tones and eyeliner with the makeup artists assigned to Jimmy and Alistair. And Jimmy and Alistair? They were shooting the breeze about nothing much also. Believe it or not, they even tried to include me in the conversation.

I concentrated on turning my curled lip into a smile of sorts and practiced some deep breathing. My makeup man interrupted a particularly zen-like breath to enquire as to how I like my bangs combed.

"How about over my eyes?" I suggested. But alas, my very short haircut wouldn't cooperate.

An excruciating fifteen minutes later we were deemed sufficiently fluffed and puffed, and A, B, and C returned to escort us down to the studio.

I suppose the interview area was meant to mimic a private living room—all comfy and cozy, with easy chairs and side tables for our water glasses.

As I took the seat to Jimmy's right, and directly across from Alistair, I listened to Belinda Bing. The anchorwoman sat behind the news desk across the expansive room, and through the ringing in my ears, I heard her say something about Jimmy's exclusive interview.

"You heard that right!" Her voice got a bit louder. "Jessica Hewitt faces off against Alistair Amesworth Pritt! Coming up!"

***

"You're on in three." Woman B hovered before me holding up three fingers. "Two." Two fingers. "One." She held up an index finger and took three giant steps backward.

And Jimmy was talking. Dare I say, it was actually comforting to hear his high-pitched overly-excitable voice? As long as he kept talking I didn't have to. And considering I had completely forgotten what I was supposed to say—

"What do you say to that, Jessie?"

"Excuse me?" I blinked at the camera as it zoomed in.

"Alistair," Jimmy indicated his other interviewee, "wants to know your justification for writing smut."

"What right have you to destroy the moral fabric of this great community?" Alistair raised a fist, and made as if to stand up, but Woman A popped up from somewhere off camera. Her right hand landed hard on his shoulder, and he was propelled back into sitting position.

But the pout on his face inspired me. I found my voice, even if I was still drawing a complete blank on the script Jimmy and I had planned.

I winged it. "I'm afraid, Mr. Pritt," I began. "What with all the energy you've devoted to studying my work, that you have quite missed the point."

"The point?"

"The plot, to be exact." I tapped my chin and contemplated Adelé Nightingale's plots. "In fact, I think you'd find the plot of my latest book most intriguing."

"Huh?" Jimmy seemed as confused as Alistair.

"*A Singular Seduction*," I clarified. "Mr. Pritt would relate to the characters."

"I think not!" Alistair pursed his indignant lips for the camera.

"Oh, perhaps not to Willow LaSwann or Kipp Jupiter," I said. "But I do believe you'd relate to Willow LaSwann's uncle." I practically shouted the word uncle. "Poor Uncle Hazard," I continued. "Poor old eccentric, over-protective, and misguided Uncle Hazard."

Alistair winced.

I pretended not to notice and spoke to Jimmy. "And now Willow is paying for the foibles and mistakes of her misguided uncle." I tut-tutted. "But Uncle Hazard did mean well."

"He did?" Jimmy asked.

"Oh, yes. Uncle Hazard was way ahead of his time. He didn't think Willow should be denied anything because of her sex. And so he left her his ranch!"

Jimmy smiled at me. "Is this a western?" he asked. "I like westerns!"

Apparently Belinda Bing and the weatherman also enjoyed the genre. They left their appointed posts to come closer as I summarized my main plot point. "Willow LaSwann is a rancher. She loves the work, but she does face certain challeng—"

"Why are we talking about this smut?" Alistair interrupted.

"Because you asked about it," Jimmy said. He turned back to me. "Go ahead, Jessie."

"Now, where was I?" I held up an index finger. "Oh, yes. I was explaining the happy ending. Adelé Nightingale insists on happy endings. So don't you worry, Mr. Pritt. Willow shall overcome. She will gain the respect and regard of her fellow ranchers, and she will keep her beloved ranch. Willow LaSwann will prevail!" I raised my fist in the air, skipped a beat for effect, and sat back. “Unlike your niece, Darla Notari.”

Alistair’s face dropped about a mile.

Woman C said something to the director about cutting to a commercial.

“Later,” I heard him say.

“What’s this about a niece?” Jimmy asked as we got back on track of our prearranged script.

“Alistair’s niece, Darla Notari,” I said loud and clear. “You remember Officer Notari, Jimmy? She was on the police force here in Clarence before she took a job in Georgia.”

Of course Jimmy remembered. I had explained the whole nine yards of motive, means, and opportunity to him an hour earlier.

“Darla Notari.” He adopted a reflective pose. “She was killed in the line of duty, wasn’t she? About a year ago?”

“That’s right,” I said. “Darla Notari was killed exactly one year ago, last Saturday night.”

Alistair gasped, and I turned slowly to face him. “You must have been quite upset about it?”

Watching Alistair Pritt squirm was what was upsetting. And I was very uncomfortable speaking in such brash terms about his niece. But I thought about Miriam Jilton. And I recollected my goal—to infuriate the man who killed her.

“The timing is interesting, isn’t it, Jimmy? Darla Notari was killed exactly one year to the day before Miriam Jilton.”

Jimmy agreed that it was interesting.

“It’s also interesting how similar the two women were,” I said. “They remind me of each other.”

“Why does Darla Notari remind you of Miriam Jilton?” Jimmy was quite adept at following our invisible script.

“They were both such outstanding citizens, both so good at their jobs.” I glared at Alistair. “They were both stellar, and they were both murdered.”

“I covered Darla Notari’s funeral,” Jimmy continued relentlessly. “Channel 15 travelled down to Atlanta, as did half the police force. We went down to pay our respects.

The public had a right to know about such a tragedy. A fine public servant like that? Someone who devoted her entire career to helping others. Someone who—"

"Stop it!" Alistair flung out his hands and knocked over his water glass. "Stop talking about her!"

Someone behind me again asked the director about a commercial break.

"Not on your life." The director twirled an index finger at the cameraman. "Keep filming or you're fired."

The cameras kept rolling, as did Jimmy. "You want us to stop talking about Miriam Jilton?" he asked Alistair.

"No, you idiot! Stop talking about Darla." He pointed at me. "How dare you even utter her name. Pornographer! Smut-monger! Murderer!"

"What!?" Jimmy said.

Alistair turned on him. "She's a murderer, you idiot! You know it as well as I do. Why are you protecting her?"

"Protecting who?" Jimmy played dumb.

"Jessie Hewitt, you idiot!" Alistair pointed at me again. "She killed that Jilton woman in cold blood!"

"Blood!" I said loudly, and both heads snapped toward me.

"What!?"

I thought fast. "The murder scene was very bloody." I kept thinking. "Exceedingly bloody. Whoever shot Miriam Jilton made a big huge bloody mess all over my car."

Alistair sprang out of his chair. "You lie!" he screamed.

Woman A tried to get him to sit back down, but he was far too wound up. "She's a pornographer!" he yelled at Jimmy. "She's a murderer! And now she's a liar!"

"How so?" Jimmy asked calmly.

"There was no blood, you idiot! She was strangled!"

I remained silent and let Jimmy do the dirty work. "Darla Notari was strangled?" he asked. "I always thought she was shot."

"No, you idiot! Miriam Jilton was strangled!"

While I waited for Alistair to catch his breath, I chatted with Jimmy. "Now here's another point I find interesting," I said.

"What's that?" he asked.

"The police haven't released the details on how exactly Miriam was murdered."

I looked up at Alistair. "And so." I paused. "The million-dollar question is, how do you know she was strangled?"

He stumbled backward, tripped over his chair, and fainted.

"Now!" the director shouted. "Now, cut to commercial!"

Chapter 38

"Can I give you a lift home?"

I glanced up from the prone figure of Alistair Pritt and into Jimmy Beak's smiling face.

When pigs fly, I thought to myself. I said no thank you and tried to stand up, but somehow the skill escaped me. Joe the cameraman rushed over, and between them, he and Jimmy got me to my feet.

I thanked the guys for their assistance and planned my escape route. Alistair required a wide berth, as did A, B, and C. All three women had unceremoniously dropped their clipboards and other apparatus and were kneeling beside him, taking turns slapping him. I got past those obstacles, avoided the water Alistair had splattered, and picked my way toward the outskirts of the studio.

The going was slow since I was still a bit unsteady on my feet, and the entire floor was strewn with a variety of wires, cables, and other assorted junk. The human obstacles were even worse. Everyone and his brother—or at least every employee of Channel 15—felt compelled to get in my way and hinder my progress.

They patted me on the back and said things like "Off-the-charts ratings!" and "Justice is served!" and "Interview of the century!"

And then there were Jimmy and Joe to contend with. The two of them kept following me and insisting I needed a lift home. "You still don't have your car," Jimmy said. "And your fiancé's too busy with his warrants to come get you."

"We'll bring you home, and then we can have tea," Joe the cameraman suggested. "Do you happen to have that green tea your mother serves?"

"I prefer Earl Grey," Jimmy informed me.

Needless to say, I was quite relieved when I saw Russell Densmore rushing toward me.

I waved to my knight in shining armor. "You-who," I sang. "Over here, Lieutenant."

Why was he ignoring me?

I tripped over a cable and landed in his path, and he stopped short.

He helped me to my feet, but his eyes were still focused on something behind me. “Are you okay?” he asked absently.

“I will be once you drive me home.”

Russell’s gaze finally met mine. “I’m sorry, Jessie,” he said. “You did great, but I can’t help you right now. I’m in charge of Pritt.”

“Bu—bu—but.”

He spoke to Jimmy. “Can you take her down to the police station?”

“No problemo.”

“Bu—bu—”

“That’s okay with you, isn’t it?” Russell looked at me. “The Captain will be there as soon as he’s done at Pritt’s place.”

The lieutenant didn’t wait for an answer, but moved off toward A, B, and C. The three women were now standing over Alistair, nudging him with the toes of their pumps.

I glanced sideways at Jimmy, who had yet to stop smiling.

***

Wilson offered me a hand as I stepped out of the Channel 15 News van and onto the curb at the police station. “Has hell frozen over?” he asked.

“You left me no other options,” I said. “Shame on Russell for choosing to guard Alistair instead of me.”

About then Joe popped out from the backdoor of the van, camera rolling.

“Beak!” Wilson shouted, and my chauffeur emerged from the driver’s side.

“No film?” Jimmy asked.

“Like, duh! You just had the interview of the century thanks to this woman.” Wilson wrapped an arm around me. “Get out of here.”

Jimmy looked at me. “I promise to make it real positive,” he said. “The public has a right to know.”

I shook my head and reminded Jimmy we had a deal.

"What is this deal?" Wilson asked. "You never did say."

"Oh, nothing," Jimmy and I sang in unison. He winked at me, waved Joe into the van, and off they drove.

"Yep," Wilson said as the van disappeared. "Hell has frozen over."

***

And speaking of startling and shocking, Wilson gave me a great big bear hug right there in front of the police station. Right there in front of—I surveyed our audience from over his shoulder—at least half the Clarence police force.

"Where did all these people come from?" I asked.

"Where did that scarf come from?"

"Why aren't you at Alistair's?"

"What's the deal you made with Jimmy?"

But the answers to our questions would have to wait, since the crowd would not. They circled in to congratulate me on a job well done.

At some point, I did manage to learn why Wilson was with me and not searching Alistair Pritt's house. Apparently he had left Tiffany Sass and the forensics team to finish up that detail.

"Sass is thorough," he said as the last few cops gave me the requisite pat on the back. "I predict we'll have evidence out the yin-yang." He elbowed his way back toward me and the crowd gave us a little space. "Between that and what you pulled off tonight, we got him. You did great, Jessie."

"But I didn't get him to say why he killed her."

Wilson assured me I had done enough. "That business about the blood was inspired."

I shrugged modestly. "I knew Alistair would love catching me in a lie."

Wilson tugged at my new scarf. "One more vice for the Queen of Smut."

I blinked twice.

"What's up?"

"Sex!" I shouted. "We need sex!"

I do believe the man actually blushed. And the cops surrounding us laughed out loud.

"Nooo!" I said. "Not we, we." I slapped Wilson's chest. "Not Wilson and me, we. I'm talking about Willow LaSwann and Kipp Jupiter!"

Wilson ignored the puzzled expressions surrounding us. "This have something to do with Willow's well?" he asked.

"Nooo!" I waved my hands impatiently. "Forget about the well. This has nothing to do with the plumbing. The plumbing is meaningless."

"It is?"

"It's my title, Wilson! It's all wrong."

"But I thought we liked *A Singular Seduction*."

"Not anymore. Don't you see? Singular implies just one. Just one sex scene!" I gave him a meaningful look. "One," I repeated, and he finally caught on.

"All wrong," he said.

"But how about *Seduction in the Shadows*?" I held up an index finger. "Now that has possibilities! Every haystack in Hogan's Hollow must cast a shadow somewhere! Shadows here, shadows there, shadows everywhere!"

"But what about Willow's secret?" Wilson asked. "About being a woman?"

"It's not just her secret anymore. It's their secret!" I jumped up and down. "Willow and Kipp will both—both!—be hiding her true identity from the townsfolk."

"You mean Kipp knows she's a woman?"

"Oh, yes! He's going to catch her right away. He'll discover her secret before page ten." I started. "No!" I was back to bouncing. "Before page five!"

"But how?"

I stopped bouncing.

Wilson grabbed my shoulders and shook me. "Think, Jessie. How will Kipp find out she's a girl?"

I slumped, and it was a good thing he was holding onto me.

"I don't know," I said in despair. "How?"

He was thinking. "I got it!" he shouted, and everyone and his brother jumped.

"You do?" we asked.

He glanced around and seemed startled that we still had an audience. "Don't you people have work to do?" he asked the cops.

"Later," several people said. "The story, Captain," several others added. They pointed at me. "Jessie's waiting."

Wilson turned back to me. "Willow will be two people," he said. "Willow and Will. She'll pretend to be twins."

I scowled. "Willow has a brother?"

"No! Don't you know what pretend means? Willow LaSwann will pretend to be both herself and her brother Will. And Will will be the one who supposedly inherited the ranch from their-slash-her Uncle Hazard. And Kipp Jupiter will think there's two of her-slash-them. And—" He stopped abruptly. "It's too convoluted, isn't it?"

I smiled into the baby blues. "Heck, no," I said. "It's inspired."

"It is?"

I reminded him convoluted plot twists were Adelé Nightingale's middle name and dove on in. "Willow will be forever changing in and out of men's and women's clothes to keep up this twins pretense. And that's how Kipp will learn the truth. He'll catch her in Will's clothes, but she'll have forgotten to bind her bosom. And, well, you get the picture."

Wilson considered the possibilities. "Once Kipp knows the truth about Willow, they can get together, right?"

"Correct." I kept thinking. "But for some reason—as yet to be disclosed—they'll still need to rendezvous in secret." I batted my eyelashes. "And you can trust Adelé Nightingale on this, Captain Rye. There is nothing quite like secret sex to get the libido flowing. Maxine Carlisle devotes two chapters to that topic!"

"Sensual and Scintillating," Wilson told his colleagues. "The Sex Scene Handbook."

"*For Today's Romance Writer*." I tapped my head with all ten fingertips. "I have got to get home, Wilson. The sex scenes are racing through Adelé's head."

"What about Auntie Abigail?"

"Auntie Who?" I asked impatiently. "Surely I've mentioned Uncle Hazard was a confirmed bachelor?"

For some reason Wilson was smiling as he moved me backward toward the nearest patrol car. He held onto the top of my head and guided me into the vehicle. At least he put me in the passenger seat, and not behind the bars in the back.

"Get her to the corner of Sullivan and Vine," he told the patrolman in the driver's seat. He twirled an index finger over his head, and the cop beside me flicked a switch on the dashboard.

I barely had time to register the flashing blue lights and siren before we peeled out.

Epilogue

"I can't believe it," Frankie Smythe stared at the red light in front of us. "I cannot believe it!"

"But it's perfectly logical," I said. "Together they'll overcome a few more pesky problems, and then they'll get married." I pointed to the green light, and Frankie hit the gas. "Willow LaSwann and Kipp Jupiter are destined for each other. They'll merge their properties into one big ranch and live happily ever after."

"Miss Jessie!" Frankie scolded. "I'm not talking about your book. I'm talking about your car." He tapped the steering wheel. "Is it really all mine?"

"Everything but the license plate." I gestured to the car lot up ahead. "But not until we pick out a new one for me. I'm thinking gold this time." I turned to my driver. "What do you think?"

Frankie made it to the next red light. "I think this is crazy."

I doubt he was referring to a gold Porsche, but to the fact that I was giving him the silver one. After consulting with Laura and Greg Smythe, I decided my old car would make an excellent high school graduation gift. Perhaps a bit extravagant, but Frankie deserved it.

And lo and behold, I could finally afford a new car for myself. Thanks to the publicity Adelé Nightingale had gotten of late, my bank account was looking healthier than ever.

"Now remember," I said as we inched forward in the traffic. "This is an early graduation gift. I won't be giving you another car next year."

"Miss Jessie! Do you really think I'll ever forget this?" He tapped the steering wheel. "Now then, about that wedding."

"You are referring to Willow and Kipp's wedding?"

"No. To your wedding. Lizzie thinks it's romantic that old—I mean older—people like you and Captain Rye are getting married." I braced myself and waited for the inevitable. "So, like, when is it?"

I stared out the passenger window. "Sometime soon," I said.

"You're stalling," Frankie told me. "Why won't you marry Captain Rye"

I suggested we concentrate on our cars.

"Why?" he asked firmly.

"Oh, for Lord's sake!" I threw my arms up. "I do love the guy, okay? But I can't see myself living way out at Lake Lookadoo in a shack. And don't get me started on the supposed plumbing. It would ward away even the scariest of the Septosauri."

"Can't you get the plumbing fixed?"

I skipped a beat. "Maybe," I said. "But then there's Wilson—Captain Rye. He doesn't want to live downtown any more than I want to live out in the boondocks."

"That's it?" Frankie was incredulous. "You're worried about where you'll live?"

"It is an important consideration," I argued as we finally, finally pulled into the car dealership.

He parked, and I quick went to open my door. But Frankie was faster. He reached out and grabbed my left arm. He was as thin as ever. But somewhere along the line the child—I mean, the young man—had acquired some strength.

I bit my lip to keep from laughing. "Kindly unhand me, Mr. Smythe."

Frankie let go of my wrist and apologized. "I told Lizzie this would come out all wrong. I'm being nosey, and now you're mad at me." He reached for his own door, but I grabbed his wrist.

"I'm not mad." I waited until he would look at me. "You can be as nosey as you want."

"Well then, you are being kind of stupid, Miss Jessie."

"Oh? And what's your brilliant solution to my housing problem?"

"Like, duh! Live in both places. Lots of people have two houses, right? Like, what's wrong with that?"

I blinked twice.

Like, nothing.

***

"Let's hope my ploy worked," I told my mother as we pulled into Wilson's driveway. "He thinks he's taking me to the fancy restaurant on the other side of the lake."

Mother informed me I'm a shameless liar, but Wilson was indeed wearing his best suit when he stepped outside to greet us.

"What do you think?" I asked as I climbed out of my brand new car.

"It's great!" His eyes got wide. "It's gold."

"But it's understated, no?"

"I have news for you, Darlin.' There's nothing understated about this car." He pointed to the Adelé license plate and hustled over to help my mother from the passenger seat.

He told her he hadn't been expecting her. No kidding. And that it was a nice surprise to see her. No kidding again.

"When did you get into town?" he asked.

"This morning." Mother took Wilson's hand and struggled out of the low seat. "I wouldn't miss this, would I?"

"Miss wha—" Wilson stopped mid-question when he noticed the rather formal dress I was wearing.

"What the—" But he stopped mid-sentence again when Karen's van pulled in behind my car. She, Candy, and Peter Harrison hopped out, and Karen leaned into the back for Snowflake's cat carrier.

"Doesn't everyone look nice?" Mother asked.

"What the—"

"I asked them to wear yellow," I explained as my neighbors walked over to greet us.

Karen wore her ubiquitous jeans and work boots, but she had replaced the usual T-shirt for a lovely yellow silk blouse. Candy wore a yellow mini dress with matching stilettos. And Peter sported a yellow tie.

Peter pumped Wilson's stunned hand, offered me a slight bow, and held an elbow out for my mother. "May I have the honor?"

Mother giggled and took his arm, and they tottered off toward the lawn overlooking Lake Lookadoo.

"What the—" This time Wilson appealed to Candy and Karen.

"It's Snowflake." Karen jiggled the cat carrier. "She wasn't about to miss this."

"Gosh, no," Candy agreed. "Especially since she's already dressed for the occasion. All white and all." She took Karen's hand, and together they maneuvered their way up to the porch. They released Snowflake into the care of Bernice and Wally and joined Mother and Peter on the lawn.

"White?" Wilson pointed to my own outfit. "You look nice." He reconsidered. "You look beautiful."

I thanked him for noticing, told him he looked handsome, too, and pointed to the driveway. "But look," I said. "Here comes The Stone Fountain gang."

Wilson stared aghast at the U-haul truck pulling up.

Matthew and Gina Stone emerged from the cab, and Kirby, Gus, and Charlie popped out of the back. Kirby stood at attention and saluted us, and then got to work helping Gus unload several flower arrangements and quite a few white folding chairs. Karen whistled, and Charlie started carrying said chairs to the lawn.

Matthew and Gina ventured over to us. While Matthew shook Wilson's hand, Gina informed me the cake had survived the trip over the dirt roads. "And we brought enough food to feed an army."

"And enough champagne to float the Titanic," Matthew added.

"Did someone say champagne?" Christopher Rye hopped out of the latest vehicle to arrive.

"What the—"

"It's your son, Wilson." I pointed. "And your parents, of course."

While Chris helped LuAnn—his grandmother and Wilson's mother—from the passenger seat, Mitchell Rye, Wilson's father, got out of the back seat and walked over.

I thanked him for making the trip from Raleigh.

"Are you kidding?" He stopped shaking his son's hand to hug me.

"We wouldn't miss this for the world," LuAnn said as she and Chris joined us.

"Way to go, Dad." Chris high-fived Wilson, and me, and jogged back to the driveway to help with the last of the chairs.

LuAnn and Mitchell joined the group assembling on the lawn.

Wilson blinked at me. "I want Chris to stand up with me. With us."

"Already taken care of," I said and pointed to the continuing action in the driveway.

"What the—"

"It's Frankie and Lizzie," I said as the silver Porsche came to a stop. I waved to the teenagers, and an SUV pulled up behind them. "And that must be Like, The Lyricals. They're the girl group Lizzie is now a part of." I smiled at Wilson. "They do oldies."

Three young women emerged from the SUV, and with Frankie and Lizzie's help, unloaded a variety of instruments.

"Lizzie and the Lyricals," Wilson said. "I like it."

"No, Wilson. It's Like, The Lyricals."

"I do like The Lyricals."

I told him to never mind, since the poor guy was confused enough. Especially when we heard the sirens.

You guessed it. Two police cars pulled up, and out popped several members of Wilson's team. Tiffany Sass threw a kiss in our direction as Russell Densmore and his wife emerged from the car behind, and everyone began their trek toward the lawn.

Wilson waved to Russell in particular. "I want Densmore—I mean, I want Russell—to stand up with us also," he said, and I told him that, too, had already been arranged.

"Did you arrange for better plumbing?" a voice said from behind us.

We turned in time to see Loretta Springfield emerge from the woods that separated her property from Wilson's.

“Not yet,” I said, but Loretta assured us her bathroom facilities were in working order if the water stopped working at Wilson’s.

“But we almost always have running water,” I said optimistically.

“We?” Wilson asked me as Loretta wandered off.

“And you must be Snowflake,” she said as she passed the porch. She waved to the three cats and made her way toward my mother.

Tessie had busied herself introducing everyone—whether she knew them or not—to everyone else—whether she knew them or not.

Wilson considered the gathering crowd. “Is that it?” he asked me.

“Oh, heck no. We couldn’t forget Louise.”

“Heck no,” Wilson said, but he was drowned out by the voice of Geez Louise Urko.

“Fantasical, fantastical, and beyond fantastical!” she shouted as she emerged from Roslynn’s car. Louise managed about a hundred more “fantasticals” before she and Roslynn landed in front of us.

“This is so, so, so romantic!” she said. “The whole nine yards of romance! How do you think of these things, Jessica!?”

“It’s that imagination of hers,” Roslynn suggested, but Louise of the limited attention span had caught sight of my mother.

“Tessie!” she shouted and hurried away.

Roslynn looked back and forth between Wilson and me. “Fantastical,” she said quietly and followed in the footsteps of Geez Louise.

“Is that it?” Wilson asked again. He may have sounded a bit desperate.

“Heck no,” I said as the Channel 15 News van pulled up.

“No!” Okay, now Wilson definitely sounded desperate. “Please tell me no.”

“No can do!” I waved to Jimmy Beak and Joe the cameraman. “Remember that deal I made with Jimmy?”

Wilson may have whimpered.

"Jimmy agreed to my showdown with Alistair," I continued. "And I gave him an exclusive on this occasion."

"The public has a right to know," Jimmy called out. He gave us a thumbs up as he and Joe started setting up their equipment at the far end of the seating area.

Wilson began squeaking.

"Don't worry," I told him. "Jimmy promised only a very positive, two-minute segment on the Weekly Wrap Up. And Joe is going to give us all the photos and film. Isn't that nice?"

"You're a little scary. You know that?"

"Speaking of which." I pointed to what I promised would be the last car.

"Yikes!"

I nodded in agreement as I beckoned to Gabby and Gordon Yates. "Believe it or not, Superintendent Yates is a justice of the peace in her spare time."

"Why am I not surprised?"

"Because nothing surprises you, Captain Rye." Gabby gave me a hug, but continued addressing Wilson. "When Jessie told me what she had planned, I told her she was missing one key person. Me!"

"You." He scowled at the legal-looking documents Gordon held.

I waited until Wilson looked up and made sure I had the full attention of the baby blues. I took a deep breath. "What do you say, Wilson? Let's just do it."

A slow grin made its way across his face. "I think the proper response is 'I do.'"

"Actually, it's 'I will,'" Gabby corrected. "But follow my instructions, and you'll do fine." She took the paperwork from the hapless Gordon. "Come along," she ordered.

Chris and Russell, and Candy and Karen had already taken their appointed places in front of the gathering.

"The rings?" Gabby asked, and Karen and Chris tapped their pockets.

Candy handed me a yellow rose, I nodded to Gabby, and she addressed the crowd. "If I could have everyone's attention please. We're about to get started."

Wilson squeezed my hand, and together we stepped forward.

My new friend Gabby was right of course. Wilson and I were indeed, about to get started.

The End

Never fear! Jessie and Wilson may live happily ever after, but Adelé Nightingale predicts more adventures along the way. And once she figures out another convoluted plot and implausible murder, she'll be sure to let you know. In the meantime, be on the lookout for *Unbelievable*, the first book in a brand new series by Cindy Blackburn. The Cassie Baxter series begins soon!

The Cue Ball Mysteries by Cindy Blackburn: Because Jessie and company can't seem to stay out of trouble.

Book One: Playing With Poison

Pool shark Jessie Hewitt usually knows where the balls will fall and how the game will end. But when a body lands on her couch, and the cute cop in her kitchen accuses her of murder, even Jessie isn't sure what will happen next. *Playing With Poison* is a cozy mystery with a lot of humor, a little romance, and far too much champagne.

Book Two: Double Shot

Jessie Hewitt thought her pool-hustling days were long gone. But when über-hunky cop Wilson Rye asks her to go undercover to catch a killer, she jumps at the chance to return to a sleazy poolroom. Jessie is confident she can handle a double homicide, but the doubly-annoying Wilson Rye is another matter altogether. What's he doing flirting with a woman half his age? Will Jessie have what it takes to deal with Tiffany La-Dee-Doo-Da Sass and solve the murders? Take a guess.

Book Three: Three Odd Balls

A romantic vacation for…five? This wasn't exactly what Jessie and Wilson had in mind when they planned their trip to the tropics. But when Jessie's delightfully spry mother, Wilson's surfer dude son, and Jessie's rabidly hyperactive New York agent decide to tag along the fun begins. What kind of trouble can these three oddest of odd balls possibly get into? Take a guess.

Playing With Poison

Chapter 1

"Going bra shopping at age fifty-two gives new meaning to the phrase fallen woman," I announced as I gazed at my reflection.

"Oh, Jessie, you always say that." Candy poked her head around the dressing room door and took a peek at the royal blue contraption she was trying to sell me. "Gosh, that looks great. It's very flattering."

I lifted an unconvinced eyebrow. "Oh, Candy, you always say that."

"No really. I hope my figure looks that nice when I'm old."

Okay, so I took that as a compliment and agreed to buy the silly bra. And before she even mentioned them, I also asked for the matching panties. To know my neighbor Candy Poppe is to have a drawer full of completely inappropriate, and often alarming, lace, silk, and satin undergarments.

I got dressed and went out to the floor.

"*Temptation at Twilight* giving you trouble?" she asked as she rang me up. Candy hasn't known me long, but she does know me well. And she's figured out I show up at Tate's whenever writer's block strikes.

I sighed dramatically. "Plot plight."

"But you know you never have issues for very long, Jessie." She wrapped my purchases in pink tissue paper and placed them in a pink Tate's shopping bag. "Even after your divorce, remember? You came in, bought a few nice things, and went on home to finish *Windswept Whispers*." She offered an encouraging nod. "So go home, put on this bra, and start writing."

I did as I was told, but wearing the ridiculous blue bra didn't help after all. The page on my computer screen remained stubbornly blank no matter how hard I stared at it. I was deciding there must be better ways to spend a

Saturday night when a knock on the door pulled me out of my funk.

"Maybe it's Prince Charming," I said to my cat. Snowflake seemed skeptical, but I got up to answer anyway.

Funny thing? It really was Prince Charming. I opened my door to find Candy Poppe's handsome to a fault fiancé standing in the hallway. But Stanley wasn't looking all that handsome. Without bothering to say hello, he pushed me aside, stumbled toward the couch, and collapsed. Prince Charming was sick.

I rushed over to where he had invited himself to lie down and knelt beside him. "Stanley?" I asked. "What's wrong?"

"Candy," he whispered, and then he died.

He died?

I blinked twice and told myself I was not seeing what I was seeing. "He's just drunk," I reassured Snowflake. "He passed out."

But then, why were his eyes open like that?

I reached for his wrist. No pulse. I checked for breathing. Nope. I shook him and called his name a few times. Nothing.

Nothing.

The gravity of the situation finally dawned on me, and I jumped up. "CPR!" I shouted at the cat.

But Snowflake doesn't know CPR. And I remembered that I don't either.

I screamed a four-letter word and lunged for the phone.

***

Twenty minutes later a Clarence police officer was standing in my living room, hovering over me, my couch, and Candy's dead fiancé. I stared down at Stanley, willing him to start breathing again, while Captain Wilson Rye kept repeating the same questions about how I knew Candy, how I knew her boyfriend, and—here was the tricky part—what he was doing lying dead on my couch. I imagined Candy would wonder about that, too.

"Ms. Hewitt? Look at me." I glanced up at a pair of blue eyes that might have been pleasant under other circumstances. "You have anywhere else we can talk?"

Hope drained from his face as he scanned my condominium, an expansive loft with an open floor plan and very few doors. At the moment the place was swarming with people wearing plastic sheeting, talking into doohickeys, and either dusting or taking samples of who knows what from every corner and crevice. Unless Officer Rye and I decided to talk in the bathroom, we were doomed to be in the midst of the action.

"I'll make some tea," I said. At least then we could sit at the kitchen counter and stare at the stove. I glanced down. A far better option than staring at poor Stanley.

"Ms. Hewitt?"

"Tea," I repeated and pointed Officer Rye toward a barstool. I turned on the kettle and sat down beside him while the plastic people bustled about behind us, continuing their search for dust bunnies.

"Let's try this again," he said. "What was your relationship with Mr. Sweetzer?"

"We had no relationship."

"Mm-hmm."

"No, really. He was Candy's boyfriend. She lives downstairs in 2B."

The kettle whistled and I got up to pour the tea. Conscious that this cop was watching my every move, I spilled more water on the counter than into the cups. But eventually I succeeded in my task and even managed to hand him a cup.

"How do you take it?" I asked.

"Excuse me?"

"Your tea. Lemon, cream, sugar?"

"Nothing, thank you." He frowned at the tea. "So you knew Sweetzer through Ms. Poppe?"

"Correct." I carried my own cup around the counter and sat down again. "She and I met a few months ago."

"Where? Here?"

I sipped my tea and thought back. I had met Candy in the bra department at Tate's of course. It was the day after my divorce was finalized, and she had sold me a dozen bras spanning every color in the rainbow. Candy had even mentioned it that afternoon.

"Ms. Hewitt?"

"We met in the foundations department at Tate's."

"The what department?"

So much for discretion. "The bra department," I said bluntly. "Candy sold me some bras."

Rye's gaze moved southward for the briefest of seconds, and I remembered the brand new, bright blue specimen lurking beneath my white shirt.

My white shirt.

If there had been a wall handy, I would have banged my head against it. Instead, I mumbled something about not expecting company.

Rye cleared his throat and suggested we move on.

"Candy and I got to talking, and I told her I was in the market for a condo, and she told me about this place." I pointed up. "I took one look at these fifteen-foot ceilings and huge windows and signed a mortgage a week later. We've been good friends ever since."

"And Stanley Sweetzer?"

"Was Candy's boyfriend. He had some hotshot job in finance, and he was madly in love with Candy."

"So what was he doing up here?"

Okay, good question. I was trying to think of a good answer when one of the plastic people interrupted. "Will someone please get this cat out of here?" she called from behind us.

I turned to see Snowflake scurrying across the floor, gleefully unraveling a roll of yellow police tape. I quick hopped down to retrieve her while the plastic people sputtered this and that about contaminating the crime scene.

"She does live here," I said. They stopped scolding and watched as I picked her up and returned to my seat.

Snowflake had other ideas, however. She switched from my lap to Rye's and immediately commenced purring.

Rye resumed the interrogation. "Did you invite Mr. Sweetzer up here?"

"Nooo, I did not. I was working. I was sitting at my desk, minding my own business, when Stanley showed up out of the blue."

"You always work Saturday nights?"

I raised an eyebrow. "Do you?"

Rye took a deep breath. "You were alone then? Before Sweetzer showed up?"

"Snowflake was here."

More deep breathing. "Did he say anything, Ms. Hewitt?"

"He looked up when he hit the couch and whispered 'Candy.'" I shook my head. "It was awful."

"Could he have mistaken you for Candy?"

I shook my head again. "She's at least twenty years younger than me, a lot shorter, and has long dark hair." I pointed to my short blond cut. "No."

"Well then, maybe he had come from Candy's." Rye twirled around and called over to a young black guy—the only person other than himself in a business suit—and introduced me to Lieutenant Russell Densmore.

The Lieutenant shook my hand, but seemed far more interested in the teacups and the cat, who continued to occupy his boss's lap. His gaze landed back on me while he listened to instructions.

"Go downstairs to 2B and get them up here," Captain Rye told him. "Someone named Candy Poppe in particular."

"She's still at work," I said, but Lieutenant Densmore left anyway.

I looked at Rye. "I really don't think Stanley came here from Candy's," I insisted. "She's at work. I saw her there myself."

"Excuse me?"

"I was in Tate's this afternoon."

Rye took another gander at my chest. "That outfit for Sweetzer's benefit?"

"My outfi—What? No!"

Despite the stupid bra, only a madman would find my typical writing attire even remotely seductive. That evening I was wearing a pair of jeans, cut off above the knee, and a discarded men's dress shirt from way back when, courtesy of my ex-husband. As usual when I'm at home, I was barefoot. Stick a corncob pipe in my mouth and point me toward the Mississippi, and I might have borne a vague resemblance to Huck Finn—a tall, thin, menopausal Huck Finn.

I folded my arms and glared. "As I keep telling you, Captain, I was not expecting company."

"Is the door downstairs always unlocked?"

"Umm, yes?"

"You are kidding, right? You live smack in the middle of downtown Clarence and leave your front door unlocked? Anyone and his brother had access to this building tonight. You realize that?"

I gritted my teeth, mustered what was left of my patience, and suggested he talk to my neighbors about it. "For all I know, they've been here for years without a lock on that door."

Rye might have enjoyed lecturing me further, but luckily Lieutenant Densmore came back and distracted him. He reported that, indeed, Candy Poppe was not at home.

"What a shocker," I mumbled.

One of the plastic people also joined us. "You were right, Captain," she said. "This definitely looks unnatural."

"Yet another shocker." My voice had gained some volume, and all three of them frowned at me. I frowned back. "This whole evening has been extremely unnatural."

Rye turned and gave directions to the plastic person—something about getting the body to the medical examiner. He told Lieutenant Densmore to go downstairs and wait for Candy. Then he scooted Snowflake onto the floor and stood up to issue orders to the rest of the crowd.

I stood up also. Everyone appeared to have finished with their dusting, and I was happy to see that Stanley had been taken away. But it was a bit disconcerting to watch my couch being hauled off.

"You wouldn't want it here anyway, would you?" the Captain asked me. We stood together and waited while everyone else gathered their equipment and departed.

Rye was the last go. "I'll be downstairs if you think of anything else, Ms. Hewitt. Or call me." He handed me his card and headed toward the door. "I can't wait to hear what Ms. Poppe has to say for herself."

"She'll have nothing to say for herself," I called after him. "She's been at work all day."

He turned at the doorway. "Stay put," he said. "That's an order."

"Shut the door behind you, Captain. That's an order."

***

I headed for the fridge, desperately in search of champagne. Given the situation, this may seem odd. But champagne became my drink of choice after my divorce, when I decided every day without my ex is a day worth celebrating. Even days with dead bodies in them. I popped the cork. Make that, especially days with dead bodies.

I opened my door to better hear what was happening below and sank down in an easy chair. Candy got home at 9:30, but Rye and Densmore quickly shuffled her into her condo, and someone closed the door.

"Most unhandy," I told Snowflake. She jumped onto my lap, and together we stared at the empty spot where my couch had been.

The Korbel bottle was nearly half empty by the time Candy's door opened again. I hopped up to eavesdrop at my own doorway and heard Rye say something about calling him if she thought of anything else. Lieutenant Densmore asked if she had any family close by.

"My parents," she answered. "But I think I'll go see Jessie now, okay?"

I didn't catch Rye's reply, but the cops finally left, and within seconds Candy was at my doorstep.

"Oh, Jessie," she cried as I pulled her inside. She stopped short. "Umm, what happened to your sofa?"

"We need to talk," I told her. I guided her toward my bed and had her lie down.

The poor woman cried for a solid ten minutes. I held her hand and waited, and eventually she asked for some champagne. Like I told Rye—Candy and I are good friends.

I went to fetch a tray, and she was sitting up when I returned to the bedroom.

"Do you feel like talking, Sweetie?" I asked as I handed her a glass.

She took a sip, and then pulled a tissue from the box on my nightstand and made a sloppy attempt to wipe the mascara from under her eyes. "Those policemen told me what happened, but I could barely listen."

"They wanted to know why Stanley was here tonight. Do you know?"

She shook her head. "They kept asking me where I was. I was at work, right?"

"At least you have a solid alibi." I frowned. "Which makes one of us."

"Captain Rye was real interested in you, Jessie. I think he likes you."

I rolled my eyes. "Would you get a grip, Candy? Rye's real interested because he thinks I killed your boyfriend."

Her face dropped and she blinked her big brown eyes. "Did someone kill Stanley?"

Okay, so Candy Poppe isn't exactly the fizziest champagne in the fridge. Even on days without dead bodies.

"It looks like Stanley was murdered," I said quietly and handed her another tissue. "Did he have any enemies?"

"That's what Captain Rye kept asking me," she whined. "But everyone loved Stanley, didn't they?"

I had my doubts but thought it best to agree. I asked about his family, and over the remains of the Korbel, we discussed his parents. Apparently Margaret and Roger Sweetzer did not approve of Candy.

"They think I was after his money," she said. She put down her empty glass. "They don't like my job either. I swear to God, his mother comes into the store twice a week to embarrass me in front of the customers. And every time Mr. Sweetzer sees me, he asks how business is and stares at my chest."

While Candy blew her nose, I stared at her chest. The woman is my friend and all, but I could see how people might get the wrong impression. On this particular occasion she was wearing her red mini dress—and I do mean mini—and had accessorized with a truckload of red baubles and beads that would have fit better on a Christmas tree than on

Candy's petite frame. An unlikely pair of red patent leather stilettos completed the ensemble.

I stifled a frown. Hopefully, Captain Rye understood she had not known her fiancé was about to die when she wiggled her curvaceous little body into that outfit.

I mumbled something about trying to get some rest. If I still had my couch, I would have slept on it and let Candy drift off on the bed. I lamented such as she got up to leave, but she assured me she would be fine and teetered out the door in those ridiculous red shoes.

About the Author

Cindy Blackburn has a confession to make–she does not play pool. It's that whole eye-hand coordination thing. What Cindy does do well is school. So when she's not writing silly stories she's teaching serious history. European history is her favorite subject, and the ancient stuff is best of all. The deader the better! A native Vermonter who hates cold weather, Cindy divides her time between the south and the north. During the school year you'll find her in South Carolina, but come summer she'll be on the porch of her lakeside shack in Vermont. Cindy has a fat cat named Betty and a cute husband named John. Betty the muse meows constantly while Cindy tries to type. John provides the technical support. Both are extremely lovable.

When Cindy isn't writing, grading papers, or feeding the cat, she likes to take long walks or paddle her kayak around the lake. Her favorite travel destinations are all in Europe, her favorite TV show is NCIS, her favorite movie is Moonstruck, her favorite color is orange, and her favorite authors (if she must choose) are Joan Hess and Spencer Quinn. Cindy dislikes vacuuming, traffic, and lima beans.

www.cueballmysteries.com

www.cueballmysteries.com/blog

@cbmysteries

8025052R00158

Made in the USA
San Bernardino, CA
25 January 2014